A Good Hanging

Also by Ian Rankin

THE INSPECTOR REBUS SERIES
Knots & Crosses
Hide & Seek
Tooth & Nail (previously published as *Wolfman*)
Strip Jack
The Black Book
Mortal Causes
Let It Bleed
Black & Blue
The Hanging Garden
Death Is Not the End (novella)
Dead Souls
Rebus: The Early Years
Set in Darkness
The Falls

OTHER NOVELS
The Flood
Watchman
Westwind

WRITING AS JACK HARVEY
Witch Hunt
Bleeding Hearts
Blood Hunt

A Good Hanging

Ian Rankin

Minotaur Books ≈ New York

A GOOD HANGING. Copyright © 1992 by Ian Rankin. All rights reserved. Printed in the United States of America. For information, address St. Martin's Press, 175 Fifth Avenue, New York, N.Y. 10010.

Both the author and publisher acknowledge first publication of 'Playback' in *Writer's Crimes 22* (Macmillan).

www.minotaurbooks.com

The Library of Congress has cataloged the hardcover edition as follows:

Rankin, Ian.
    A good hanging : short stories / Ian Rankin.—1st U.S. ed.
        p. cm.
    ISBN 978-0-312-28027-7
    1. Rebus, Inspector (Fictitious character)—Fiction. 2. Detective and mystery stories, English. 3. Police—Scotland—Fiction. 4. Edinburgh (Scotland)—Fiction. I. Title.
    PR6068.A57 G66 2002
    823'.914—dc22

                                           2003269104

ISBN 978-0-312-65351-4 (trade paperback)

First published in Great Britain by Century

First Minotaur Books Paperback Edition: December 2010

10 9 8 7 6 5 4 3 2 1

To my editor, Euan Cameron,
who had faith from the first

Contents

A Good Hanging

Playback

It was the perfect murder.

Perfect, that is, so far as the Lothian and Borders Police were concerned. The murderer had telephoned in to confess, had then panicked and attempted to flee, only to be caught leaving the scene of the crime. End of story.

Except that now he was pleading innocence. Pleading, yelling and screaming it. And this worried Detective Inspector John Rebus, worried him all the way from his office to the four-storey tenement in Leith's trendy dockside area. The tenements here were much as they were in any working-class area of Edinburgh, except that they boasted colour-splashed roller blinds or Chinese-style bamboo affairs at their windows, and their grimy stone facades had been power-cleaned, their doors now boasting intruder-proof intercoms. A far cry from the greasy Venetian blinds and kicked-in passageways of the tene-ments in Easter Road or Gorgie, or even in nearby parts of Leith itself, the parts the developers were ignoring as yet.

The victim had worked as a legal secretary, this much Rebus knew. She had been twenty-four years old. Her name was Moira Bitter. Rebus smiled at that. It was a guilty smile, but at this hour of the morning any smile he could raise was something of a miracle.

He parked in front of the tenement, guided by a uniformed officer who had recognised the badly dented front bumper of Rebus's car. It was rumoured that the dent had come from knocking down too many old ladies, and who was Rebus to deny it? It was the stuff of legend and it

1

gave him prominence in the fearful eyes of the younger recruits.

A curtain twitched in one of the ground-floor windows and Rebus caught a glimpse of an elderly lady. Every tenement, it seemed, tarted up or not, boasted its elderly lady. Living alone, with one dog or four cats for company, she was her building's eyes and ears. As Rebus entered the hallway, a door opened and the old lady stuck out her head.

'He was going to run for it,' she whispered. 'But the bobby caught him. I saw it. Is the young lass dead? Is that it?' Her lips were pursed in keen horror. Rebus smiled at her but said nothing. She would know soon enough. Already she seemed to know as much as he did himself. That was the trouble with living in a city the size of a town, a town with a village mentality.

He climbed the four flights of stairs slowly, listening all the while to the report of the constable who was leading him inexorably towards the corpse of Moira Bitter. They spoke in an undertone: stairwell walls had ears.

'The call came at about 5 a.m., sir,' explained PC MacManus. 'The caller gave his name as John MacFarlane and said he'd just murdered his girlfriend. He sounded distressed by all accounts, and I was radioed to investigate. As I arrived, a man was running down the stairs. He seemed in a state of shock.'

'Shock?'

'Sort of disorientated, sir.'

'Did he say anything?' asked Rebus.

'Yes, sir, he told me, "Thank God you're here. Moira's dead." I then asked him to accompany me upstairs to the flat in question, called in for assistance, and the gentleman was arrested.'

Rebus nodded. MacManus was a model of efficiency, not a word out of place, the tone just right. Everything by rote and without the interference of too much thought. He would go far as a uniformed officer, but Rebus doubted the young man would ever make CID. When they reached the fourth floor, Rebus paused for breath then walked into the flat.

The hall's pastel colour scheme extended to the living-room and bedroom. Mute colours, subtle and warming. There was nothing subtle about the blood though. The blood was copious. Moira Bitter lay sprawled across her bed, her chest a riot of colour. She was wearing apple-green pyjamas, and her hair was silky blonde. The police pathologist was examining her head.

'She's been dead about three hours,' he informed Rebus. 'Stabbed three or four times with a small sharp instrument, which, for the sake of convenience, I'm going to term a knife. I'll examine her properly later on.'

Rebus nodded and turned to MacManus, whose face had a sickly grey tinge to it.

'Your first time?' Rebus asked. The constable nodded slowly. 'Never mind,' Rebus continued. 'You never get used to it anyway. Come on.'

He led the constable out of the room and back into the small hallway. 'This man we've arrested, what did you say his name was?'

'John MacFarlane, sir,' said the constable, taking deep breaths. 'He's the deceased's boyfriend apparently.'

'You said he seemed in a state of shock. Was there anything else you noticed?'

The constable frowned, thinking. 'Such as, sir?' he said at last.

'Blood,' said Rebus coolly. 'You can't stab someone in the heat of the moment without getting blood on you.'

MacManus said nothing. Definitely not CID material and perhaps realising it for the very first time. Rebus turned from him and entered the living-room. It was almost neurotically tidy. Magazines and newspapers in their rack beside the sofa. A chrome and glass coffee table bearing nothing more than a clean ashtray and a paperback romance. It could have come straight from an Ideal Home exhibition. No family photographs, no clutter. This was the lair of an individualist. No ties with the past, a present ransacked wholesale from Habitat and Next. There was no evidence of a struggle. No evidence of an encounter of any kind: no glasses or coffee cups. The killer had not loitered, or else had been very tidy about his business.

Rebus went into the kitchen. It, too, was tidy. Cups and plates stacked for drying beside the empty sink. On the draining-board were knives, forks, teaspoons. No murder weapon. There were spots of water in the sink and on the draining-board itself, yet the cutlery and crockery were dry. Rebus found a dishtowel hanging up behind the door and felt it. It was damp. He examined it more closely. There was a small smudge on it. Perhaps gravy or chocolate. Or blood. Someone had dried something recently, but what?

He went to the cutlery drawer and opened it. Inside, amidst the various implements was a short-bladed chopping knife with a heavy black handle. A quality knife, sharp and gleaming. The other items in the drawer were bone dry, but this chopping knife's wooden handle was damp to the touch. Rebus was in no doubt: he had found his murder weapon.

Clever of MacFarlane though to have cleaned and put away the knife. A cool and calm action. Moira Bitter had been dead three hours. The call to the police station had come an hour ago. What had MacFarlane done during the intervening two hours? Cleaned the flat? Washed and dried the dishes? Rebus looked in the kitchen's swing-bin, but found no other clues, no broken ornaments, nothing that might hint at a struggle. And if there had been no struggle, if the murderer had gained access to the tenement and to Moira Bitter's flat without forcing an entry ... if all this were true, Moira had known her killer.

Rebus toured the rest of the flat, but found no other clues. Beside the telephone in the hall stood an answering machine. He played the tape, and heard Moira Bitter's voice.

'Hello, this is Moira. I'm out, I'm in the bath, or I'm otherwise engaged.' (A giggle.) 'Leave a message and I'll get back to you, unless you sound boring.'

There was only one message. Rebus listened to it, then wound back the tape and listened again.

'Hello, Moira, it's John. I got your message. I'm coming over. Hope you're not "otherwise engaged". Love you.'

John MacFarlane: Rebus didn't doubt the identity of the caller. Moira sounded fresh and fancy-free in her message. But did MacFarlane's response hint at jealousy? Perhaps she *had* been otherwise engaged when he'd arrived. He lost his temper, blind rage, a knife lying handy. Rebus had seen it before. Most victims knew their attackers. If that were not the case, the police wouldn't solve so many crimes. It was a blunt fact. You double bolted your door against the psychopath with the chainsaw, only to be stabbed in the back by your lover, husband, son or neighbour.

John MacFarlane was as guilty as hell. They would find blood on his clothes, even if he'd tried cleaning it off. He had stabbed his girlfriend, then calmed down and called in to report the crime, but had grown frightened at the end and had attempted to flee.

The only question left in Rebus's mind was the why? The why and those missing two hours.

Edinburgh through the night. The occasional taxi rippling across setts and lone shadowy figures slouching home with hands in pockets, shoulders hunched. During the night hours, the sick and the old died peacefully, either at home or in some hospital ward. Two in the morning until four: the dead hours. And then some died horribly, with terror in their eyes. The taxis still rumbled past, the night people kept moving. Rebus let his car idle at traffic lights, missing the change to green, only coming to his senses as amber

turned red again. Glasgow Rangers were coming to town on
Saturday. There would be casual violence. Rebus felt
comfortable with the thought. The worst football hooligan
could probably not have stabbed with the same ferocity as
Moira Bitter's killer. Rebus lowered his eyebrows. He was
rousing himself to fury, keen for confrontation. Confrontation with the murderer himself.

John MacFarlane was crying as he was led into the
interrogation room, where Rebus had made himself look
comfortable, cigarette in one hand, coffee in the other.
Rebus had expected a lot of things, but not tears.

'Would you like something to drink?' he asked. MacFarlane shook his head. He had slumped into the chair on the
other side of the desk, his shoulders sagging, head bowed,
and the sobs still coming from his throat. He mumbled
something.

'I didn't catch that,' said Rebus.

'I said I didn't do it,' MacFarlane answered quietly.
'How could I do it? I love Moira.'

Rebus noted the present tense. He gestured towards the
tape machine on the desk. 'Do you have any objections to
my making a recording of this interview?' MacFarlane
shook his head again. Rebus switched on the machine. He
flicked ash from his cigarette onto the floor, sipped his
coffee, and waited. Eventually, MacFarlane looked up. His
eyes were stinging red. Rebus stared hard into those eyes,
but still said nothing. MacFarlane seemed to be calming.
Seemed, too, to know what was expected of him. He asked
for a cigarette, was given one, and started to speak.

'I'd been out in my car. Just driving, thinking.'

Rebus interrupted him. 'What time was this?'

'Well,' said MacFarlane, 'ever since I left work, I
suppose. I'm an architect. There's a competition on just
now to design a new art gallery and museum complex in
Stirling. Our partnership's going in for it. We were

discussing ideas most of the day, you know, brainstorming.'
He looked up at Rebus again, and Rebus nodded.
Brainstorm: now there was an interesting word.

'And after work,' MacFarlane continued, 'I was so fired
up I just felt like driving. Going over the different options
and plans in my head. Working out which was strongest –'

He broke off, realising perhaps that he was talking in a
rush, without thought or caution. He swallowed and
inhaled some smoke. Rebus was studying MacFarlane's
clothes. Expensive leather brogues, brown corduroy trousers, a thick white cotton shirt, the kind cricketers wore,
open at the neck, a tailor-made tweed jacket. MacFarlane's
3-Series BMW was parked in the police garage, being
searched. His pockets had been emptied, a Liberty print tie
confiscated in case he had ideas about hanging himself. His
brogues, too, were without their laces, these having been
confiscated along with the tie. Rebus had gone through the
belongings. A wallet, not exactly bulging with money but
containing a fair spread of credit cards. There were more
cards, too, in MacFarlane's personal organiser. Rebus
flipped through the diary pages, then turned to the sections
for notes and for addresses. MacFarlane seemed to lead a
busy but quite normal social life.

Rebus studied him now, across the expanse of the old
table. MacFarlane was well-built, handsome if you liked
that sort of thing. He looked strong, but not brutish.
Probably he would make the local news headlines as
'Secretary's Yuppie Killer'. Rebus stubbed out his cigarette.

'We know you did it, John. That's not in dispute. We
just want to know why.'

MacFarlane's voice was brittle with emotion. 'I swear I
didn't, I swear.'

'You're going to have to do better than that.' Rebus
paused again. Tears were dripping onto MacFarlane's
corduroys. 'Go on with your story,' he said.

7

MacFarlane shrugged. 'That's about it,' he said, wiping his nose with the sleeve of his shirt.

Rebus prompted him. 'You didn't stop off anywhere for petrol or a meal or anything like that?' He sounded sceptical. MacFarlane shook his head.

'No, I just drove until my head was clear. I went all the way to the Forth Road Bridge. Turned off and went into Queensferry. Got out of the car to have a look at the water. Threw a few stones in for luck.' He smiled at the irony. 'Then drove round the coast road and back into Edinburgh.'

'Nobody saw you? You didn't speak to anyone?'

'Not that I can remember.'

'And you didn't get hungry?' Rebus sounded entirely unconvinced.

'We'd had a business lunch with a client. We took him to The Eyrie. After lunch there, I seldom need to eat until the next morning.'

The Eyrie was Edinburgh's most expensive restaurant. You didn't go there to eat, you went there to spend money. Rebus was feeling peckish himself. The canteen did a fine bacon buttie.

'When did you last see Miss Bitter alive?'

At the word 'alive', MacFarlane shivered. It took him a long time to answer. Rebus watched the tape revolving. 'Yesterday morning,' MacFarlane said at last. 'She stayed the night at my flat.'

'How long have you known her?'

'About a year. But I only started going out with her a couple of months ago.'

'Oh? And how did you know her before that?'

MacFarlane paused. 'She was Kenneth's girlfriend,' he said at last.

'Kenneth being –'

MacFarlane's cheeks reddened before he spoke. 'My best

8

friend,' he said. 'Kenneth was my best friend. You could say I stole her from him. These things happen, don't they?'

Rebus raised an eyebrow. 'Do they?' he said. MacFarlane bowed his head again.

'Can I have a coffee?' he asked quietly. Rebus nodded, then lit another cigarette.

MacFarlane sipped the coffee, holding it in both hands like a shipwreck survivor. Rebus rubbed his nose and stretched, feeling tired. He checked his watch. Eight in the morning. What a life. He had eaten two bacon rolls and a string of rind curled across the plate in front of him. MacFarlane had refused food, but finished the first cup of coffee in two gulps and gratefully accepted a second.

'So,' Rebus said, 'you drove back into town.'

'That's right.' MacFarlane took another sip of coffee. 'I don't know why, but I decided to check my answering machine for calls.'

'You mean when you got home?'

MacFarlane shook his head. 'No, from the car. I called home from my car-phone and got the answering machine to play back any messages.'

Rebus was impressed. 'That's clever,' he said.

MacFarlane smiled again, but the smile soon vanished. 'One of the messages was from Moira,' he said. 'She wanted to see me.'

'At that hour?' MacFarlane shrugged. 'Did she say why she wanted to see you?'

'No. She sounded ... strange.'

'Strange?'

'A bit ... I don't know, distant maybe.'

'Did you get the feeling she was on her own when she called?'

'I've no idea.'

'Did you call her back?'

'Yes. Her answering machine was on. I left a message.'

'Would you say you're the jealous type, Mr Mac-Farlane?'

'What?' MacFarlane sounded surprised by the question. He seemed to give it serious thought. 'No more so than the next man,' he said at last.

'Why would anyone want to kill her?'

MacFarlane stared at the table, shaking his head slowly.

'Go on,' said Rebus, sighing, growing impatient. 'You were saying how you got her message.'

'Well, I went straight to her flat. It was late, but I knew if she was asleep I could always let myself in.'

'Oh?' Rebus was interested. 'How?'

'I had a spare key,' MacFarlane explained.

Rebus got up from his chair and walked to the far wall and back, deep in thought.

'I don't suppose,' he said, 'you've got any idea *when* Moira made that call?'

MacFarlane shook his head. 'But the machine will have logged it,' he said. Rebus was more impressed than ever. Technology was a wonderful thing. What's more, he was impressed by MacFarlane. If the man was a murderer, then he was a very good one, for he had fooled Rebus into thinking him innocent. It was crazy. There was nothing to point to him not being guilty. But all the same, a feeling was a feeling, and Rebus most definitely had a feeling.

'I want to see that machine,' he said. 'And I want to hear the message on it. I want to hear Moira's last words.'

It was interesting how the simplest cases could become so complex. There was still no doubt in the minds of those around Rebus – his superiors and those below him – that John MacFarlane was guilty of murder. They had all the proof they needed, every last bit of it circumstantial.

MacFarlane's car was clean: no bloodstained clothes

stashed in the boot. There were no prints on the chopping-knife, though MacFarlane's prints were found elsewhere in the flat, not surprising given that he'd visited that night, as well as on many a previous one. No prints either on the kitchen sink and taps, though the murderer had washed a bloody knife. Rebus thought that curious. And as for motive: jealousy, a falling-out, a past indiscretion discovered. The CID had seen them all.

Murder by stabbing was confirmed and the time of death narrowed down to a quarter of an hour either side of three in the morning. MacFarlane claimed that at that time he was driving towards Edinburgh, but had no witnesses to corroborate the claim. There was no blood to be found on MacFarlane's clothing, but, as Rebus himself knew, that didn't mean the man wasn't a killer.

More interesting, however, was that MacFarlane denied making the call to the police. Yet someone – in fact, whoever murdered Moira Bitter – *had* made it. And more interesting even than this was the telephone answering machine.

Rebus went to MacFarlane's flat in Liberton to investigate. The traffic was busy coming into town, but quiet heading out. Liberton was one of Edinburgh's many anonymous middle-class districts, substantial houses, small shops, a busy thoroughfare. It looked innocuous at midnight, and was even safer by day.

What MacFarlane had termed a 'flat' comprised, in fact, the top two storeys of a vast, detached house. Rebus roamed the building, not sure if he was looking for anything in particular. He found little. MacFarlane led a rigorous and regimented life and had the home to accommodate such a lifestyle. One room had been turned into a makeshift gymnasium, with weightlifting equipment and the like. There was an office for business use, a study for private use. The main bedroom was decidedly masculine in taste, though a framed painting of a naked woman had been removed from one wall and tucked behind a chair. Rebus thought he detected Moira Bitter's influence at work.

In the wardrobe were a few pieces of her clothing and a pair of her shoes. A snapshot of her had been framed and placed on MacFarlane's bedside table. Rebus studied the photograph for a long time, then sighed and left the bedroom, closing the door after him. Who knew when John MacFarlane would see his home again?

The answering machine was in the living-room. Rebus played the tape of the previous night's calls. Moira Bitter's voice was clipped and confident, her message to the point: 'Hello.' Then a pause. 'I need to see you. Come round as soon as you get this message. Love you.'

MacFarlane had told Rebus that the display unit on the machine showed time of call. Moira's call registered at 3.50 a.m., about forty-five minutes after her death. There was room for some discrepancy, but not three-quarters of an hour's worth. Rebus scratched his chin and pondered. He played the tape again. 'Hello.' Then the pause. 'I need to see you.' He stopped the tape and played it again, this time with the volume up and his ear close to the machine. That pause was curious and the sound quality on the tape was poor. He rewound and listened to another call from the same evening. The quality was better, the voice much clearer. Then he listened to Moira again. Were these recording machines infallible? Of course not. The time displayed could have been tampered with. The recording itself could be a fake. After all, whose word did he have that this *was* the voice of Moira Bitter? Only John MacFarlane's. But John MacFarlane had been caught leaving the scene of a murder. And now Rebus was being presented with a sort of an alibi for the man. Yes, the tape could well be a fake, used by MacFarlane to substantiate his story, but stupidly not put into use until after the time of death. Still, from what Rebus had heard from Moira's own answering machine, the voice was certainly similar to her own. The lab boys could sort it out with their clever machines. One technician in particular owed him a rather large favour.

Rebus shook his head. This still wasn't making much sense. He played the tape again and again.

'Hello.' Pause. 'I need to see you.'

'Hello.' Pause. 'I need to see you.'

'Hello.' Pause. 'I need –'

And suddenly it became a little clearer in his mind. He ejected the tape and slipped it into his jacket pocket, then picked up the telephone and called the station. He asked to speak to Detective Constable Brian Holmes. The voice, when it came on the line, was tired but amused.

'Don't tell me,' Holmes said, 'let me guess. You want me to drop everything and run an errand for you.'

'You must be psychic, Brian. Two errands really. Firstly, last night's calls. Get the recording of them and search for one from John MacFarlane, claiming he'd just killed his girlfriend. Make a copy of it and wait there for me. I've got another tape for you, and I want them both taken to the lab. Warn them you're coming –'

'And tell them it's priority, I know. It's *always* priority. They'll say what they always say: give us four days.'

'Not this time,' Rebus said. 'Ask for Bill Costain and tell him Rebus is collecting on his favour. He's to shelve what he's doing. I want a result today, not next week.'

'What's the favour you're collecting on?'

'I caught him smoking dope in the lab toilets last month.'

Holmes laughed. 'The world's going to pot,' he said. Rebus groaned at the joke and put down the receiver. He needed to speak with John MacFarlane again. Not about lovers this time, but about friends.

Rebus rang the doorbell a third time and at last heard a voice from within.

'Jesus, hold on! I'm coming.'

The man who answered the door was tall, thin, with wire-framed glasses perched on his nose. He peered at Rebus and ran his fingers through his hair.

'Mr Thomson?' Rebus asked. 'Kenneth Thomson?'

'Yes,' said the man, 'that's right.'

Rebus flipped open his ID. 'Detective Inspector John Rebus,' he said by way of introduction. 'May I come in?'

Kenneth Thomson held open the door. 'Please do,' he said. 'Will a cheque be all right?'

'A cheque?'

'I take it you're here about the parking tickets,' said Thomson. 'I'd have got round to them eventually, believe me. It's just that I've been hellish busy, and what with one thing and another ...'

'No, sir,' said Rebus, his smile as cold as a church pew, 'nothing to do with parking fines.'

'Oh?' Thomson pushed his glasses back up his nose and looked at Rebus. 'Then what's the problem?'

'It's about Miss Moira Bitter,' said Rebus.

'Moira? What about her?'

'She's dead, sir.'

Rebus had followed Thomson into a cluttered room overflowing with bundles of magazines and newspapers. A hi-fi sat in one corner, and covering the wall next to it were shelves filled with cassette tapes. These had an orderly look to them, as though they had been indexed, each tape's spine carrying an identifying number.

Thomson, who had been clearing a chair for Rebus to sit on, froze at the detective's words.

'Dead?' he gasped. 'How?'

'She was murdered, sir. We think John MacFarlane did it.'

'John?' Thomson's face was quizzical, then sceptical, then resigned. 'But why?'

14

'We don't know that yet, sir. I thought you might be able
to help.'

'Of course I'll help if I can. Sit down, please.'

Rebus perched on the chair, while Thomson pushed
aside some newspapers and settled himself on the sofa.

'You're a writer, I believe,' said Rebus.

Thomson nodded distractedly. 'Yes,' he said. 'Freelance
journalism, food and drink, travel, that sort of thing. Plus
the occasional commission to write a book. That's what I'm
doing now, actually. Writing a book.'

'Oh? I like books myself. What's it about?'

'Don't laugh,' said Thomson, 'but it's a history of the
haggis.'

'The haggis?' Rebus couldn't disguise a smile in his
voice, warmer this time: the church pew had been given a
cushion. He cleared his throat noisily, glancing around the
room, noting the piles of books leaning precariously against
walls, the files and folders and newsprint cuttings. 'You
must do a lot of research,' he said appreciatively.

'Sometimes,' said Thomson. Then he shook his head. 'I
still can't believe it. About Moira, I mean. About John.'

Rebus took out his notebook, more for effect than
anything else. 'You were Miss Bitter's lover for a while,' he
stated.

'That's right, Inspector.'

'But then she went off with Mr MacFarlane.'

'Right again.' A hint of bitterness had crept into
Thomson's voice. 'I was very angry at the time, but I got
over it.'

'Did you still see Miss Bitter?'

'No.'

'What about Mr MacFarlane?'

'No again. We spoke on the telephone a couple of times.
It always seemed to end in a shouting match. We used to be
like, well, it's a cliché, I suppose, but we used to be like
brothers.'

15

'Yes,' said Rebus, 'so Mr MacFarlane told me.'

'Oh?' Thomson sounded interested. 'What else did he say?'

'Not much really.' Rebus rose from his perch and went to the window, holding aside the net curtain to stare out onto the street below. 'He said you'd known each other for years.'

'Since school,' Thomson added.

Rebus nodded. 'And he said you drove a black Ford Escort. That'll be it down there, parked across the street?'

Thomson came to the window. 'Yes,' he agreed, uncertainly, 'that's it. But I don't see what –'

'I noticed it as I was parking my own car,' Rebus continued, brushing past Thomson's interruption. He let the curtain fall and turned back into the room. 'I noticed you've got a car alarm. I suppose you must get a lot of burglaries around here.'

'It's not the most salubrious part of town,' Thomson said. 'Not all writers are like Jeffrey Archer.'

'Did money have anything to do with it?' Rebus asked. Thomson paused.

'With what, Inspector?'

'With Miss Bitter leaving you for Mr MacFarlane. He's not short of a bob or two, is he?'

Thomson's voice rose perceptibly. 'Look, I really can't see what this has to do with –'

'Your car was broken into a few months ago, wasn't it?' Rebus was examining a pile of magazines on the floor now. 'I saw the report. They stole your radio and your car phone.'

'Yes.'

'I notice you've replaced the car phone.' He glanced up at Thomson, smiled, and continued browsing.

'Of course,' said Thomson. He seemed confused now, unable to fathom where the conversation was leading.

'A journalist would need a car phone, wouldn't he?'

16

Rebus observed. 'So people could keep in touch, contact him at any time. Is that right?'

'Absolutely right, Inspector.'

Rebus threw the magazine back onto the pile and nodded slowly. 'Great things, car phones.' He walked over towards Thomson's desk. It was a small flat. This room obviously served a double purpose as study and living-room. Not that Thomson entertained many visitors. He was too aggressive for many people, too secretive for others. So John MacFarlane had said.

On the desk there was more clutter, though in some appearance of organisation. There was also a neat word processor, and beside it a telephone. And next to the telephone sat an answering machine.

'Yes,' Rebus repeated. 'You need to be in contact.' Rebus smiled towards Thomson. 'Communication, that's the secret. And I'll tell you something else about journalists.'

'What?' Unable to comprehend Rebus's direction, Thomson's tone had become that of someone bored with a conversation. He shoved his hands deep into his pockets.

'Journalists are hoarders.' Rebus made this sound like some great wisdom. His eyes took in the room again. 'I mean, near-pathological hoarders. They can't bear to throw things away, because they never know when something might become useful. Am I right?'

Thomson shrugged.

'Yes,' said Rebus, 'I bet I am. Look at these cassettes, for example.' He went to where the rows of tapes were neatly displayed. 'What are they? Interviews, that sort of thing?'

'Mostly, yes,' Thomson agreed.

'And you still keep them, even though they're years old?'

Thomson shrugged again. 'So I'm a hoarder.'

But Rebus had noticed something on the top shelf, some brown cardboard boxes. He reached up and lifted one down. Inside were more tapes, marked with months and

17

years. But these tapes were smaller. Rebus gestured with the box towards Thomson, his eyes seeking an explanation.

Thomson smiled uneasily. 'Answering machine messages,' he said.

'You keep these, too?' Rebus sounded amazed.

'Well,' Thomson said, 'someone may agree to something over the phone, an interview or something, then deny it later. I need them as records of promises made.'

Rebus nodded, understanding now. He replaced the brown box on its shelf. He still had his back to Thomson when the telephone rang, a sharp electronic sound.

'Sorry,' Thomson apologised, going to answer it.

'Not at all.'

Thomson picked up the receiver. 'Hello?' He listened, then frowned. 'Of course,' he said finally, holding the receiver out towards Rebus. 'It's for you, Inspector.'

Rebus raised a surprised eyebrow and accepted the receiver. It was, as he had known it would be, Detective Constable Holmes.

'Okay,' Holmes said. 'Costain no longer owes you that favour. He's listened to both tapes. He hasn't run all the necessary tests yet, but he's pretty convinced.'

'Go on.' Rebus was looking at Thomson, who was sitting, hands clasping knees, on the arm of the chair.

'The call we received last night,' said Holmes, 'the one from John MacFarlane admitting to the murder of Moira Bitter, originated from a portable telephone.'

'Interesting,' said Rebus, his eyes on Thomson. 'And what about the other one?'

'Well, the tape you gave me seems to be twice-removed.'

'What does that mean?'

'It means,' said Holmes, 'that according to Costain it's not just a recording, it's the recording of a recording.'

Rebus nodded, satisfied.

'Okay, thanks, Brian.' He put down the receiver.

'Good news or bad?' Thomson asked.

'A bit of both,' answered Rebus thoughtfully. Thomson had risen to his feet.

'I feel like a drink, Inspector. Can I get you one?'

'It's a bit early for me, I'm afraid,' Rebus said, looking at his watch. It was eleven o'clock: opening time. 'All right,' he said, 'just a small one.'

'The whisky's in the kitchen,' Thomson explained. 'I'll just be a moment.'

'Fine, sir, fine.'

Rebus listened as Thomson left the room and headed off towards the kitchen. He stood beside the desk, thinking through what he now knew. Then, hearing Thomson returning from the kitchen, floor-boards bending beneath his weight, he picked up the wastepaper basket from below the desk, and, as Thomson entered the room, proceeded to empty the contents in a heap on the sofa.

Thomson stood in the doorway, a glass of whisky in each hand, dumbstruck. 'What on earth are you doing?' he spluttered at last. But Rebus ignored him and started to pick through the now strewn contents of the bin, talking as he searched.

'It was pretty close to being fool-proof, Mr Thomson. Let me explain. The killer went to Moira Bitter's flat and talked her into letting him in despite the late hour. He murdered her quite callously, let's make no mistake about that. I've never seen so much premeditation in a case before. He cleaned the knife and returned it to its drawer. He was wearing gloves, of course, knowing John MacFarlane's fingerprints would be all over the flat, and he cleaned the knife precisely to disguise the fact that he *had* worn gloves. MacFarlane, you see, had not.'

Thomson took a gulp from one glass, but otherwise seemed rooted to the spot. His eyes had become vacant, as though picturing Rebus's story in his mind.

'MacFarlane,' Rebus continued, still rummaging, 'was summoned to Moira's flat. The message did come from her. He knew her voice well enough not to be fooled by someone else's voice. The killer sat outside Moira's flat, sat waiting for MacFarlane to arrive. Then the killer made one last call, this one to the police, in the guise of an hysterical MacFarlane. We know this last call was made on a car phone. The lab boys are very clever that way. The police are hoarders, too, you see, Mr Thomson. We make recordings of emergency calls made to us. It won't be hard to voice-print that call and try to match it to John MacFarlane. But it won't be John MacFarlane, will it?' Rebus paused for effect. 'It'll be you.'

Thomson gave a thin smile, but his grip on the two glasses had grown less steady, and whisky was dribbling from the angled lip of one of them.

'Ah-ha.' Rebus had found what he was looking for in the contents of the bin. With a pleased-as-punch grin on his unshaven, sleepless face, he pinched forefinger and thumb together and lifted them for his own and Thomson's inspection. He was holding a tiny sliver of brown recording tape.

'You see,' he continued, 'the killer had to lure MacFarlane to the murder scene. Having killed Moira, he went to his car, as I've said. There he had his portable telephone and a cassette recorder. He was a hoarder. He had kept all his answering machine tapes, including messages left by Moira at the height of their affair. He found the message he needed and he spliced it. He played this message to John MacFarlane's answering machine. All he had to do after that was wait. The message MacFarlane received was "Hello. I need to see you." There was a pause after the "hello". And that pause was where the splice was made in the tape, excising this.' Rebus looked at the sliver of tape. 'The one word "Kenneth". "Hello, Kenneth, I need to see you." It was Moira Bitter talking to you, Mr Thomson, talking to you a long time ago.'

Thomson hurled both glasses at once, so that they

arrowed in towards Rebus, who ducked. The glasses collided above his head, shards raining down on him. Thomson had reached the front door, had hauled it open even, before Rebus was on him, lunging, pushing the younger man forwards through the doorway and onto the tenement landing. Thomson's head hit the metal rails with a muted chime and he let out a single moan before collapsing. Rebus shook himself free of glass, feeling one or two tiny pieces nick him as he brushed a hand across his face. He brought a hand to his nose and inhaled deeply. His father had always said whisky would put hairs on his chest. Rebus wondered if the same miracle might be effected on his temples and the crown of his head ...

It had been the perfect murder.

Well, almost. But Kenneth Thomson had reckoned without Rebus's ability actually to believe someone innocent despite the evidence against him. The case against John MacFarlane had been overwhelming. Yet Rebus, feeling it to be wrong, had been forced to invent other scenarios, other motives and other means to the fairly chilling end. It wasn't enough that Moira had died – died at the hands of someone she knew. MacFarlane had to be implicated in her murder. The killer had been out to tag them both. But it was Moira the killer hated, hated because she had broken a friendship as well as a heart.

Rebus stood on the steps of the police station. Thomson was in a cell somewhere below his feet, somewhere below ground level. Confessing to everything. He would go to jail, while John MacFarlane, perhaps not realising his luck, had already been freed.

The streets were busy now. Lunchtime traffic, the reliable noises of the everyday. The sun was even managing to burst from its slumber. All of which reminded Rebus that his day was over. Time, all in all he felt, for a short visit home, a shower and a change of clothes, and, God and the Devil willing, some sleep.

The Dean Curse

The locals in Barnton knew him either as 'the Brigadier' or as 'that Army type who bought the West Lodge'. West Lodge was a huge but until recently neglected detached house set in a walled acre and a half of grounds and copses. Most locals were relieved that its high walls hid it from general view, the house itself being too angular, too gothic for modern tastes. Certainly, it was very large for the needs of a widower and his unsmiling daughter. Mrs MacLennan, who cleaned for the Brigadier, was pumped for information by curious neighbours, but could say only that Brigadier-General Dean had had some renovations done, that most of the house was habitable, that one room had become a library, another a billiard-room, another a study, another a makeshift gymnasium and so on. The listeners would drink this in deeply, yet it was never enough. What about the daughter? What about the Brigadier's background? What happened to his wife?

Shopkeepers too were asked for their thoughts. The Brigadier drove a sporty open-topped car which would pull in noisily to the side of the road to allow him to pop into this or that shop for a few things, including, each day at the same time, a bottle of something or other from the smarter of the two off-licences.

The grocer, Bob Sladden, reckoned that Brigadier-General Dean had been born nearby, even that he had lived for a few childhood years in West Lodge and so had retired there because of its carefree connections. But Miss Dalrymple, who at ninety-three was as old as anyone in that part of Barnton, could not recall any family named Dean living at West Lodge. Could not, indeed, recall any Deans ever living in this 'neck' of Barnton, with the exception of Sam Dean. But when pressed about Sam Dean, she merely shook her head and said, 'He was no good, that one, and got what he deserved. The Great War saw to him.' Then she would nod slowly, thoughtfully, and nobody would be any further forward.

Speculation grew wilder as no new facts came to light, and in The Claymore public bar one afternoon, a bar never patronised by the Brigadier (and who'd ever heard of an Army man not liking his drink?), a young out-of-work plasterer named Willie Barr came up with a fresh proposition.

'Maybe Dean isn't his real name.'

But everyone around the pool table laughed at that and Willie just shrugged, readying to play his next shot. 'Well,' he said, 'real name or not, I wouldn't climb over that daughter of his to get to any of you lot.'

Then he played a double off the cushion, but missed. Missed not because the shot was difficult or he'd had too many pints of Snakebite, but because his cue arm jerked at the noise of the explosion.

It was a fancy car all right, a Jaguar XJS convertible, its bodywork a startling red. Nobody in Barnton could mistake it for anyone else's car. Besides, everyone was used to it revving to its loud roadside halt, was used to its contented ticking-over while the Brigadier did his shopping. Some complained – though never to his face – about the noise, about the fumes from the exhaust. They couldn't say why he never switched off the ignition. He always seemed to want to be ready for a quick getaway. On this particular afternoon, the getaway was quicker even than usual, a squeal of tyres as the car jerked out into the road and sped past the shops. Its driver seemed ready actually to disregard the red stop light at the busy junction. He never got the chance. There was a ball of flames where the car had been and the heart-stopping sound of the explosion. Twisted metal flew into the air, then down again, wounding passers-by, burning skin. Shop windows blew in, shards of fine glass finding soft targets. The traffic lights turned to green, but nothing moved in the street.

For a moment, there was a silence punctuated only by the arrival on terra firma of bits of speedometer, headlamp, even steering-wheel. Then the screaming started, as people realised they'd been wounded. More curdling still though were the silences, the dumb horrified faces of people who would never forget this moment, whose shock would disturb each wakeful night.

And then there was a man, standing in a doorway, the doorway of what had been the wine merchant's. He carried a bottle with him, carefully wrapped in green paper, and his mouth was open in surprise. He dropped the bottle with a crash when he realised his car was not where he had left it, realising that the roaring he had heard and thought he recognised was that of his own car being driven away. At his feet, he saw one of his driving gloves lying on the pavement in front of him. It was still smouldering. Only five minutes before, it had been lying on the leather of his passenger seat. The wine merchant was standing beside him now, pale and shaking, looking in dire need of a drink. The Brigadier nodded towards the carcass of his sleek red Jaguar.

'That should have been me,' he said. Then: 'Do you mind if I use your telephone?'

John Rebus threw *The Dain Curse* up in the air, sending it spinning towards his living-room ceiling. Gravity caught up with it just short of the ceiling and pulled it down hard, so that it landed open against the uncarpeted floor. It was a cheap copy, bought secondhand and previously much read.

But not by Rebus; he'd got as far as the beginning of the third section, 'Quesada', before giving up, before tossing what many regard as Hammett's finest novel into the air. Its pages fell away from the spine as it landed, scattering chapters. Rebus growled. The telephone had, as though prompted by the book's demise, started ringing. Softly, insistently. Rebus picked up the apparatus and studied it. It was six o'clock on the evening of his first rest-day in what seemed like months. Who would be phoning him? Pleasure or business? And which would he prefer it to be? He put the receiver to his ear.

'Yes?' His voice was non-committal.

'DI Rebus?' It was work then. Rebus grunted a response. 'DC Coupar here, sir. The Chief thought you'd be interested.' There was a pause for effect. 'A bomb's just gone off in Barnton.'

Rebus stared at the sheets of print lying all around him. He asked the Detective Constable to repeat the message.

'A bomb, sir. In Barnton.'

'What? A World War Two leftover you mean?'

'No, sir. Nothing like that. Nothing like that at all.'

There was a line of poetry in Rebus's head as he drove out towards one of Edinburgh's many quiet middle-class districts, the sort of place where nothing happened, the sort of place where crime was measured in a yearly attempted break-in or the theft of a bicycle. That was Barnton. The line of poetry hadn't been written about Barnton. It had been written about Slough.

It's my own fault, Rebus was thinking, for being disgusted at how far-fetched that Hammett book was. Entertaining, yes, but you could strain credulity only so far, and Dashiell Hammett had taken that strain like the anchor-man on a tug-o'-war team, pulling with all his might. Coincidence after coincidence, plot after plot, corpse following corpse like something off an assembly line.

Far-fetched, definitely. But then what was Rebus to make of his telephone call? He'd checked: it wasn't 1st April. But then he wouldn't put it past Brian Holmes or one of his other colleagues to pull a stunt on him just because he was having a day off, just because he'd carped on about it for the previous few days. Yes, this had Holmes' fingerprints all over it. Except for one thing.

The radio reports. The police frequency was full of it; and when Rebus switched on his car radio to the local commercial channel, the news was there, too. Reports of an explosion in Barnton, not far from the roundabout. It is thought a car has exploded. No further details, though there are thought to be many casualties. Rebus shook his head and drove, thinking of the poem again, thinking of anything that would stop him focussing on the truth of the news. A car bomb? *A car bomb?* In Belfast, yes, maybe even on occasion in London. But here in Edinburgh? Rebus blamed himself. If only he hadn't cursed Dashiell Hammett, if only he hadn't sneered at his book, at its exaggerations and its melodramas, if only ... Then none of this would have happened.

But of course it would. It had.

The road had been blocked off. The ambulances had left with their cargo. Onlookers stood four deep behind the orange and white tape of the hastily erected cordon. There was just the one question: how many dead? The answer seemed to be: just the one. The driver of the car. An Army bomb disposal unit had materialised from somewhere and, for want of anything else to do, was checking the shops either side of the street. A line of policemen, aided so far as Rebus could judge by more Army personnel, was moving slowly up the road, mostly on hands and knees, in what an outsider might regard as some bizarre slow-motion race. They carried with them polythene bags, into which they dropped anything they found. The whole scene was one of brilliantly organised confusion and it didn't take Rebus longer than a couple of minutes to detect the mastermind behind it all – Superintendent 'Farmer' Watson. 'Farmer' only behind his back, of course, and a nickname which matched both his north-of-Scotland background and his at times agricultural methods. Rebus decided to skirt around his superior officer and glean what he could from the various less senior officers present.

He had come to Barnton with a set of preconceptions and it took time for these to be corrected. For example, he'd premised that the person in the car, the as-yet-unidentified deceased, would be the car's owner and that this person would have been the target of the bomb attack (the evidence all around most certainly pointed to a bomb, rather than spontaneous combustion, say, or any other more likely explanation). Either that or the car might be stolen or borrowed, and the driver some sort of terrorist, blown apart by his own device before he could leave it at its intended destination. There were certainly Army installations around Edinburgh: barracks, armouries, listening posts. Across the Forth lay what was left of Rosyth naval dockyard, as well as the underground installation at Pitreavie. There were targets. Bomb meant terrorist meant target. That was how it always was.

But not this time. This time there was an important difference. The apparent target escaped, by dint of leaving his car for a couple of minutes to nip into a shop. But while he was in the shop someone had tried to steal his car, and that person was now drying into the tarmac beneath the knees of the crawling policemen. This much Rebus learned before Superintendent Watson caught sight of him, caught sight of him smiling wryly at the car thief's luck. It wasn't every day you got the chance to steal a Jaguar XJS ... but what a day to pick.

'Inspector!' Farmer Watson beckoned for Rebus to join him, which Rebus, ironing out his smile, did.

Before Watson could start filling him in on what he already knew, Rebus himself spoke.

'Who was the target, sir?'

'A man called Dean.' Meaningful pause. 'Brigadier-General Dean, retired.'

Rebus nodded. 'I thought there were a lot of Tommies about.'

'We'll be working with the Army on this one, John. That's how it's done, apparently. And then there's Scotland Yard, too. Their anti-terrorist people.'

'Too many cooks if you ask me, sir.'

Watson nodded. 'Still, these buggers are supposed to be specialised.'

'And we're only good for solving the odd drunk driving or domestic, eh, sir?'

The two men shared a smile at this. Rebus nodded towards the wreck of the car. 'Any idea who was behind the wheel?'

Watson shook his head. 'Not yet. And not much to go on either. We may have to wait till a mum or girlfriend reports him missing.'

'Not even a description?'

'None of the passers-by is fit to be questioned. Not yet anyway.'

'So what about Brigadier-General Whassisname?'

'Dean.'

'Yes. Where is he?'

'He's at home. A doctor's been to take a look at him, but he seems all right. A bit shocked.'

'A bit? Someone rips the arse out of his car and he's a *bit* shocked?' Rebus sounded doubtful. Watson's eyes were fixed on the advancing line of debris collectors.

'I get the feeling he's seen worse.' He turned to Rebus. 'Why don't you have a word with him, John? See what you think.'

29

Rebus nodded slowly. 'Aye, why not,' he said. 'Anything for a laugh, eh, sir?'

Watson seemed stuck for a reply, and by the time he'd formed one Rebus had wandered back through the cordon, hands in trouser pockets, looking for all the world like a man out for a stroll on a balmy summer's evening. Only then did the Superintendent remember that this was Rebus's day off. He wondered if it had been such a bright idea to send him off to talk to Brigadier-General Dean. Then he smiled, recalling that he had brought John Rebus out here precisely because something didn't quite feel right. If he could feel it, Rebus would feel it too, and would burrow deep to find its source – as deep as necessary and, perhaps, deeper than was seemly for a Superintendent to go.

Yes, there were times when even Detective Inspector John Rebus came in useful.

It was a big house. Rebus would go further. It was bigger than the last hotel he'd stayed in, though of a similar style: closer to Hammer Films than *House and Garden*. A hotel in Scarborough it had been; three days of lust with a divorced school-dinner lady. School-dinner ladies hadn't been like that in Rebus's day ... or maybe he just hadn't been paying attention.

He paid attention now. Paid attention as an Army uniform opened the door of West Lodge to him. He'd already had to talk his way past a mixed guard on the gate – an apologetic PC and two uncompromising squaddies. That was why he'd started thinking back to Scarborough – to stop himself punching those squaddies in their square-chinned faces. The closer he came to Brigadier-General Dean, the more aggressive and unlovely the soldiers seemed. The two on the gate were like lambs compared to the one on the main door of the house, yet he in his turn was meekness itself compared to the one who led Rebus into a well-appointed living-room and told him to wait.

Rebus hated the Army – with good reason. He had seen the soldier's lot from the inside and it had left him with a resentment so huge that to call it a 'chip on the shoulder' was to do it an injustice. Chip? Right now it felt like a whole transport cafe! There was only one thing for it. Rebus made for the sideboard, sniffed the contents of the decanter sitting there and poured himself an inch of whisky. He was draining the contents of the glass into his mouth when the door opened.

Rebus had brought too many preconceptions with him today. Brigadier-Generals were squat, ruddy-faced men, with stiff moustaches and VSOP noses, a few silvered wisps of Brylcreemed hair and maybe even a walking stick. They retired in their seventies and babbled of campaigns over dinner.

Not so Brigadier-General Dean. He looked to be in his mid- to late-fifties. He stood over six feet tall, had a youthful face and vigorous dark hair. He was slim too, with no sign of a retirement gut or a port drinker's red-veined cheeks. He looked twice as fit as Rebus felt and for a moment the policeman actually caught himself straightening his back and squaring his shoulders.

'Good idea,' said Dean, joining Rebus at the sideboard. 'Mind if I join you?' His voice was soft, blurred at the edges, the voice of an educated man, a civilised man. Rebus tried hard to imagine Dean giving orders to a troop of hairy-fisted Tommies. Tried, but failed.

'Detective Inspector Rebus,' he said by way of introduction. 'Sorry to bother you like this, sir, but there are a few questions –'

Dean nodded, finishing his own drink and offering to replenish Rebus's.

'Why not?' agreed Rebus. Funny thing though: he could

31

swear this whisky wasn't whisky at all but whiskey – Irish whiskey. Softer than the Scottish stuff, lacking an edge.

Rebus sat on the sofa, Dean on a well-used armchair. The Brigadier-General offered a toast of *slainte* before starting on his second drink, then exhaled noisily.

'Had to happen sooner or later, I suppose,' he said.

'Oh?'

Dean nodded slowly. 'I worked in Ulster for a time. Quite a long time. I suppose I was fairly high up in the tree there. I always knew I was a target. The Army knew, too, of course, but what can you do? You can't put bodyguards on every soldier who's been involved in the conflict, can you?'

'I suppose not, sir. But I assume you took precautions?'

Dean shrugged. 'I'm not in *Who's Who* and I've got an unlisted telephone number. I don't even use my rank much, to be honest.'

'But some of your mail might be addressed to Brigadier-General Dean?'

A wry smile. 'Who gave you that impression?'

'What impression, sir?'

'The impression of rank. I'm not a Brigadier-General. I retired with the rank of Major.'

'But the –'

'The what? The locals? Yes, I can see how gossip might lead to exaggeration. You know how it is in a place like this, Inspector. An incomer who keeps himself to himself. A military air. They put two and two together then multiply it by ten.'

Rebus nodded thoughtfully. 'I see.' Trust Watson to be wrong even in the fundamentals. 'But the point I was trying to make about your mail still stands, sir. What I'm wondering, you see, is how they found you.'

Dean smiled quietly. 'The IRA are quite sophisticated these days, Inspector. For all I know, they could have hacked into a computer, bribed someone in the know, or maybe it was just a fluke, sheer chance.' He shrugged. 'I suppose we'll have to think of moving somewhere else now, starting all over again. Poor Jacqueline.'

'Jacqueline being?'

'My daughter. She's upstairs, terribly upset. She's due to start university in October. It's her I feel sorry for.'

Rebus looked sympathetic. He felt sympathetic. One thing about Army life and police life – both could have a devastating effect on your personal life.

'And your wife, sir?'

'Dead, Inspector. Several years ago.' Dean examined his now empty glass. He looked his years now, looked like someone who needed a rest. But there was something other about him, something cool and hard. Rebus had met all types in the Army – and since. Veneers could no longer fool him, and behind Major Dean's sophisticated veneer he could glimpse something other, something from the man's past. Dean hadn't just been a good soldier. At one time he'd been lethal.

'Do you have any thoughts on how they might have found you, sir?'

'Not really.' Dean closed his eyes for a second. There was resignation in his voice. 'What matters is that they *did* find me.' His eyes met Rebus's. 'And they can find me again.'

Rebus shifted in his seat. Christ, what a thought. What a, well, time-bomb. To always be watching, always expecting, always fearing. And not just for yourself.

'I'd like to talk to Jacqueline, sir. It may be that she'll have some inkling as to how they were able to –'

But Dean was shaking his head. 'Not just now, Inspector. Not yet. I don't want her – well, you understand. Besides, I'd imagine that this will all be out of your hands by tomorrow. I believe some people from the Anti-Terrorist Branch are on their way up here. Between them and the Army ... well, as I say, it'll be out of your hands.'

Rebus felt himself prickling anew. But Dean was right,

wasn't he? Why strain yourself when tomorrow it would be someone else's weight? Rebus pursed his lips, nodded, and stood up.

'I'll see you to the door,' said the Major, taking the empty glass from Rebus's hand.

As they passed into the hallway, Rebus caught a glimpse of a young woman – Jacqueline Dean presumably. She had been hovering by the telephone-table at the foot of the staircase, but was now starting up the stairs themselves, her hand thin and white on the bannister. Dean, too, watched her go. He half-smiled, half-shrugged at Rebus.

'She's upset,' he explained unnecessarily. But she hadn't looked upset to Rebus. She had looked like she was moping.

The next morning, Rebus went back to Barnton. Wooden boards had been placed over some of the shop windows, but otherwise there were few signs of yesterday's drama. The guards on the gate to West Lodge had been replaced by beefy plainclothes men with London accents. They carried portable radios, but otherwise might have been bouncers, debt collectors or bailiffs. They radioed the house. Rebus couldn't help thinking that a shout might have done the job for them, but they were in love with technology; you could see that by the way they held their radio-sets. He'd seen soldiers holding a new gun the same way.

'The guvnor's coming down to see you,' one of the men said at last. Rebus kicked his heels for a full minute before the man arrived.

'What do you want?'

'Detective Inspector Rebus. I talked with Major Dean yesterday and –'

The man snapped. 'Who told you his rank?'

'Major Dean himself. I just wondered if I might –'

'Yes, well there's no need for that, Inspector. We're in charge now. Of course you'll be kept informed.'

The man turned and walked back through the gates with a steady, determined stride. The guards were smirking as they closed the gates behind their 'guvnor'. Rebus felt like a snubbed schoolboy, left out of the football game. Sides had been chosen and there he stood, unwanted. He could smell London on these men, that cocky superiority of a self-chosen elite. What did they call themselves? C13 or somesuch, the Anti-Terrorist Branch. Closely linked to Special Branch, and everyone knew the trade name for Special Branch – Smug Bastards.

The man had been a little younger than Rebus, well-groomed and accountant-like. More intelligent, for sure, than the gorillas on the gate, but probably well able to handle himself. A neat pistol might well have been hidden under the arm of his close-fitting suit. None of that mattered. What mattered was that the captain was leaving Rebus out of his team. It rankled; and when something rankled, it rankled hard.

Rebus had walked half a dozen paces away from the gates when he half-turned and stuck his tongue out at the guards. Then, satisfied with this conclusion to his morning's labours, he decided to make his own inquiries. It was eleven-thirty. If you want to find out about someone, reasoned a thirsty Rebus, visit his local.

The reasoning, in this case, proved false: Dean had never been near The Claymore.

'The daughter came in though,' commented one young man. There weren't many people in the pub at this early stage of the day, save a few retired gentlemen who were in conversation with three or four reporters. The barman, too, was busy telling his life story to a young female hack, or rather, into her tape recorder. This made getting served difficult, despite the absence of a lunchtime scrum. The young man had solved this problem, however, reaching behind the bar to refill his glass with a mixture of cider and lager, leaving money on the bartop.

35

'Oh?' Rebus nodded towards the three-quarters full glass. 'Have another?'

'When this one's finished I will.' He drank greedily, by which time the barman had finished with his confessions – much (judging by her face) to the relief of the reporter. 'Pint of Snakebite, Paul,' called the young man. When the drink was before him, he told Rebus that his name was Willie Barr and that he was unemployed.

'You said you saw the daughter in here?' Rebus was anxious to have his questions answered before the alcohol took effect on Barr.

'That's right. She came in pretty regularly.'

'By herself?'

'No, always with some guy.'

'One in particular, you mean?'

But Willie Barr laughed, shaking his head. 'A different one every time. She's getting a bit of a name for herself. And,' he raised his voice for the barman's benefit, 'she's not even eighteen, I'd say.'

'Were they local lads?'

'None I recognised. Never really spoke to them.' Rebus swirled his glass, creating a foamy head out of nothing.

'Any Irish accents among them?'

'In here?' Barr laughed. 'Not in here. Christ, no. Actually, she hasn't been in for a few weeks, now that I think of it. Maybe her father put a stop to it, eh? I mean, how would it look in the Sunday papers? Brigadier's daughter slumming it in Barnton.'

Rebus smiled. 'It's not exactly a slum though, is it?'

'True enough, but her boyfriends ... I mean, there was more of the car mechanic than the estate agent about them. Know what I mean?' He winked. 'Not that a bit of rough ever hurt *her* kind, eh?' Then he laughed again and suggested a game or two of pool, a pound a game or a fiver if the detective were a betting man.

But Rebus shook his head. He thought he knew now why

Willie Barr was drinking so much: he was flush. And the reason he was flush was that he'd been telling his story to the papers – for a price. *Brigadier's Daughter Slumming It*. Yes, he'd been telling tales all right, but there was little chance of them reaching their intended audience. The Powers That Be would see to that.

Barr was helping himself to another pint as Rebus made to leave the premises.

It was late in the afternoon when Rebus received his visitor, the Anti-Terrorist accountant.

'A Mr Matthews to see you,' the Desk Sergeant had informed Rebus, and 'Matthews' he remained, giving no hint of rank or proof of identity. He had come, he said, to 'have it out' with Rebus.

'What were you doing in The Claymore?'

'Having a drink.'

'You were asking questions. I've already told you, Inspector Rebus, we can't have –'

'I know, I know.' Rebus raised his hands in a show of surrender. 'But the more furtive you lot are, the more interested I become.'

Matthews stared silently at Rebus. Rebus knew that the man was weighing up his options. One, of course, was to go to Farmer Watson and have Rebus warned off. But if Matthews were as canny as he looked, he would know this might have the opposite effect from that intended. Another option was to talk to Rebus, to ask him what he wanted to know.

'What do you want to know?' Matthews said at last.

'I want to know about Dean.'

Matthews sat back in his chair. 'In strictest confidence?'

Rebus nodded. 'I've never been known as a clipe.'

'A clipe?'

'Someone who tells tales,' Rebus explained. Matthews was thoughtful.

'Very well then,' he said. 'For a start, Dean is an alias, a very necessary one. During his time in the Army Major Dean worked in Intelligence, mostly in West Germany but also for a time in Ulster. His work in both spheres was very important, crucially important. I don't need to go into details. His last posting was West Germany. His wife was killed in a terrorist attack, almost certainly IRA. We don't think they had targeted her specifically. She was just in the wrong place with the wrong number plates.'

'A car bomb?'

'No, a bullet. Through the windscreen, point-blank. Major Dean asked to be ... he was invalided out. It seemed best. We provided him with a change of identity, of course.'

'I thought he looked a bit young to be retired. And the daughter, how did she take it?'

'She was never told the full details, not that I'm aware of. She was in boarding school in England.' Matthews paused. 'It was for the best.'

Rebus nodded. 'Of course, nobody'd argue with that. But why did − Dean − choose to live in Barnton?'

Matthews rubbed his left eyebrow, then pushed his spectacles back up his sharply sloping nose. 'Something to do with an aunt of his,' he said. 'He spent holidays there as a boy. His father was Army, too, posted here, there and everywhere. Never the most stable upbringing. I think Dean had happy memories of Barnton.'

Rebus shifted in his seat. He couldn't know how long Matthews would stay, how long he would continue to answer Rebus's questions. And there were so many questions.

'What about the bomb?'

'Looks like the IRA, all right. Standard fare for them, all the hallmarks. It's still being examined, of course, but we're pretty sure.'

'And the deceased?'

'No clues yet. I suppose he'll be reported missing sooner or later. We'll leave that side of things to you.'

'Gosh, thanks.' Rebus waited for his sarcasm to penetrate, then, quickly: 'How does Dean get on with his daughter?'

Matthews was caught off-guard by the question. He blinked twice, three times, then glanced at his wristwatch.

'All right, I suppose,' he said at last, making show of scratching a mark from his cuff. 'I can't see what ... Look, Inspector, as I say, we'll keep you fully informed. But meantime –'

'Keep out of your hair?'

'If you want to put it like that.' Matthews stood up. 'Now I really must be getting back –'

'To London?'

Matthews smiled at the eagerness in Rebus's voice. 'To Barnton. Don't worry, Inspector, the more *you* keep out of *my* hair, the quicker I can get out of yours. Fair enough?' He shot a hand out towards Rebus, who returned the almost painful grip.

'Fair enough,' said Rebus. He ushered Matthews from the room and closed the door again, then returned to his seat. He slouched as best he could in the hard, uncomfortable chair and put his feet up on the desk, examining his scuffed shoes. He tried to feel like Sam Spade, but failed. His legs soon began to ache and he slid them from the surface of the desk. The coincidences in Dashiell Hammett had nothing on the coincidence of someone nicking a car seconds before it exploded. Someone must have been watching, ready to detonate the device. But if they were watching, how come they didn't spot that Dean, the intended victim, wasn't the one to drive off?

Either there was more to this than met the eye, or else there was less. Rebus was wary – very wary. He'd already made far too many prejudgments, had already been proved wrong too many times. Keep an open mind, that was the secret. An open mind and an inquiring one. He nodded his head slowly, his eyes on the door.

'Fair enough,' he said quietly. 'I'll keep out of your hair, Mr Matthews, but that doesn't necessarily mean I'm leaving the barber's.'

The Claymore might not have been Barnton's most salubrious establishment, but it was as Princes Street's Caledonian Hotel in comparison with the places Rebus visited that evening. He began with the merely seedy bars, the ones where each quiet voice seemed to contain a lifetime's resentment, and then moved downwards, one rung of the ladder at a time. It was slow work; the bars tended to be in a ring around Edinburgh, sometimes on the outskirts or in the distant housing schemes, sometimes nearer the centre than most of the population would dare to think.

Rebus hadn't made many friends in his adult life, but he had his network of contacts and he was as proud of it as any grandparent would be of their extended family. They were like cousins, these contacts; mostly they knew each other, at least by reputation, but Rebus never spoke to one about another, so that the extent of the chain could only be guessed at. There were those of his colleagues who, in Major Dean's words, added two and two, then multiplied by ten. John Rebus, it was reckoned, had as big a net of 'snitches' as any copper on the force bar none.

It took four hours and an outlay of over forty pounds before Rebus started to catch a glimpse of a result. His basic question, though couched in vague and imprecise terms, was simple: have any car thieves vanished off the face of the earth since yesterday?

One name was uttered by three very different people in three distinct parts of the city: Brian Cant. The name meant little to Rebus.

'It wouldn't,' he was told. 'Brian only shifted across here

from the west a year or so ago. He's got form from when he was a nipper, but he's grown smart since then. When the Glasgow cops started sniffing, he moved operations.' The detective listened, nodded, drank a watered-down whisky, and said little. Brian Cant grew from a name into a description, from a description into a personality. But there was something more.

'You're not the only one interested in him,' Rebus was told in a bar in Gorgie. 'Somebody else was asking questions a wee while back. Remember Jackie Hanson?'

'He used to be CID, didn't he?'

'That's right, but not any more …'

Not just any old banger for Brian Cant: he specialised in 'quality motors'. Rebus eventually got an address: a third-floor tenement flat near Powderhall race-track. A young man answered the door. His name was Jim Cant, Brian's younger brother. Rebus saw that Jim was scared, nervous. He chipped away at the brother quickly, explaining that he was there because he thought Brian might be dead. That he knew all about Cant's business, but that he wasn't interested in pursuing this side of things, except insofar as it might shed light on the death. It took a little more of this, then the brother opened up.

'He said he had a customer interested in a car,' Jim Cant explained. 'An Irishman, he said.'

'How did he know the man was Irish?'

'Must have been the voice. I don't think they met. Maybe they did. The man was interested in a specific car.'

'A red Jaguar?'

'Yeah, convertible. Nice cars. The Irishman even knew where there was one. It seemed a cinch, that's what Brian kept saying. A cinch.'

'He didn't think it would be hard to steal?'

'Five seconds' work, that's what he kept saying. I thought it sounded too easy. I told him so.' He bent over in his chair, grabbing at his knees and sinking his head between them. 'Ach, Brian, what the hell have you done?'

Rebus tried to comfort the young man as best he could with brandy and tea. He drank a mug of tea himself, wandering through the flat, his mind thrumming. Was he blowing things up out of all proportion? Maybe. He'd made mistakes before, not so much errors of judgment as errors of jumping the gun. But there was something about all of this ... Something.

'Do you have a photo of Brian?' he asked as he was leaving. 'A recent one would be best.' Jim Cant handed him a holiday snap.

'We went to Crete last summer,' he explained. 'It was magic.' Then, holding the door open for Rebus: 'Don't I have to identify him or something?'

Rebus thought of the scrapings which were all that remained of what may or may not have been Brian Cant. He shook his head. 'I'll let you know,' he said. 'If we need you, we'll let you know.'

The next day was Sunday, day of rest. Rebus rested in his car, parked fifty yards or so along the road from the gates to West Lodge. He put his radio on, folded his arms and sank down into the driver's seat. This was more like it. The Hollywood private eye on a stakeout. Only in the movies, a stakeout could be whittled away to a few minutes' footage. Here, it was measured in a slow ticking of seconds ... minutes ... quarter hours.

Eventually, the gates opened and a figure hurried out, fairly trotting along the pavement as though released from bondage. Jacqueline Dean was wearing a denim jacket, short black skirt and thick black tights. A beret sat awkwardly on her cropped dark hair and she pressed the palm of her hand to it from time to time to stop it sliding off altogether. Rebus locked his car before following her. He kept to the other side of the road, wary not so much from fear that she might spot him but because C13 might have put a tail on her, too.

She stopped at the local newsagent's first and came out heavy-laden with Sunday papers. Rebus, making to cross the road, a Sunday-morning stroller, studied her face. What was the expression he'd thought of the first time he'd seen her? Yes, *moping*. There was still something of that in her liquid eyes, the dark shadows beneath. She was making for the corner shop now. Doubtless she would appear with rolls or bacon or butter or milk. All the things Rebus seemed to find himself short of on a Sunday, no matter how hard he planned.

He felt in his jacket pockets, but found nothing of comfort there, just the photograph of Brian Cant. The window of the corner shop, untouched by the blast, contained a dozen or so personal ads, felt-tipped onto plain white postcards. He glanced at these, and past them, through the window itself to where Jacqueline was making her purchases. Milk and rolls: elementary, my dear Conan Doyle. Waiting for her change, she half-turned her head towards the window. Rebus concentrated on the postcards. 'Candy, Masseuse' vied for attention with 'Pram and carry-cot for sale', 'Babysitting considered', and 'Lada, seldom used'. Rebus was smiling, almost despite himself, when the door of the shop tinkled open.

'Jacqueline?' he said. She turned towards him. He was holding open his ID. 'Mind if I have a word, Miss Dean?'

Major Dean was pouring himself a glass of Irish whiskey when the drawing-room door opened.

'Mind if I come in?' Rebus's words were directed not at Dean but at Matthews, who was seated in a chair by the window, one leg crossed over the other, hands gripping the arm-rests. He looked like a nervous businessman on an airplane, trying not to let his neighbour see his fear.

'Inspector Rebus,' he said tonelessly. 'I thought I could feel my scalp tingle.'

Rebus was already in the room. He closed the door behind him. Dean gestured with the decanter, but Rebus shook his head.

'How did you get in?' Matthews asked.

'Miss Dean was good enough to escort me through the gate. You've changed the guard detail again. She told them I was a friend of the family.'

Matthews nodded. 'And are you, Inspector? Are you a friend of the family?'

'That depends on what you mean by friendship.'

Dean had seated himself on the edge of his chair, steadying the glass with both hands. He didn't seem quite the figure he had been on the day of the explosion. A reaction, Rebus didn't doubt. There had been a quiet euphoria on the day; now came the aftershock.

'Where's Jacqui?' Dean asked, having paused with the glass to his lips.

'Upstairs,' Rebus explained. 'I thought it would be better if she didn't hear this.'

Matthews' fingers plucked at the arm-rests. 'How much does she know?'

'Not much. Not yet. Maybe she'll work it out for herself.'

'So, Inspector, we come to the reason why you're here.'

'I'm here,' Rebus began, 'as part of a murder inquiry. I thought that's why you were here, too, Mr Matthews. Maybe I'm wrong. Maybe you're here to cover up rather than bring to light.'

Matthews' smile was momentary. But he said nothing.

'I didn't go looking for the culprits,' Rebus went on. 'As you said, Mr Matthews, that was *your* department. But I did wonder who the victim was. The accidental victim, as I thought. A young car thief called Brian Cant, that would be my guess. He stole cars to order. A client asked him for a red open-top Jag, even told him where he might find one. The client told him about Major Dean. Very specifically about Major Dean, right down to the fact that every day he'd nip into the wine-shop on the main street.' Rebus turned to Dean. 'A bottle of Irish a day, is it, sir?'

Dean merely shrugged and drained his glass.

'Anyway, that's what your daughter told me. So all Brian Cant had to do was wait near the wine-shop. You'd get out of your car, leave it running, and while you were in the shop he could drive the car away. Only it bothered me that the client — Cant's brother tells me he spoke with an Irish accent — knew so much, making it easy for Cant. What was stopping this person from stealing the car himself?'

'And the answer came to you?' Matthews suggested, his voice thick with irony.

Rebus chose to avoid his tone. He was still watching Dean. 'Not straight away, not even then. But when I came to the house, I couldn't help noticing that Miss Dean seemed a bit strange. Like she was waiting for a phone call from someone and that someone had let her down. It's easy to be specific now, but at the time it just struck me as odd. I asked her about it this morning and she admitted it's because she's been jilted. A man she'd been seeing, and seeing regularly, had suddenly stopped calling. I asked her about him, but she couldn't be very helpful. They never went to his flat, for example. He drove a flashy car and had plenty of money, but she was vague about what he did for a living.'

Rebus took a photograph from his pocket and tossed it into Dean's lap. Dean froze, as though it were some hair-trigger grenade.

'I showed her a photograph of Brian Cant. Yes, that was the name of her boyfriend — Brian Cant. So you see, it was small wonder she hadn't heard from him.'

Matthews rose from the chair and stood before the window itself, but nothing he saw there seemed to please him, so he turned back into the room. Dean had found the courage to lift the photograph from his leg and place it on the floor. He got up too, and made for the decanter.

'For Christ's sake,' Matthews hissed, but Dean poured regardless.

Rebus's voice was level. 'I always thought it was a bit of a coincidence, the car being stolen only seconds before exploding. But then the IRA use remote control devices, don't they? So that someone in the vicinity could have triggered the bomb any time they liked. No need for all these long-term timers and what have you. I was in the SAS once myself.'

Matthews raised an eyebrow. 'Nobody told me that,' he said, sounding impressed for the first time.

'So much for Intelligence, eh?' Rebus answered. 'Speaking of which, you told me that Major Dean here was in Intelligence. I think I'd go further. Covert operations, that sort of thing? Counter–intelligence, subversion?'

'Now you're speculating, Inspector.'

Rebus shrugged. 'It doesn't really matter. What matters is that someone had been spying on Brian Cant, an ex-policeman called Jackie Hanson. He's a private detective these days. He won't say anything about his clients, of course, but I think I can put two and two together without multiplying the result. He was working for you, Major Dean, because you were interested in Brian Cant. Jacqueline was serious about him, wasn't she? So much so that she might have forsaken university. She tells me they were even talking of moving in together. You didn't want her to leave. When you found out what Cant did for a ... a living, I suppose you'd call it, you came up with a plan.' Rebus was enjoying himself now, but tried to keep the pleasure out of his voice.

'You contacted Cant,' he went on, 'putting on an Irish accent. Your Irish accent is probably pretty good, isn't it,

Major? It would need to be, working in counter-intelligence. You told him all about a car – your car. You offered him a lot of money if he'd steal it for you and you told him precisely when and where he might find it. Cant was greedy. He didn't think twice.' Rebus noticed that he was sitting very comfortably in his own chair, whereas Dean looked ... the word that sprang to mind was 'rogue'. Matthews, too, was sparking internally, though his surface was all metal sheen, cold bodywork.

'You'd know how to make a bomb, that goes without saying. Wouldn't you, Major? Know thine enemy and all that. Like I say, I was in the SAS myself. What's more, you'd know how to make an IRA device, or one that looked like the work of the IRA. The remote was in your pocket. You went into the shop, bought your whiskey, and when you heard the car being driven off, you simply pressed the button.'

'Jacqueline.' Dean's voice was little more than a whisper. 'Jacqueline.' He rose to his feet, walked softly to the door and left the room. He appeared to have heard little or nothing of Rebus's speech. Rebus felt a pang of disappointment and looked towards Matthews, who merely shrugged.

'You cannot, of course, prove any of this, Inspector.'

'If I put my mind to it I can.'

'Oh, I've no doubt, no doubt.' Matthews paused. 'But will you?'

'He's mad, you've got to see that.'

'Mad? Well, he's unstable. Ever since his wife ...'

'No reason for him to murder Brian Cant.' Rebus helped himself to a whisky now, his legs curiously shaky. 'How long have you known?'

Matthews shrugged again. 'He tried a similar trick in Germany, apparently. It didn't work that time. So what do we do now? Arrest him? He'd be unfit to plead.'

'However it happens,' Rebus said, 'he's got to be made safe.'

'Absolutely.' Matthews was nodding agreement. He came to the sideboard. 'A hospital, somewhere he can be treated. He was a good soldier in his day. I've read his record. A good soldier. Don't worry, Inspector Rebus, he'll be "made safe" as you put it. He'll be taken care of.' A hand landed on Rebus's forearm. 'Trust me.'

Rebus trusted Matthews – about as far as he could spit into a Lothian Road headwind. He had a word with a reporter friend, but the man wouldn't touch the story. He passed Rebus on to an investigative journalist who did some ferreting, but there was little or nothing to be found. Rebus didn't know Dean's real name. He didn't know Matthews' first name or rank or even, to be honest, that he had been C13 at all. He might have been Army, or have inhabited that indefinite smear of operations somewhere between Army, Secret Service and Special Branch.

By the next day, Dean and his daughter had left West Lodge and a fortnight later it appeared in the window of an estate agent on George Street. The asking price seemed surprisingly low, if your tastes veered towards *The Munsters*. But the house would stay in the window for a long time to come.

Dean haunted Rebus's dreams for a few nights, no more. But how did you make safe a man like that? The Army had designed a weapon and that weapon had become mis-adjusted, its sights all wrong. You could dismantle a weapon. You could dismantle a man, too, come to that. But each and every piece was still as lethal as the whole. Rebus put aside fiction, put aside Hammett and the rest and of an evening read psychology books instead. But then they too, in their way, were fiction, weren't they? And so, too, in time became the case that was not a case of the man who had never been.

Being Frank

It wasn't easy, being Frank.

That's what everybody called him, when they weren't calling him a dirty old tramp or a scrounger or a layabout. Frank, they called him. Only the people at the hostel and at the Social Security bothered with his full name: Francis Rossetti Hyslop. Rossetti, he seemed to remember, not after the painter but after his sister the poet, Christina. Most often, a person – a person in authority – would read that name from the piece of paper they were holding and then look up at Frank, not quite in disbelief, but certainly wondering how he'd come so low.

He couldn't tell them that he was climbing higher all the time. That he preferred to live out of doors. That his face was weatherbeaten, not dirty. That a plastic bag was a convenient place to keep his possessions. He just nodded and shuffled his feet instead, the shuffle which had become his trademark.

'Here he comes,' his companions would cry. 'Here comes The Shuffler!' Alias Frank, alias Francis Rossetti Hyslop.

He spent much of the spring and autumn in Edinburgh. Some said he was mad, leaving in the summer months. That, after all, was when the pickings were richest. But he didn't like to bother the tourists, and besides, summer was for travelling. He usually walked north, through Fife and into Kinross or Perthshire, setting up camp by the side of a loch or up in the hills. And when he got bored, he'd move on. He was seldom moved on by gamekeepers or the police. Some of them he knew of old, of course. But others he encountered seemed to regard him more and more as some rare species, or, as one had actually said, a 'national monument'.

It was true, of course. Tramp meant to walk and that's what tramps used to do. The term 'gentleman of the road' used to be accurate. But the tramp was being replaced by the beggar: young, fit men who didn't move from the city and who were unrelenting in their search for spare change. That had never been Frank's way. He had his regulars of course, and often he only had to sit on a bench in The Meadows, a huge grassy plain bordered by tree-lined paths, and wait for the money to appear in his lap.

That's where he was when he heard the two men talking. It was a bright day, a lunchtime and there were few spaces to be had on the meagre supply of Meadows benches. Frank was sitting on one, arms folded, eyes closed, his legs stretched out in front of him with one foot crossed over the other. His three carrier bags were on the ground beside him, and his hat lay across his legs – not because he was hot especially, but because you never knew who might drop a coin in while you were dozing, or pretending to doze.

Maybe his was the only bench free. Maybe that's why the men sat down beside him. Well, 'beside him' was an exaggeration. They squeezed themselves onto the furthest edge of the bench, as far from him as possible. They couldn't be comfortable, squashed up like that and the thought brought a moment's smile to Frank's face.

But then they started to talk, not in a whisper but with voices lowered. The wind, though, swept every word into Frank's right ear. He tried not to tense as he listened, but it was difficult. Tried not to move, but his nerves were jangling.

'It's war,' one said. 'A council of war.'

War? He remembered reading in a newspaper recently about terrorists. Threats. A politician had said something about vigilance. Or was it vigilantes? A council of war: it sounded ominous. Maybe they were teasing him, trying to scare him from the bench so that they could have it for themselves. But he didn't think so. They were speaking in undertones; they didn't think he could hear. Or maybe they simply knew that it didn't matter whether an old tramp heard them or not. Who would believe him?

This was especially true in Frank's case. Frank believed that there was a worldwide conspiracy. He didn't know who was behind it, but he could see its tentacles stretching out across the globe. Everything was connected, that was the secret. Wars were connected by arms manufacturers, the same arms manufacturers who made the guns used in robberies, who made the guns used by crazy people in America when they went on the rampage in a shopping-centre or hamburger restaurant. So already you had a connection between hamburgers and dictators. Start from there and the thing just grew and grew.

And because Frank had worked this out, he wondered from time to time if *they* were after him. The dictators, the arms industry, or maybe even the people who made the buns for the hamburger chains. Because he *knew*. He wasn't crazy; he was sure of that.

'If I was,' he told one of his regulars, 'I wouldn't wonder if I was or not, would I?'

And she'd nodded, agreeing with him. She was a student at the university. A lot of students became regulars. They lived in Tollcross, Marchmont, Morningside, and had to pass through The Meadows on their way to the university buildings in George Square. She was studying psychology, and she told Frank something.

'You've got what they call an active fantasy life.'

Yes, he knew that. He made up lots of things, told himself stories. They whiled away the time. He pretended he'd been an RAF pilot, a spy, minor royalty, a slave-trader in Africa, a poet in Paris. But he *knew* he was making all these stories up, just as he knew that there really was a conspiracy.

And these two men were part of it.

'Rhodes,' one of them was saying now.

A council of war in Rhodes. So there was a Greek connection, too. Well, that made sense. He remembered stories about the generals and their junta. The terrorists were using Greece as their base. And Edinburgh was called the 'Athens of the north'. Yes! Of course! That's why they were basing themselves in Edinburgh too. A symbolic gesture. Had to be.

But who would believe him? That was the problem, being Frank. He'd told so many stories in the past, given the police so much information about the conspiracy, that now they just laughed at him and sent him on his way. Some of them thought he was looking for a night in the cells and once or twice they'd even obliged, despite his protests.

No, he didn't want to spend another night locked up. There was only one thing for it. He'd follow the men and see what he could find. Then he'd wait until tomorrow. They were talking about tomorrow, too, as if it was the start of their campaign. Well, tomorrow was Sunday and with a bit of luck if Frank hung around The Meadows, he'd bump into another of his regulars, one who might know exactly what to do.

Sunday morning was damp, blustery. Not the sort of day for a constitutional. This was fine by John Rebus: it meant there'd be fewer people about on Bruntsfield Links. Fewer men chipping golf-balls towards his head with a wavering cry of 'Fore!' Talk about crazy golf! He knew the Links had been used for this purpose for years and years, but all the same there were so many paths cutting through that it was a miracle no one had been killed.

He walked one circuit of the Links, then headed as usual

across Melville Drive and into The Meadows. Sometimes he'd stop to watch a kickabout. Other times, he kept his head down and just walked, hoping for inspiration. Sunday was too close to Monday for his liking and Monday always meant a backlog of work. Thinking about it never did any good, of course, but he found himself thinking of little else.

'Mr Rebus!'

But then The Meadows offered other distractions, too.

'Mr Rebus!'

'Hello, Frank.'

'Sit yourself down.'

Rebus lowered himself onto the bench. 'You look excited about something.'

Frank nodded briskly. Though he was seated, he shuffled his feet on the earth, making little dance movements. Then he looked around him, as though seeking interlopers.

Oh no, thought Rebus, here we go again.

'War,' Frank whispered. 'I heard two men talking about it.'

Rebus sighed. Talking to Frank was like reading one of the Sunday rags – except sometimes the stories *he* told were more believable. Today didn't sound like one of those days.

'Talking about war? Which war?'

'Terrorism, Mr Rebus. Has to be. They've had a council of war at Rhodes. That's in Greece.'

'They were Greek, were they?'

Frank wrinkled his face. 'I don't think so. I can give you a description of them though. They were both wearing suits. One was short and bald, the other one was young, taller, with black hair.'

'You don't often see international terrorists wearing suits these days, do you?' Rebus commented. Actually, he thought to himself, that's a lie: they're becoming more smartly dressed all the time.

In any case, Frank had an answer ready. 'Need a disguise though, don't they? I followed them.'

'Did you?' A kickabout was starting nearby. Rebus concentrated on the kick-off. He liked Frank, but there were times ...

'They went to a bed and breakfast near the Links.'

'Did they now?' Rebus nodded slowly.

'And they said it was starting *today*. Today, Mr Rebus.'

'They don't hang about, do they? Anything else?'

Frank frowned, thinking. 'Something about lavatories, or laboratories. Must have been laboratories, mustn't it? And money, they talked about that. Money they needed to set it up. That's about it.'

'Well, thanks for letting me know, Frank. I'll keep my ears open, see if I can hear any whispers. But listen, don't go following people in future. It could be dangerous, understand?'

Frank appeared to consider this. 'I see what you mean,' he said at last, 'but I'm tougher than I look, Mr Rebus.'

Rebus was standing now. 'Well, I'd better be getting along.' He slipped his hands into his pockets. The right hand emerged again holding a pound note. 'Here you go, Frank.' He began to hand the money over, then withdrew it again. Frank knew what was coming and grinned.

'Just one question,' Rebus said, as he always did. 'Where do you go in the winter?'

It was a question a lot of his cronies asked him. 'Thought you were dead,' they'd say each spring as he came walking back into their lives. His reply to Rebus was the same as ever: 'Ah, that would be telling, Mr Rebus. That's *my* secret.'

The money passed from one hand to the other and Rebus sauntered off towards Jawbone Walk, kicking a stone in front of him. Jawbone because of the whale's jawbone which made an arch at one end of the path. Frank knew that. Frank knew lots of things. But he knew, too, that

Rebus hadn't believed him. Well, more fool him. For over a year now they'd played this little game: where did Frank go in the winter? Frank wasn't sure himself why he didn't just say, I go to my sister's place in Dunbar. Maybe because it was the truth. Maybe because it *was* a secret.

Rebus looked to him like a man with secrets, too. Maybe one day Rebus would set out for a walk and never return home, would just keep on walking the way Frank himself had done. What was it the girl student had said?

'Sometimes I think we're *all* gentlemen of the road. It's just that most of us haven't got the courage to take that first step.'

Nonsense: that first step was the easiest. It was the hundredth, the thousandth, the millionth that was hard. But not as hard as going back, never as hard as that.

Rebus had counted the steps up to his second-floor flat many, many times. It always added up to the same number. So how come with the passing years there seemed to be more? Maybe it was the height of each step that was changing. Own up, John. For once, own up: it's *you* that's changing. You're growing older and stiffer. You never used to pause on the first-floor landing, never used to linger outside Mrs Cochrane's door, breathing in that smell unique to blackcurrant bushes and cat-pee.

How could one cat produce that amount of odour? Rebus had seen it many a time: a fat, smug-looking creature with hard eyes. He'd caught it on his own landing, turning guiltily to look at him before sprinting for the next floor up. But it was inside Mrs Cochrane's door just now. He could hear it mewling, clawing at the carpet, desperate to be outside. He wondered. Maybe Mrs Cochrane was ill? He'd noticed that recently her brass nameplate had become tarnished. She wasn't bothering to polish it any more. How old was she anyway? She seemed to have come with the tenement, almost as if they'd constructed the thing around her. Mr and Mrs Costello on the top floor had been here nigh-on twenty-five years, but they said she'd been here when they arrived. Same brass nameplate on her door. Different cat, of course, and a husband, too. Well, he'd been dead by the time Rebus and his wife – now ex-wife – had moved here, what, was it ten years ago now?

Getting old, John. Getting old. He clamped his left hand onto the bannister and somehow managed the last flight of steps to his door.

He started a crossword in one of the newspapers, put some jazz on the hi-fi, drank a pot of tea. Just another Sunday. Day of rest. But he kept catching glimpses of the week ahead. No good. He made another pot of tea and this time added a dollop of J&B to the mixture in his mug. Better. And then, naturally, the doorbell rang.

Jehovah's Witnesses. Well, Rebus had an answer ready for them. A friend in the know had said that Roman Catholics are taught how to counter the persuasive arguments of the JWs. Just tell them you're a Catholic and they'll go away.

'I'm Catholic,' he said. They didn't go away. There were two of them, dressed in dark suits. The younger one stood a little behind the older one. This didn't matter, since he was a good foot taller than his elder. He was holding a briefcase. The chief, however, held only a piece of paper. He was frowning, glancing towards this. He looked at Rebus, sizing him up, then back to the paper. He didn't appear to have heard what Rebus said.

'I'm Catholic,' Rebus repeated, but hollowly.

The man shook his head. Maybe they were foreign missionaries, come to convert the heathen. He consulted his scrap of paper again.

'I think this is the wrong address,' he said. 'There isn't a Mr Bakewell here?'

'Bakewell?' Rebus started to relax. A simple mistake; they weren't JWs. They weren't salesmen or cowboy builders or tinkers. Simply, they'd got the wrong flat. 'No,' he said. 'No Mr Bakewell here. And his tart's not here either.'

Oh, they laughed at that. Laughed louder than Rebus had expected. They were still laughing as they made their apologies and started back downstairs. Rebus watched them until they were out of sight. He'd stopped laughing almost before they'd begun. He checked that his keys were in his pocket, then slammed shut his door – but with himself still out on the landing.

Their footsteps sent sibilant echoes up towards the skylight. What was it about them? If pressed, he couldn't have said. There was just *something*. The way the smaller, older man had seemed to weigh him up in a moment, then mentioned Bakewell. The way the younger man had laughed so heartily, as if it were such a release. A release of what? Tension, obviously.

The footsteps had stopped. Outside Mrs Cochrane's door. Yes, that was the ting-ting-ting of her antiquated doorbell, the kind you pulled, tightening and releasing the spring on a bell inside the door. The door which was now being pulled open. The older man spoke.

'Mrs Cochrane?' Well, they'd got that name right. But then it was on her nameplate, wasn't it? *Anyone* could have guessed at it.

'Aye.' Mrs Cochrane, Rebus knew, was not unique in making this sound not only questioning but like a whole sentence. Yes, I'm Mrs Cochrane, and who might you be and what do you want?

'Councillor Waugh.'

Councillor! No, no, there was no problem: Rebus had paid his Poll Tax, always put his bin-bags out the night before, never earlier. They might be after Bakewell, but Rebus was in the clear.

'It's about the roadworks.'

'Roadworks?' echoed Mrs Cochrane.

Roadworks? thought Rebus.

'Yes, roadworks. Digging up the roads. You made a complaint about the roads. I've come to talk to you about it.'

'Roadworks? Here, you mean?'

He was patient, Rebus had to grant him that. 'That's right, Mrs Cochrane. The road outside.'

There was a bit more of this, then they all went indoors to talk over Mrs Cochrane's grievances. Rebus opened his own door and went in, too. Then, realising, he slapped his hand against his head. These were the two men Shuffling Frank had been talking about! Of course they were, only Frank had misheard: council of war was Councillor Waugh; Rhodes was roads. What else had Frank said? Something about money: well, that might be the money for the repairs. That it was all planned to start on Sunday: and here they were, on Sunday, ready to talk to the residents about roadworks.

What roadworks? The road outside was clear, and Rebus hadn't heard any gossip concerning work about to start. Something else Frank had heard them say. Lavatories or laboratories. Of course, his own cherished conspiracy theory had made him plump for 'laboratories', but what if he'd misheard again? Where did lavatories fit into the scheme? And if, as seemed certain, these were the two men, what was a local councillor doing staying at a bed and breakfast? Maybe he owned it, of course. Maybe it was run by his wife.

Rebus was a couple of paces further down his hall when it hit him. He stopped dead. Slow, John, slow. Blame the whisky, maybe. And Jesus, wasn't it so obvious when you thought of it? He went back to his door opened it quietly, and slipped out onto the landing.

There was no such thing as silent movement on an Edinburgh stairwell. The sound of shoe on stone, a sound like sandpaper at work, was magnified and distorted, bouncing off the walls upwards and downwards. Rebus slipped off his shoes and left them on his landing, then started downstairs. He listened outside Mrs Cochrane's door. Muffled voices from the living-room. The layout of her flat was the same as Rebus's own: a long hallway off which were half a dozen doors, the last of which – actually around a corner – led to the living-room. He crouched down and pushed open the letterbox. The cat was just inside the door and it swiped at him with its paw. He let the hinge fall back.

Then he tried the doorhandle, which turned. The door opened. The cat swept past him and down the stairs. Rebus began to feel that the odds were going his way. The door was open just wide enough to allow him to squeeze inside. Open it an inch or two further, he knew, and it creaked with the almightiest groan. He tiptoed into the hallway. Councillor Waugh's voice boomed from the living-room.

'Bowel trouble. Terrible in a man so young.'

Yes, he'd no doubt be explaining why his assistant was taking so long in the lavatory: that was the excuse they always made. Well, either that or a drink of water. Rebus passed the toilet. The door wasn't locked and the tiny closet was empty. He pushed open the next door along – Mrs Cochrane's bedroom: The young man was closing the wardrobe doors.

'Well,' said Rebus, 'I hope you didn't think *that* was the toilet.'

The man jerked around. Rebus filled the doorway. There was no way past him; the only way to get out was to go through him, and that's what the man tried, charging at the doorway, head low. Rebus stood back a little, giving himself room and time, and brought his knee up hard, aiming for the bridge of the nose but finding mouth instead. Well, it was an imprecise science, wasn't it? The man flew backwards like a discarded ragdoll and fell onto the bed. Flat out, to Rebus's satisfaction.

They'd heard the noise of course, and the 'councillor' was already on his way. But he, too, would need to get past Rebus to reach the front door. He stopped short. Rebus nodded slowly.

'Very wise,' he said. 'Your colleague's going to need some new teeth when he wakes up. I'm a police officer by the way. And you, "councillor", are under arrest.'

'Arresting the councillor?' This from Mrs Cochrane, who had appeared in the hall.

'He's no more a councillor than I am, Mrs Cochrane. He's a conman. His partner's been raking through your bedroom.'

'What?' She went to look.

'Bakewell,' Rebus said, smiling. They would try the same ruse at every door where they didn't fancy their chances. Sorry, wrong address, and on to the next potential sucker until they found someone old enough or gullible enough. Rebus was trying to remember if Mrs Cochrane had a telephone. Yes, there was one in her living-room, wasn't there? He gestured to his prisoner.

'Let's go back into the living-room,' he said. Rebus could call the station from there ...

Mrs Cochrane was back beside him. 'Blood on my good quilt,' she muttered. Then she saw that Rebus was in his stocking-soles. 'You'll get chilblains, son,' she said. 'Mark my words. You should take better care of yourself. Living on your own like that. You need somebody to look after you. Mark my words. He told me he was a councillor. Would you credit it? And me been wanting to talk to them for ages about the dogs' mess on the Links.'

'Hello, Shuffler.'

'Mr Rebus! Day off is it? Don't usually see you around here during the week.'

Frank was back on his bench, a newspaper spread out on his lap. One of yesterday's papers. It contained a story about some black magic conspiracy in the United States. Wealthy people, it was reckoned, influential people, taking part in orgies and rituals. Yes, and the arms manufacturers would be there, too. That's how they got to know the politicians and the bankers. It all connected.

'No, I'm off to work in a minute. Just thought I'd stop by. Here.' He was holding out a ten-pound note. Frank looked at it suspiciously, moved his hand towards it, and took it. What? Didn't Rebus even want to ask him the question?

'You were right,' Rebus was saying. 'What you told me about those two men, dead right. Well, nearly dead right. Keep your ears open, Frank. And in future, I'll try to keep *my* ears open when you talk to me.'

And then he turned and was walking away, back across the grass towards Marchmont. Frank stared at the money. Ten pounds. Enough to finance another long walk. He needed a long walk to clear his head. Now that they'd had the council of war at Rhodes, the laboratories would be making potions for satanic rituals. They'd put the politicians in a trance, and ... No, no, it didn't bear thinking about.

'Mr Rebus!' he called. 'Mr Rebus! I go to my sister's! She lives in Dunbar! That's where I go in the winter!'

But if the distant figure heard him, it made no sign. Just kept on walking. Frank shuffled his feet. Ten pounds would buy a transistor radio, or a pair of shoes, a jacket, or a new hat, maybe a little camping stove. That was the problem with having money: you ended up with decisions to make. And if you bought anything, where would you put it? He'd need either to ditch something, or to start on another carrier-bag.

That was the problem, being Frank.

Concrete Evidence

'It's amazing what you find in these old buildings,' said the contractor, a middle-aged man in safety helmet and overalls. Beneath the overalls lurked a shirt and tie, the marks of his station. He was the chief, the gaffer. Nothing surprised him any more, not even unearthing a skeleton.

'Do you know,' he went on, 'in my time, I've found everything from ancient coins to a pocket-watch. How old do you reckon he is then?'

'We're not even sure it *is* a he, not yet. Give us a chance, Mr Beesford.'

'Well, when can we start work again?'

'Later on today.'

'Must be gey old though, eh?'

'How do you make that out?'

'Well, it's got no clothes on, has it? They've perished. Takes time for that to happen, plenty of time ...'

Rebus had to concede, the man had a point. Yet the concrete floor beneath which the bones had been found ... *it* didn't look so old, did it? Rebus cast an eye over the cellar again. It was situated a storey or so beneath road-level, in the basement of an old building off the Cowgate. Rebus was often in the Cowgate; the mortuary was just up the road. He knew that the older buildings here were a veritable warren, long narrow tunnels ran here, there and, it seemed, everywhere, semi-cylindrical in shape and just about high enough to stand up in. This present building was being given the full works – gutted, new drainage system, rewiring. They were taking out the floor in the cellar to lay new drains and also because there seemed to be damp – certainly there was a fousty smell to the place – and its cause needed to be found.

They were expecting to find old drains, open drains perhaps. Maybe even a trickle of a stream, something which would lead to damp. Instead, their pneumatic drills found what remained of a corpse, perhaps hundreds of years old. Except, of course, for that concrete floor. It couldn't be more than fifty or sixty years old, could it? Would clothing deteriorate to a visible nothing in so short a time? Perhaps the damp could do that. Rebus found the cellar oppressive. The smell, the shadowy lighting provided by portable lamps, the dust.

But the photographers were finished, and so was the pathologist, Dr Curt. He didn't have too much to report at this stage, except to comment that he preferred it when skeletons were kept in cupboards, not confined to the cellar. They'd take the bones away, along with samples of the earth and rubble around the find, and they'd see what they would see.

'Archaeology's not really my line,' the doctor added. 'It may take me some time to bone up on it.' And he smiled his usual smile.

It took several days for the telephone call to come. Rebus picked up the receiver.

'Hello?'

'Inspector Rebus? Dr Curt here. About our emaciated friend.'

'Yes?'

'Male, five feet ten inches tall, probably been down there between thirty and thirty-five years. His left leg was broken at some time, long before he died. It healed nicely. But the little finger on his left hand had been dislocated and it did *not* heal so well. I'd say it was crooked all his adult life. Perfect for afternoon tea in Morningside.'

'Yes?' Rebus knew damned well Curt was leading up to something. He knew, too, that Curt was not a man to be hurried.

'Tests on the soil and gravel around the skeleton show traces of human tissue, but no fibres or anything which might have been clothing. No shoes, socks, underpants, nothing. Altogether, I'd say he was buried there in the altogether.'

'But did he die there?'

'Can't say.'

'All right, what did he die *of*?'

There was an almost palpable smile in Curt's voice. 'Inspector, I thought you'd never ask. Blow to the skull, a blow of considerable force to the back of the head. Murder, I'd say. Yes, definitely murder.'

There were, of course, ways of tracing the dead, of coming to a near-infallible identification. But the older the crime, the less likely this outcome became. Dental records, for example. They just weren't *kept* in the 50s and 60s the way they are today. A dentist practising then would most probably be playing near-full-time golf by now. And the record of a patient who hadn't been in for his check-up since 1960? Discarded, most probably. Besides, as Dr Curt pointed out, the man's teeth had seen little serious work, a few fillings, a single extraction.

The same went for medical records, which didn't stop Rebus from checking. A broken left leg, a dislocated left pinkie. Maybe some aged doctor would recall? But then again, maybe not. Almost certainly not. The local papers and radio were interested, which was a bonus. They were given what information the police had, but no memories seemed to be jogged as a result.

Curt had said he was no archaeologist; well, Rebus was no historian either. He knew other cases – contemporary cases – were yammering for his attention. The files stacked up on his desk were evidence enough of that. He'd give this one a few days, a few hours of his time. When the dead ends started to cluster around him, he'd drop it and head back for the here and now.

Who owned the building back in the 1950s? That was easy enough to discover: a wine importer and merchant. Pretty much a one-man operation, Hillbeith Vintners had held the premises from 1948 until 1967. And yes, there was a Mr Hillbeith, retired from the trade and living over in Burntisland, with a house gazing out across silver sands to the grey North Sea.

He still had a cellar, and insisted that Rebus have a 'wee taste' from it. Rebus got the idea that Mr Hillbeith liked visitors – a socially acceptable excuse for a drink. He took his time in the cellar (there must have been over 500 bottles in there) and emerged with cobwebs hanging from his cardigan, holding a dusty bottle of something nice. This he opened and sat on the mantelpiece. It would be half an hour or so yet at the very least before they could usefully have a glass.

Mr Hillbeith was, he told Rebus, seventy-four. He'd been in the wine trade for nearly half a century and had 'never regretted a day, not a day, nor even an hour'. Lucky you, Rebus thought to himself.

'Do you remember having that new floor laid in the cellar, Mr Hillbeith?'

'Oh, yes. That particular cellar was going to be for best claret. It was just the right temperature, you see, and there was no vibration from passing buses and the like. But it was damp, had been ever since I'd moved in. So I got a building firm to take a look. They suggested a new floor and some other alterations. It all seemed fairly straightforward and their charges seemed reasonable, so I told them to go ahead.'

'And when was this, sir?'

'1960. The spring of that year. There you are, I've got a

great memory where business matters are concerned.' His small eyes beamed at Rebus through the thick lenses of their glasses. 'I can even tell you how much the work cost me ... and it was a pretty penny at the time. All for nothing, as it turned out. The cellar was still damp, and there was always that *smell* in it, a very unwholesome smell. I couldn't take a chance with the claret, so it became the general stock-room, empty bottles and glasses, packing-cases, that sort of thing.'

'Do you happen to recall, Mr Hillbeith, was the smell there *before* the new floor was put in?'

'Well, certainly there was *a* smell there before the floor was laid, but the smell afterwards was different somehow.' He rose and fetched two crystal glasses from the china cabinet, inspecting them for dust. 'There's a lot of nonsense talked about wine, Inspector. About decanting, the type of glasses you must use and so on. Decanting can help, of course, but I prefer the feel of the bottle. The bottle, after all, is part of the wine, isn't it?' He handed an empty glass to Rebus. 'We'll wait a few minutes yet.'

Rebus swallowed drily. It had been a long drive. 'Do you recall the name of the firm, sir, the one that did the work?'

Hillbeith laughed. 'How could I forget? Abbot & Ford, they were called. I mean, you just don't forget a name like that, do you? Abbot & Ford. You see, it sounds like Abbotsford, doesn't it? A small firm they were, mind. But you may know one of them, Alexander Abbot.'

'Of Abbot Building?'

'The same. He went on to make quite a name for himself, didn't he? Quite a fortune. Built up quite a company, too, but he started out small like most of us do.'

'How small, would you say?'

'Oh, small, small. Just a few men.' He rose and stretched an arm towards the mantelpiece. 'I think this should be ready to taste, Inspector. If you'll hold out your glass –'

Hillbeith poured slowly, deliberately, checking that no

lees escaped into the glass. He poured another slow, generous measure for himself. The wine was reddish-brown. 'Robe and disc not too promising,' he muttered to himself. He gave his glass a shake and studied it. 'Legs not promising either.' He sighed. 'Oh dear.' Finally, Hillbeith sniffed the glass anxiously, then took a swig.

'Cheers,' said Rebus, indulging in a mouthful. A mouthful of vinegar. He managed to swallow, then saw Hillbeith spit back into the glass.

'Oxidisation,' the old man said, sounding cruelly tricked. 'It happens. I'd best check a few more bottles to assess the damage. Will you stay, Inspector?' Hillbeith sounded keen.

'Sorry, sir,' said Rebus, ready with his get-out clause. 'I'm still on duty.'

Alexander Abbot, aged fifty-five, still saw himself as the force behind the Abbot Building Company. There might be a dozen executives working furiously beneath him, but the company had grown from *his* energy and from *his* fury. He was Chairman, and a busy man too. He made this plain to Rebus at their meeting in the executive offices of ABC. The office spoke of business confidence, but then in Rebus's experience this meant little in itself. Often, the more dire straits a company was in, the healthier it tried to look. Still, Alexander Abbot seemed happy enough with life.

'In a recession,' he explained, lighting an overlong cigar, 'you trim your workforce pronto. You stick with regular clients, good payers, and don't take on too much work from clients you don't know. They're the ones who're likely to welch on you or go bust, leaving nothing but bills. Young businesses ... they're always hit hardest in a recession, no back-up you see. Then, when the recession's over for another few years, you dust yourself off and go touting for business again, re-hiring the men you laid off. That's where we've always had the edge over Jack Kirkwall.'

Kirkwall Construction was ABC's main competitor in

the Lowlands, when it came to medium-sized contracts. Doubtless Kirkwall was the larger company. It, too, was run by a 'self-made' man, Jack Kirkwall. A larger-than-life figure. There was, Rebus quickly realised, little love lost between the two rivals.

The very mention of Kirkwall's name seemed to have dampened Alexander Abbot's spirits. He chewed on his cigar like it was a debtor's finger.

'You started small though, didn't you, sir?'

'Oh aye, they don't come much smaller. We were a pimple on the bum of the construction industry at one time.' He gestured to the walls of his office. 'Not that you'd guess it, eh?'

Rebus nodded. 'You were still a small firm back in 1960, weren't you?'

'1960. Let's think. We were just starting out. It wasn't ABC then, of course. Let's see. I think I got a loan from my dad in 1957, went into partnership with a chap called Hugh Ford, another self-employed builder. Yes, that's right. 1960, it was Abbot & Ford. Of course it was.'

'Do you happen to remember working at a wine merchant's in the Cowgate?'

'When?'

'The spring of 1960.'

'A wine merchant's?' Abbot furrowed his brow. 'Should be able to remember that. Long time ago, mind. A wine merchant's?'

'You were laying a new floor in one of his cellars, amongst other work. Hillbeith Vintners.'

'Oh, aye, Hillbeith, it's coming back now. I remember him. Little funny chap with glasses. Gave us a case of wine when the job was finished. Nice of him, but the wine was a bit off as I remember.'

'How many men were working on the job?'

Abbot exhaled noisily. 'Now you're asking. It was over thirty years ago, Inspector.'

'I appreciate that, sir. Would there be any records?'

Abbot shook his head. 'There might have been up to about ten years ago, but when we moved into this place a lot of the older stuff got chucked out. I regret it now. It'd be nice to have a display of stuff from the old days, something we could set up in the reception. But no, all the Abbot & Ford stuff got dumped.'

'So you don't remember how many men were on that particular job? Is there anyone else I could talk to, someone who might –'

'We were small back then, I can tell you that. Mostly using casual labour and part-timers. A job that size, I wouldn't think we'd be using more than three or four men, if that.'

'You don't recall anyone going missing? Not turning up for work, that sort of thing?'

Abbot bristled. 'I'm a stickler for time-keeping, Inspector. If anyone had done a bunk, I'd remember, I'm pretty sure of that. Besides, we were careful about who we took on. No lazy buggers, nobody who'd do a runner halfway through a job.'

Rebus sighed. Here was one of the dead ends. He rose to his feet. 'Well, thanks anyway, Mr Abbot. It was good of you to find time to see me.' The two men shook hands, Abbot rising to his feet.

'Not at all, Inspector. Wish I could help you with your little mystery. I like a good detective story myself.' They were almost at the door now.

'Oh,' said Rebus, 'just one last thing. Where could I find your old partner Mr Ford?'

Abbot's face lost its animation. His voice was suddenly that of an old man. 'Hugh died, Inspector. A boating accident. He was drowned. Hell of a thing to happen. Hell of a thing.'

Two dead ends.

* * *

Mr Hillbeith's telephone call came later that day, while Rebus was ploughing through the transcript of an interview with a rapist. His head felt full of foul-smelling glue, his stomach acid with caffeine.

'Is that Inspector Rebus?'

'Yes, hello, Mr Hillbeith. What can I do for you?' Rebus pinched the bridge of his nose and screwed shut his eyes.

'I was thinking all last night about that skeleton.'

'Yes?' In between bottles of wine, Rebus didn't doubt.

'Well, I was trying to think back to when the work was being done. It might not be much, but I definitely recall that there were four people involved. Mr Abbot and Mr Ford worked on it pretty much full-time, and there were two other men, one of them a teenager, the other in his forties. They worked on a more casual basis.'

'You don't recall their names?'

'No, only that the teenager had a nickname. Everyone called him by that. I don't think I ever knew his real name.'

'Well, thanks anyway, Mr Hillbeith. I'll get back to Mr Abbot and see if what you've told me jogs his memory.'

'Oh, you've spoken to him then?'

'This morning. No progress to report. I didn't realise Mr Ford had died.'

'Ah, well, that's the other thing.'

'What is?'

'Poor Mr Ford. Sailing accident, wasn't it?'

'That's right.'

'Only I remember that, too. You see, that accident happened just after they'd finished the job. They kept talking about how they were going to take a few days off and go fishing. Mr Abbot said it would be their first holiday in years.'

Rebus's eyes were open now. 'How soon was this after they'd finished your floor?'

'Well, directly after, I suppose.'

'Do you remember Mr Ford?'

'Well, he was very quiet. Mr Abbot did all the talking, really. A very quiet man. A hard worker though, I got that impression.'

'Did you notice anything about his hands? A misshapen pinkie?'

'Sorry, Inspector, it *was* a long time ago.'

Rebus appreciated that. 'Of course it was, Mr Hillbeith. You've been a great help. Thank you.'

He put down the receiver. A long time ago, yes, but still murder, still calculated and cold-blooded murder. Well, a path had opened in front of him. Not much of a path perhaps, a bit overgrown and treacherous. Nevertheless ... Best foot forward, John. Best foot forward.

Of course, he kept telling himself, he was still ruling possibilities out rather than ruling them in, which was why he wanted to know a little more about the boating accident. He didn't want to get the information from Alexander Abbot.

Instead, the morning after Hillbeith's phone-call, Rebus went to the National Library of Scotland on George IV Bridge. The doorman let him through the turnstile and he climbed an imposing staircase to the reading room. The woman on the desk filled in a one-day reader's card for him, and showed him how to use the computer. There were two banks of computers, being used by people to find the books they needed. Rebus had to go into the reading room and find an empty chair, note its number and put this on his slip when he'd decided which volume he required. Then he went to his chair and sat, waiting.

There were two floors to the reading room, both enveloped by shelves of reference books. The people working at the long desks downstairs seemed bleary. Just another morning's graft for them; but Rebus found it all fascinating. One person worked with a card index in front of him, to which he referred frequently. Another seemed asleep, head resting on arms. Pens scratched across countless sheets of paper. A few souls, lost for inspiration, merely chewed on their pens and stared at the others around them, as Rebus was doing.

Eventually, his volume was brought to him. It was a bound edition of the *Scotsman*, containing every issue for the months from January to June, 1960. Two thick leather buckles kept the volume closed. Rebus unbuckled these and began to turn the pages.

He knew what he was looking for, and pretty well where to find it, but that didn't stop him browsing through football reports and front page headlines. 1960. He'd been busy trying to lose his virginity and supporting Hearts. Yes, a long time ago.

The story hadn't quite made the front page. Instead, there were two paragraphs on page three. 'Drowning Off Lower Largo.' The victim, Mr Hugh Ford, was described as being twenty-six years of age (a year old than the survivor, Mr Alex Abbot) and a resident of Duddingston, Edinburgh. The men, on a short fishing-holiday, had taken a boat out early in the morning, a boat hired from a local man, Mr John Thomson. There was a squall, and the boat capsized. Mr Abbot, a fair swimmer, had made it back to the shore. Mr Ford, a poor swimmer, had not. Mr Ford was further described as a 'bachelor, a quiet man, shy according to Mr Abbot, who was still under observation at the Victoria Hospital, Kirkcaldy'. There was a little more, but not much. Apparently, Ford's parents were dead, but he had a sister, Mrs Isabel Hammond, somewhere out in Australia.

Why hadn't Abbot mentioned any of this? Maybe he wanted to forget. Maybe it still gave him the occasional bad dream. And of course he would have forgotten all about the Hillbeith contract precisely because this tragedy happened so soon afterwards. So soon. Just the one line of print really bothered Rebus; just that one sentence niggled.

'Mr Ford's body has still not been recovered.'

73

* * *

Records might get lost in time, but not by Fife Police. They sent on what they had, much of it written in fading ink on fragile paper, some of it typed – badly. The two friends and colleagues, Abbot and Ford, had set out on Friday evening to the Fishing-Net Hotel in Largo, arriving late. As arranged, they'd set out early next morning on a boat they'd hired from a local man, John Thomson. The accident had taken place only an hour or so after setting out. The boat was recovered. It had been overturned, but of Ford there was no sign. Inquiries were made. Mr Ford's belongings were taken back to Edinburgh by Mr Abbot, after the latter was released from hospital, having sustained a bump to the head when the boat went over. He was also suffering from shock and exhaustion. Mr Ford's sister, Mrs Isabel Hammond, was never traced.

They had investigated a little further. The business run jointly by Messrs Abbot and Ford now became Mr Abbot's. The case-notes contained a good amount of information and suspicion – between the lines, as it were. Oh yes, they'd investigated Alexander Abbot, but there had been no evidence. They'd searched for the body, had found none. Without a body, they were left with only their suspicions and their nagging doubts.

'Yes,' Rebus said quietly to himself, 'but what if you were looking for the body in the wrong place?' The wrong place at the wrong time. The work on the cellar had ended on Friday afternoon and by Saturday morning Hugh Ford had ceased to exist.

The path Rebus was on had become less overgrown, but it was still rock-strewn and dangerous, still a potential dead-end.

The Fishing-Net Hotel was still in existence, though apparently much changed from its 1960 incarnation. The present owners told Rebus to arrive in time for lunch if he could and it would be on the house. Largo was north of Burntisland but on the same coastline. Alexander Selkirk, the original of Defoe's Robinson Crusoe, had a connection with the fishing village. There was a small statue of him somewhere which Rebus had been shown as a boy (but only after much hunting, he recalled). Largo was picturesque, but then so were most, if not all, of the coastal villages in Fife's 'East Neuk'. But it was not yet quite the height of the tourist season and the customers taking lunch at the Fishing-Net Hotel were businessmen and locals.

It was a good lunch, as picturesque as its surroundings but with a bit more flavour. And afterwards, the owner, an Englishman for whom life in Largo was a long-held dream come true, offered to show Rebus round, including 'the very room your Mr Ford stayed in the night before he died'.

'How can you be sure?'

'I looked in the register.'

Rebus managed not to look too surprised. The hotel had changed hands so often since 1960, he despaired of finding anyone who would remember the events of that weekend.

'The register?'

'Yes, we were left a lot of old stuff when we bought this place. The store-rooms were choc-a-bloc. Old ledgers and what have you going back to the 1920s and 30s. It was easy enough to find 1960.'

Rebus stopped in his tracks. 'Never mind showing me Mr Ford's room, would you mind letting me see that register?'

He sat at a desk in the manager's office with the register open in front of him, while Mr Summerson's finger stabbed the line. 'There you are, Inspector, H. Ford. Signed in at 11.50 p.m., address given as Duddingston. Room number seven.'

It wasn't so much a signature as a blurred scrawl and

75

above it, on a separate line, was Alexander Abbot's own
more flowing signature.

'Bit late to arrive, wasn't it?' commented Rebus.

'Agreed.'

'I don't suppose there's anyone working here nowadays
who worked in the hotel back then?'

Summerson laughed quietly. 'People do retire in this
country, Inspector.'

'Of course, I just wondered.' He remembered the
newspaper story. 'What about John Thomson? Does the
name mean anything to you?'

'Old Jock? Jock Thomson? The fisherman?'

'Probably.'

'Oh, yes, he's still about. You'll almost certainly find him
down by the dockside or else in the Harbour Tavern.'

'Thanks. I'd like to take this register with me if I may?'

Jock Thomson sucked on his pipe and nodded. He looked
the archetype of the 'old salt', from his baggy cord trousers
to his chiselled face and silvery beard. The only departure
from the norm was, perhaps, the Perrier water in front of
him on a table in the Harbour Tavern.

'I like the fizz,' he explained after ordering it, 'and
besides, my doctor's told me to keep off the alcohol. Total
abstinence, he said, total abstinence. Either the booze goes,
Jock, or the pipe does. No contest.'

And he sucked greedily on the pipe. Then complained
when his drink arrived without 'the wee slice of lemon'.
Rebus returned to the bar to fulfil his mission.

'Oh aye,' said Thomson, 'remember it like it was
yesterday. Only there's not much to remember, is there?'

'Why do you say that?'

'Two inexperienced laddies go out in a boat. Boat tips.
End of story.'

'Was the weather going to be bad that morning?'

'Not particularly. But there *was* a squall blew up. Blew

76

up and blew out in a matter of minutes. Long enough though.'

'How did the two men seem?'

'How do you mean?'

'Well, were they looking forward to the trip?'

'Don't know, I never saw them. The younger one, Abbot was it? He phoned to book a boat from me, said they'd be going out early, six or thereabouts. I told him he was daft, but he said there was no need for me to be on the dockside, if I'd just have the boat ready and tell him which one it was. And that's what I did. By the time I woke up that morning, he was swimming for the shore and his pal was food for the fish.'

'So you never actually saw Mr Ford?'

'No, and I only saw the lad Abbot afterwards, when the ambulance was taking him away.'

It was fitting into place almost too easily now. And Rebus thought, sometimes these things are only visible with hindsight, from a space of years. 'I don't suppose,' he ventured, 'you know anyone who worked at the hotel back then?'

'Owner's moved on,' said Thomson, 'who knows where to. It might be that Janice Dryman worked there then. Can't recall if she did.'

'Where could I find her?'

Thomson peered at the clock behind the bar. 'Hang around here ten minutes or so, you'll bump into her. She usually comes in of an afternoon. Meantime, I'll have another of these if you're buying.'

Thomson pushed his empty glass over to Rebus. Rebus, most definitely, was buying.

Miss Dryman – 'never married, never really saw the point' – was in her early fifties. She worked in a gift-shop in town and after her stint finished usually nipped into the Tavern for a soft drink and 'a bit of gossip'. Rebus asked what she would like to drink.

'Lemonade, please,' she said, 'with a drop of whisky in it.' And she laughed with Jock Thomson, as though this were an old and cherished joke between them. Rebus, not used to playing the part of straight-man, headed yet again for the bar.

'Oh yes,' she said, her lips poised above the glass. 'I was working there at the time all right. Chambermaid and general dogsbody, that was me.'

'You wouldn't see them arrive though?'

Miss Dryman looked as though she had some secret to impart. '*Nobody* saw them arrive, I know that for a fact. Mrs Dennis who ran the place back then, she said she'd be buggered if she'd wait up half the night for a couple of fishermen. They knew what rooms they were in and their keys were left at reception.'

'What about the front door?'

'Left unlocked, I suppose. The world was a safer place back then.'

'Aye, you're right there,' added Jock Thomson, sucking on his sliver of lemon.

'And Mr Abbot and Mr Ford knew this was the arrangement?'

'I suppose so. Otherwise it wouldn't have worked, would it?'

So Abbot knew there'd be nobody around at the hotel, not if he left it late enough before arriving.

'And what about in the morning?'

'Mrs Dennis said they were up and out before she knew anything about it. She was annoyed because she'd already cooked the kippers for their breakfast before she realised.'

So nobody saw them in the morning either. In fact ...

'In fact,' said Rebus, 'nobody saw Mr Ford at all. Nobody at the hotel, not you, Mr Thomson, nobody.' Both drinkers conceded this.

'I saw his stuff though,' said Miss Dryman.

'What stuff?'

'In his room, his clothes and stuff. That morning. I didn't know anything about the accident and I went in to clean.'

'The bed had been slept in?'

'Looked like it. Sheets all rumpled. And his suitcase was on the floor, only half unpacked. Not that there was much *to* unpack.'

'Oh?'

'A single change of clothes, I'd say. I remember them because they seemed mucky, you know, not fresh. Not the sort of stuff *I'd* take on holiday with me.'

'What? Like he'd been working in them?'

She considered this. 'Maybe.'

'No point wearing clean clothes for fishing,' Thomson added. But Rebus wasn't listening.

Ford's clothes, the clothes he had been working in while laying the floor. It made sense. Abbot bludgeoned him, stripped him and covered his body in fresh cement. He'd taken the clothes away with him and put them in a case, opening it in the hotel room, ruffling the sheets. Simple, but effective. Effective these past thirty years. The motive? A falling out perhaps, or simple greed. It was a small company, but growing, and perhaps Abbot hadn't wanted to share. Rebus placed a five-pound note on the table.

'To cover the next couple of rounds,' he said, getting to his feet. 'I'd better be off. Some of us are still on duty.'

There were things to be done. He had to speak to his superior, Chief Inspector Lauderdale. And that was for starters. Maybe Ford's Australian sister could be traced this time round. There had to be someone out there who could acknowledge that Ford had suffered from a broken leg in youth, and that he had a crooked finger. So far, Rebus could think of only one person – Alexander Abbot.

Somehow, he didn't think Abbot could be relied on to tell the truth, the whole truth.

Then there was the hotel register. The forensics lab could ply their cunning trade on it. Perhaps they'd be able to say for certain that Ford's signature was merely a bad rendition of Abbot's. But again, he needed a sample of Ford's handwriting in order to substantiate that the signature was not genuine. Who did he know who might possess such a document? Only Alexander Abbot. Or Mr Hillbeith, but Mr Hillbeith had not been able to help.

'No, Inspector, as I told you, it was Mr Abbot who handled all the paperwork, all that side of things. If there is an invoice or a receipt, it will be in his hand, not Mr Ford's. I don't recall ever seeing Mr Ford writing anything.'

No through road.

Chief Inspector Lauderdale was not wholly sympathetic. So far all Rebus had to offer were more suppositions to add to those of the Fife Police at the time. There was no proof that Alexander Abbot had killed his partner. No proof that the skeleton was Hugh Ford. Moreover, there wasn't even much in the way of circumstantial evidence. They could bring in Abbot for questioning, but all he had to do was plead innocence. He could afford a good lawyer; and even bad lawyers weren't stupid enough to let the police probe too deeply.

'We need proof, John,' said Lauderdale, 'concrete evidence. The simplest proof would be that hotel signature. If we prove it's not Ford's, then we have Abbot at that hotel, Abbot in the boat and Abbot shouting that his friend has drowned, *all* without Ford having been there. That's what we need. The rest of it, as it stands, is rubbish. You know that.'

Yes, Rebus knew. He didn't doubt that, given an hour alone with Abbot in a darkened alley, he'd have his confession. But it didn't work like that. It worked through the law. Besides, Abbot's heart might not be too healthy. BUSINESSMAN, 55, DIES UNDER QUESTIONING. No, it had to be done some other way.

The problem was, there *was* no other way. Alexander Abbot was getting away with murder. Or was he? Why did his story have to be false? Why did the body have to be Hugh Ford's? The answer was: because the whole thing seemed to fit. Only, the last piece of the jigsaw had been lost under some sofa or chair a long time ago, so long ago now that it might remain missing forever.

He didn't know why he did it. If in doubt, retrace your steps ... something like that. Maybe he just liked the atmosphere. Whatever, Rebus found himself back in the National Library, waiting at his desk for the servitor to bring him his bound volume of old news. He mouthed the words of 'Yesterday's Papers' to himself as he waited. Then, when the volume appeared, he unbuckled it with ease and pulled open the pages. He read past the April editions, read through into May and June. Football results, headlines – and what was this? A snippet of business news, barely a filler at the bottom right-hand corner of a page. About how the Kirkwall Construction Company was swallowing up a couple of smaller competitors in Fife and Midlothian.

'The 1960s will be a decade of revolution in the building industry,' said Managing Director Mr Jack Kirkwall, 'and Kirkwall Construction aims to meet that challenge through growth and quality. The bigger we are, the better we are. These acquisitions strengthen the company, and they're good news for the workforce, too.'

It was the kind of sentiment which had lasted into the 1980s. Jack Kirkwall, Alexander Abbot's bitter rival. Now there was a man Rebus ought to meet ...

The meeting, however, had to be postponed until the

following week. Kirkwall was in hospital for a minor operation.

'I'm at that age, Inspector,' he told Rebus when they finally met, 'when things go wrong and need treatment or replacing. Just like any bit of well-used machinery.'

And he laughed, though the laughter, to Rebus's ears, had a hollow centre. Kirkwall looked older than his sixty-two years, his skin saggy, complexion wan. They were in his living-room, from where, these days, he did most of his work.

'Since I turned sixty, I've only really wandered into the company headquarters for the occasional meeting. I leave the daily chores to my son, Peter. He seems to be managing.' The laughter this time was self-mocking.

Rebus had suggested a further postponement of the meeting, but when Jack Kirkwall knew that the subject was to be Alexander Abbot, he was adamant that they should go ahead.

'Is he in trouble then?'

'He might be,' Rebus admitted. Some of the colour seemed to reappear in Kirkwall's cheeks and he relaxed a little further into his reclining leather chair. Rebus didn't want to give Kirkwall the story. Kirkwall and Abbot were still business rivals, after all. Still, it seemed, enemies. Given the story, Kirkwall might try some underhand tactic, some rumour in the media, and if it got out that the story originally came from a police inspector, well. Hello, being sued and goodbye, pension.

No, Rebus didn't want that. Yet he did want to know whether Kirkwall knew anything, knew of any reason why Abbot might wish, might *need* to kill Ford.

'Go on, Inspector.'

'It goes back quite a way, sir. 1960, to be precise. Your firm was at that time in the process of expansion.'

'Correct.'

'What did you know about Abbot & Ford?'

Kirkwall brushed the palm of one hand over the knuckles of the other. 'Just that they were growing, too. Of course, they were younger than us, much smaller than us. ABC still is much smaller than us. But they were cocky, they were winning some contracts ahead of us. I had my eye on them.'

'Did you know Mr Ford at all?'

'Oh yes. Really, he was the cleverer of the two men. I've never had much respect for Abbot. But Hugh Ford was quiet, hardworking. Abbot was the one who did the shouting and got the firm noticed.'

'Did Mr Ford have a crooked finger?'

Kirkwall seemed bemused by the question. 'I've no idea,' he said at last. 'I never actually met the man, I merely knew *about* him. Why? Is it important?'

Rebus felt at last that his meandering, narrowing path had come to the lip of a chasm. Nothing for it but to turn back.

'Well,' he said, 'it would have clarified something.'

'You know, Inspector, my company *was* interested in taking Abbot & Ford under our wing.'

'Oh?'

'But then with the accident, that tragic accident. Well, Abbot took control and he wasn't at all interested in any offer we had to make. Downright rude, in fact. Yes, I've always thought that it was such a *lucky* accident so far as Abbot was concerned.'

'How do you mean, sir?'

'I mean, Inspector, that Hugh Ford was on our side. He wanted to sell up. But Abbot was against it.'

So, Rebus had his motive. Well, what did it matter? He was still lacking that concrete evidence Lauderdale demanded.

'... Would it show up from his handwriting?'

Rebus had missed what Kirkwall had been saying. 'I'm sorry, sir, I didn't catch that.'

'I said, Inspector, if Hugh Ford had a crooked finger, would it show from his handwriting?'

'Handwriting?'

'Because I had his agreement to the takeover. He'd written to me personally to tell me. Had gone behind Abbot's back, I suppose. I bet Alex Abbot was mad as hell when he found out about that.' Kirkwall's smile was vibrant now. 'I always thought that accident was a bit too lucky where Abbot was concerned. A bit too neat. No proof though. There was never any proof.'

'Do you still have the letter?'

'What?'

'The letter from Mr Ford, do you still have it?'

Rebus was tingling now, and Kirkwall caught his excitement. 'I never throw anything away, Inspector. Oh yes, I've got it. It'll be upstairs.'

'Can I see it? I mean, can I see it now?'

'If you like,' Kirkwall made to stand up, but paused. '*Is* Alex Abbot in trouble, Inspector?'

'If you've still got that letter from Hugh Ford, then, yes, sir, I'd say Mr Abbot could be in very grave trouble indeed.'

'Inspector, you've made an old man very happy.'

It was the letter against Alex Abbot's word, of course, and he denied everything. But there was enough now for a trial. The entry in the hotel, while it was *possibly* the work of Alexander Abbot was *certainly* not the work of the man who had written the letter to Jack Kirkwall. A search warrant gave the police the powers to look through Abbot's home and the ABC headquarters. A contract, drawn up between Abbot and Ford when the two men had gone into partnership, was discovered to be held in a solicitor's safe. The signature matched that on the letter to Jack Kirkwall. Kirkwall himself appeared in court to give evidence. He seemed to Rebus a different man altogether from the person he'd met previously: sprightly, keening, enjoying life to the full.

From the dock, Alexander Abbot looked on almost reproachfully, as if this were just one more business trick in a life full of them. Life, too, was the sentence of the judge.

Seeing Things

To be honest, if you were going to see Christ anywhere in Edinburgh, the Hermitage was perfect.

Or, to give it its full title, the Hermitage of Braid, named after the Braid Burn which trickled through the narrow, bushy wilderness between Blackford Hill and Braid Hills Road. Across this road, the Hermitage became a golf course, its undulations cultivated and well-trodden, but on sunny weekend afternoons, the Hermitage itself was as wild a place as your imagination wished it to be. Children ran in and out of the trees or threw sticks into the burn. Lovers could be seen hand-in-hand as they tackled the tricky descent from Blackford Hill. Dogs ran sniffing to stump and post, watched, perhaps, by punks seated atop an outcrop. Can would be tipped to mouth, the foam savoured. Picnic parties would debate the spot most sheltered from the breeze.

It was sometimes hard to believe that the place was in Edinburgh, that the main entrance to the Hermitage was just off the busy Comiston Road at the southern reach of Morningside. The protesters – such as they were – had held vigil at these gates for a couple of days, singing songs and handing out their 'No Popery' pamphlets. Occasionally a megaphone would appear, so that they could deliver their rant. A seller of religious nick-nacks and candles had set up his pitch across the road from the protesters, and at a canny distance along the road from them. The megaphone was most often directed towards him, there being no other visible target.

A rant was occurring as Inspector John Rebus arrived. Would the day of judgment be like this, he wondered, accepting a leaflet. Would the loudest voices belong to the saved? *Megaphones will be provided*, he thought to himself as he passed through the gates. He studied the leaflet. No Popery, indeed.

'Why ever not?' And so asking, he crumpled the paper and tossed it into the nearest wastepaper-bin. The voice followed him as though it had a mission and he was it.

'There must be NO idolatry! There is but ONE God and it is HE ye should worship! Do not turn YOUR face to graven IMAGES! The Good Book is the ONLY truth ye NEED!'

Rave on ...

They were a minority of course, far outweighed by the curious who came to see. But they in their turn looked as though they might be outnumbered very soon by the shrine-builders. Rebus liked to think of himself as a Christian, albeit with too many questions and doubts to ally himself with either side, Catholic or Protestant. He could not escape the fact that he had been born a Protestant; but his mother, a religious woman, had died young, and his father had been indifferent.

Rebus hadn't even been aware of any difference between Catholic and Protestant until he'd started school. His pre-schooldays best friend was a Catholic, a boy called Miles Skelly. Come their first day at school, the boys had been split up, sent to schools on different sides of town. Parted like this daily, they soon grew to have new friends and stopped playing together.

That had been Rebus's first lesson in 'the divide'. But he had nothing against Catholics. The Protestant community might call them 'left-footers', but Rebus himself kicked a ball with his left foot. He did, however, mistrust the shrine mentality. It made him uneasy: statues which wept or bled or moved. Sudden visions of the Virgin Mary. A face imprinted on a shroud.

A faith should be just that, Rebus reasoned. And if you held belief, what need had you of miracles, especially ones that seemed more the province of the Magic Circle than of the divine? So the closer he came to the spot itself, the shakier became his legs. There was a tangle of undergrowth, and in front of it a stunted tree. Around this tree had been arranged candles, small statues, photographs, written prayers, flowers, all in the last two or three days. It was quite a transformation. A knot of people knelt nearby, but at a respectful distance. Their heads were bowed in prayer. Others sat, arms out behind them, supporting themselves on the grass. They wore beatific smiles, as though they could hear or see something Rebus couldn't. He listened hard, but heard only whispers of prayer, the distant barking of dogs. He looked, but saw only a tree, though it had to be admitted that the sunlight seemed to catch it in a particularly striking way, picking it out from the undergrowth behind it.

There was a rustling from beyond the tree itself. Rebus moved around the congregation – there was no other word for the gathering – towards the undergrowth, where several police cadets were on their hands and knees, not in worship this time but searching the ground.

'Anything?'

One of the figures straightened up, pressing his fingers into his spine as he exhaled. Rebus could hear the vertebrae crackling.

'Nothing, sir, not a blasted thing.'

'Language, Holmes, language. Remember, this is a holy site.'

Detective Constable Brian Holmes managed a wry smile. He'd been smiling a lot this morning. For once he'd been put in charge and it didn't matter to him that he was in a damp copse, or that he was in charge of a shower of disgruntled cadets, or that he had twigs in his hair. He was in charge. Not even John Rebus could take that away from him.

Except that he could. And did.

'All right,' Rebus said, 'that's enough. We'll have to make do with what we've got. Or rather, what the lab boys have got.'

The cadets rose mercifully to their feet. One or two brushed white chalky powder from their knees, others scraped at dirt and grass stains. 'Well done, lads,' Rebus admitted. 'Not very exciting, I know, but that's what police work is all about. So if you're joining for thrills and spills, think again.'

That should have been *my* speech, Holmes thought to himself as the cadets grinned at Rebus's words. They would agree with anything he said, anything he did. He was an Inspector. He was *the* Inspector Rebus. Holmes felt himself losing height and density, becoming like a patch of low mist or a particularly innocuous shadow. Rebus was in charge now. The cadets had all but forgotten their former leader. They had eyes for only one man, and that man was ordering them to go and drink some tea.

'What's up, Brian?'

Holmes, watching the cadets shuffle away, realised Rebus was speaking to him. 'Sorry?'

'You look like you've found a tanner and lost a shilling.'

Holmes shrugged. 'I suppose I'm thinking about how I could have had one-and-six. No news yet on the blood?'

'Just that it's every bit as messianic as yours and mine.'

'What a surprise.'

Rebus nodded towards the clearing. 'Try telling them that. They'll have an answer for you.'

'I know. I've already been ticked off for desecration. You know they've started posting an all-night guard?'

'What for?'

'In case the Wee Frees chop down the tree and run away with it.'

They stared at one another, then burst out laughing. Hands quickly went to mouths to stifle the sound. Desecration upon desecration.

'Come on,' said Rebus, 'you look like you could do with a cuppa yourself. My treat.'

'Now that *is* a miracle,' said Holmes, following his superior out of the trees. A tall, muscled man was approaching. He wore denims and a white T-shirt. A large wooden cross swung from his neck, around which was also tied a red kerchief. His beard was as thick and black as his hair.

'Are you police officers?'

'Yes,' Rebus said.

'Then I think you should know, they're trying to steal the tree.'

'Steal it, sir?'

'Yes, steal it. We've got to keep watch twenty-four hours. Last night, one of them had a knife, but there were too many of us, thank God.'

'And you are?'

'Steven Byrne.' He paused. 'Father Steven Byrne.'

Rebus paused too, digesting this new information. 'Well, Father, would you recognise this man again? The one with the knife?'

'Yes, probably.'

'Well, we could go down to the station and have a look at some photographs.'

Father Byrne seemed to be appraising Rebus. Acknowledging that he was being taken seriously, he nodded slowly. 'Thank you, I don't think that'll be necessary. But I thought you ought to know. Things might turn nasty.'

Rebus bit back a comment about turning the other cheek. 'Not if we can help it,' he said instead. 'If you see the man again, Father, let us know straight away. Don't try anything on your own.'

Father Byrne looked around him. 'There aren't so many telephones around here.' His eyes were twinkling with humour. An attractive man, thought Rebus. Even a touch charismatic.

'Well,' he said, 'we'll try to make sure a patrol car comes by and checks on things. How would that be?'

Father Byrne nodded. Rebus made to move away. 'Bless you,' he heard the man saying. Rebus kept walking, but for some reason his cheeks had turned deep red. But it was right and proper, after all, wasn't it? Right that he should be blessed.

'Blessed are the peacemakers,' he quoted, as the megaphone came back into range.

The story was a simple one. Three girls had been in the Hermitage one late afternoon. School over, they'd decided to cut through the park, climb Blackford Hill and come down the other side towards their homes. A long way round for a short-cut, as Rebus had put it at the time.

They were sensible girls, from good Catholic homes. They were fifteen and all had future plans that included university and a career as well as marriage. They didn't seem inclined to fantasy or exaggeration. They stuck to the same story throughout. They'd been about thirty yards or so from the tree when they'd seen a man. One second he wasn't there, the next he was. Dressed in white and with a glow all around him. Long wavy dark hair and a beard. A very pale face, they were definite about that. He leaned with one hand against the tree, the other to his side. His right side – again, all three concurred on this. Then he took the hand away, and they saw that there was blood on his side. A dark red patch. They gasped. They looked to each other for confirmation that they'd seen what they had seen. When they looked again, the figure had vanished.

They ran to their separate homes, but over dinner the story came out in each of the three households. Disbelieved, perhaps, for a moment. But then why would the girls lie? The parents got together and went to the Hermitage. They were shown the place, the tree. There was no sign of anyone. But then one of the mothers shrieked before crossing herself.

'Look at that!' she cried. 'Just look at it!'

It was a smeared red mark, still wet on the bark of the tree. Blood.

The parents went to the police and the police made an initial search of the area, but in the meantime, the neighbour of one of the families telephoned a friend who was a stringer on a Sunday newspaper. The paper ran the story of the 'Hermitage Vision' and the thing began to grow. The blood, it was said, hadn't dried. And this was true, though as Rebus knew it could well have something to do with the reaction of blood and bark. Footprints were found, but so many and so varied that it was impossible to say when they'd been made or by whom. The parents, for example, had searched the area thoroughly, destroying a lot of potential evidence. There were no bloodstains on the ground. No patients with side wounds had been treated in any of the city's hospitals or by any doctor.

The description of the figure was vague: tallish, thinnish, the long hair and beard of course – but was the hair brown or black? The girls couldn't be sure. Dressed in white – 'like a gown', one of them remembered later. But by then the story had become public property; how far would that distort her memories of the evening? And as for the glow. Well, Rebus had seen how the sun hit that particular spot. Imagine a lowish sun, creeping towards evening. That would explain the glow – to a rational man.

But then the zealous – of both sides – appeared. The believers and the doubters, carrying candles or toting megaphones. It was a quiet time for news: the media loved it. The girls photographed well. When they appeared on TV, the trickle of visitors to the site became a flood. Coachloads headed north from Wales and England. Organised parties were arriving from Ireland. A Parisian magazine had picked up on the mystery; so, it was rumoured, had a Bible-thumping cable channel from the USA.

Rebus wanted to raise his hands and turn back the tide. Instead of which that tide rolled straight over him. Superintendent Watson wanted answers.

'I don't like all this hocus-pocus,' he said, with Presbyterian assuredness and an Aberdonian lilt. 'I want something tangible. I want an explanation, one I can *believe*. Understood?'

Understood. Rebus understood it; so did Chief Inspector Lauderdale. Chief Inspector Lauderdale understood that *he* wanted Rebus to do something about it. Rebus understood that hands were being washed; that his alone were to work on the case. If in doubt, delegate. That was where Brian Holmes and his cadets entered the picture. Having found no new clues – no clues *period* – Rebus decided to back off. Media interest was already dying. Some local historian would now and again come up with a 'fact' or a 'theory' and these would revive the story for a while – the hermit who'd lived in the Hermitage, executed for witchcraft in 1714 and said still to haunt the place, that sort of thing, but it couldn't last. It was like poking at embers without feeding them. A momentary glow, no more. When the media interest died, so would that of the fringe lunatics. There had already been copycat 'visions' in Cornwall, Caerphilly and East Croydon. The Doubting Thomases were appearing. What's more, the blood had gone, washed away in an overnight deluge which also extinguished the candles around the tree.

A recurrence of the 'vision' was needed if the thing were not to die. Rebus prayed each night for a quick and merciful release. It didn't come. Instead there was a 4 a.m. phone call.

'This better be worth it.'

'It is.'

'Go on then.'

'How soon can you get to the Hermitage?'

Rebus sat up in bed. 'Talk to me.'

'They've found a body, Well, that's putting it a bit strongly. Let's say they've found a trunk.'

A trunk it was, and not the sort you stuck travel labels on either.

'Dear God in heaven,' Rebus whispered, staring at the thing. 'Who found it?'

Holmes didn't look too good himself. 'One of the tree people,' he said. 'Wandered over here looking for a place to do his number twos. Had a torch with him. Found this. I think you could say he's in a state of shock. Apparently, so are his trousers.'

'I can't say I blame them.' A generator hummed in the background, providing juice for the three tall halogen lamps which lit the clearing. Some uniformed officers were cordoning off the area with strips of orange tape. 'So nobody's touched it?'

'Nobody's been near it.'

Rebus nodded, satisfied. 'Better keep it that way till forensics get here. Where the hell's the pathologist?'

Holmes nodded over Rebus's shoulder. 'Speak of the devil,' he said.

Rebus turned. Two men in sombre Crombie-style coats were walking briskly towards the scene. One carried a black surgeon's bag, the other had his hands firmly in his pockets, protection from the chill air. The halogen had fooled a few of the local birds, who were chirping their hearts out. But morning wasn't far away.

Chief Inspector Lauderdale nodded curtly towards

Rebus, reckoning this greeting enough under the circumstances. The pathologist, Dr Curt, was, however (and despite his name), as voluble as ever.

'Top of the morning to you, Inspector.' Rebus, knowing Dr Curt of old, waited for the inevitable joke. The doctor obliged, gesturing towards the body. 'Not often I get a trunk call these days.'

Rebus, as was expected of him, groaned. The doctor beamed. Rebus knew what came next: the corny newspaper headlines. Again, Dr Curt obliged. 'Corpse in the coppice baffles cops,' he mused brightly, donning overshoes and coveralls before making for the corpse itself.

Chief Inspector Lauderdale looked stunned. He shuffled closer to Rebus. 'Is he always like this?'

'Always.'

The doctor had crouched down to inspect the body. He asked for the position of the lamps to be changed, then started his examination. But there was time for a last twist of the head towards Rebus.

'I'm afraid we're too late,' Dr Curt called out. 'Poor chap's dead.'

Chuckling to himself, he set to work, bringing a tape-recorder out of his case and mumbling into it from time to time.

Lauderdale watched for a minute. It was about fifty-nine seconds too long. He turned to Rebus again. 'What can you tell me?'

'About Dr Curt? Or about the deceased?'

'About the deceased.'

Rebus pushed fingers through his hair, scratching at the scalp. He was mentally listing the bad puns still available to Dr Curt – he got legless, he's out of 'arm's way, lost his head, hadn't paid his bills so got cut off, was for the chop anyway, had no bleeding right, worked as a hack, take a butcher's at him ...

'Inspector?'

Rebus started. 'What?'

Lauderdale stared at him hard.

'Oh,' Rebus said, remembering. 'Well, he's naked of course. And they haven't severed *every* limb, so we know for sure that it *is* a he. Nothing else yet, sir. Come first light, we'll search the area for the missing appendages. One thing I'm pretty sure of, he wasn't butchered here.'

'Oh?'

'No blood, sir. Not that I can see.'

'Gentlemen!' It was Curt, calling to them, waving his arm for them to join him. They, too, had to slip on the elastic shoes, like ill-fitting polythene bags, and the coveralls. The forensics people would want to cover every inch of the ground around the victim's body. It didn't do to leave erroneous 'clues' like fibres from your jacket or a dropped coin.

'What is it, Doctor?'

'First, let me tell you that he's male, aged anywhere between thirty-five and fifty. Either dissolute thirty-five or a fairly well-preserved fifty. Stocky, too, unless the legs are in ridiculous proportion to the trunk. I can give a better guesstimate once we've had him on the slab.' His smile seemed directed at Lauderdale especially. 'Been dead a day or more. He was brought here in this condition, of course.'

'Of course,' said Lauderdale. 'No blood.'

The doctor nodded, still smiling. 'But there's something else. Look here.' He pointed to what was left of the right shoulder. 'Do you see this damage?' He circled the shoulder with his finger. They had to bend closer to see what he was talking about. The shoulder had been attacked with a knife, like someone had tried to peel it. It all looked clumsy and amateurish compared to the other neat examples.

'A tattoo,' Rebus said. 'Got to be.'

'Quite right, Inspector. They've tried removing it. *After* they dumped the trunk here. They must have spotted that there was still part of the tattoo left, enough to help us identify the victim. So ...' He moved his finger from the shoulder stump to the ground beneath it. Rebus could just make out the shreds of skin.

'We can piece it back together,' Rebus stated.

'Of course we can!' The doctor stood up. 'They must think we're stupid. They go to all this trouble, then leave something like that.' He shook his head slowly. Rebus held his breath, waiting. The doctor's face brightened. 'It's years since I last did a jigsaw,' he said, opening his bag, placing his things back in it, and closing it with a loud snap. 'An open and shut case,' he said, moving back towards the cordon.

After he'd gone, off to his slab to await delivery of the body, Lauderdale lingered to see that everything was running smoothly. It was, as Rebus assured him. Lauderdale then bid him goodnight. Rebus didn't think anyone had ever 'bid' him goodnight before; wasn't sure anyone had *ever* bid anyone goodnight, outside of books and plays. It was especially strange to be bid goodnight at dawn. He could swear there was a cock crowing in the distance, but who in Morningside would keep chickens?

He looked for Holmes and found him over beside the tree-dwellers. Overnight, a guard-duty worked in shifts, two or three people at a time for two hours at a stretch. Holmes was chatting, seeming casual. He shifted his weight from foot to foot, as though cramp or cold were seeping through his socks.

Hadn't a leg to stand on: that was another one Dr Curt could have used.

'You seem very cheerful this morning, Inspector. But then each morning is a cause for celebration in itself.' Intent on Holmes, Rebus hadn't noticed the other figure who, like him, was making his way towards the tree. Dressed in jeans, tartan shirt and lumber jacket, but with the same wooden cross. It was Father Byrne. Sky-blue eyes, piercing eyes, the pupils like tiny points of ink. The smile spreading from the lips and mouth towards the eyes and cheeks. The man's very beard seemed to take part in the process.

'I don't know about cheerful, Father Byrne —'

'Please, call me Steven.'

'Well, as I was saying, I don't know about cheerful. You know there was a murder last night?'

Now the eyes opened wide. 'A murder? Here?'

'Well, not strictly speaking, no. But the body was dumped here. We'll need to talk to anyone who was here yesterday. They may have seen something.'

Holmes waved a notebook. 'I've already collected some names and addresses.'

'Good lad. Have there been any more threats, Father?'

'Threats?'

'You remember, the man with the knife.'

'No, not that I know of.'

'Well, I really would like you to come down the station and see if you can pick him out from some photographs.'

'Now?'

'Sometime today.' Rebus paused. 'At your convenience.'

Father Byrne caught the meaning of the pause. 'Well, of course. If you think it will help. I'll come this morning. But you don't think …? Surely not.'

Rebus shrugged. 'Probably just a coincidence, Father. But you have to admit, it *is* quite a coincidence. Someone comes down here with a knife. Some days later, a body appears not three hundred yards away. Yes, coincidence.' That pause again. 'Wouldn't you say?'

But Father Byrne didn't seem to have an answer for that.

No, it was no coincidence, Rebus was sure of that. Fine, if you were going to dump a body the Hermitage was as good a spot as any. But not in a clearing, where it would be stumbled upon sooner rather than later. And not so close to the famous tree, where, as everyone knew, people were to be found round-the-clock, making dumping a body nearby a risky procedure. Too risky. There had to be a reason. There had to be some meaning. Some message.

Yes, some *message*.

And wasn't three hundred yards a long way to go for number twos? Well, that one was cleared up quickly. The man admitted that he hadn't gone off alone. He'd gone with his girlfriend. After finding the body, the man had sent her home. Partly because she was in shock; partly to avoid any 'slur on her character'. Father Byrne passed this news on to Rebus when he came to the station to look through the mug-shots — without success.

A new sort of tourist now visited the Hermitage, to view a new kind of 'shrine'. They wanted to see the spot where the trunk had been discovered. Locals still brought their dogs, and lovers still followed the route of the burn; but they wore fixed looks on their faces, as though unwilling to accept that the Hermitage, *their* Hermitage, had become something else, something they never believed it could be.

Rebus, meantime, played with a jigsaw. The tattoo was coming together, though it was a slow business. Errors were made. And one error, once made, led to more pieces being placed incorrectly, until the whole thing had to be broken up and started again. Blue was the predominant colour, along with some patches of red. The dark, inked lines tended to be straight. It looked like a professional job. Tattoo parlours were visited, but the description given was too vague as yet. Rebus showed yet another configuration of the pieces to Brian Holmes: it was the fifth such photograph in a week. The lab had provided their own dotted outline of how they thought the design might continue. Holmes nodded.

'It's a Kandinsky,' he said. 'Or one of his followers. Solid bars of colour. Yes, definitely a Kandinsky.'

Rebus was amazed. 'You mean Kandinsky did this tattoo?'

Holmes looked up from the photograph, grinned sheepishly. 'Sorry, I was making a joke. Or trying to. Kandinsky was a painter.'

'Oh,' Rebus sounded disappointed. 'Yes,' he said, 'yes, of course he was. Right.'

Feeling guilty at having raised his superior's hopes, Holmes concentrated all the harder on the photo. 'Could be a swastika,' he offered. 'Those lines ...'

'Yes.' Rebus turned the photograph towards him, then slapped a hand against it. 'No!' Holmes flinched. 'No, Brian, not a swastika ... a Union Jack! It's a bloody Union Jack!'

Once the lab had the design in front of them, it was a straightforward job of following it in their reconstruction. Not just a Union Jack, though, as they found. A Union Jack with the letters UFF slurred across it, and a machine gun half-hidden behind the letters.

'Ulster Freedom Fighters,' Rebus murmured. 'Right, let's get back to those tattoo parlours.'

A CID officer in Musselburgh came up with the break. A tattooist there thought he recognised the design as the work of Tam Finlayson, but Finlayson had retired from the business some years ago, and tracing him was hard work. Rebus even feared for a moment that the man might be dead and buried. He wasn't. He was living with his daughter and son-in-law in Brighton.

A Brighton detective visited the address and telephoned Edinburgh with details. Shown the photograph, Finlayson had flinched, then had taken, as the daughter put it, 'one of his turns'. Pills were administered and finally Finlayson was in a state to talk. But he was scared, there was no doubt of that. Reassured, though, by the information that the tattoo belonged to a corpse, the tattooist owned up. Yes, it was his work. He'd done it maybe fifteen years before. And the customer? A young man called Philips. Rab Philips. Not a terrorist, just a tearaway looking for a cause.

'Rab Philips?' Rebus stared at his telephone. '*The* Rab Philips?' Who else? A dim, small-time villain who'd spent enough time in prison, that university of life, to become a clever small-time villain. And who had grown, matured, if you like, into a big-game player. Well, not quite Premier League, but not Sunday kickabout either. He'd certainly been keeping himself to himself these past couple of years. No gossip on the street about him; no dirt; no news at all really.

Well, there was news now. Pubs and clubs were visited, drinks bought, occasionally an arm twisted and the information began to trickle in. Philips' home was searched, his wife questioned. Her story was that he'd told her he was going to London for a few days on a business trip. Rebus nodded calmly and handed her a photograph.

'Is that Rab's tattoo?'

She went pale. Then she went into hysterics.

Meanwhile, Philips' cronies and 'associates' had been rounded up and questioned. One or two were released and picked up again, released and picked up. The message was clear: CID thought they knew more than they were telling and unless they told what they knew, this process would go on indefinitely. They were nervous, of course, and who could blame them? They couldn't know who would now take over their ex-boss's terrain. There were people out there with grudges and knives. The longer they hung about in police stations, the more of a liability they would appear.

They told what they knew, or as much as CID needed to know. That was fine by Rebus. Rab Philips, they said, had started shifting drugs. Nothing serious, mostly cannabis, but in hefty quantities. Edinburgh CID had done much to clear up the hard drug problem in the city, mainly by clearing out the dealers. New dealers would always appear, but they were small-fry. Rab Philips, though, had been so quiet for so long that he was not a suspect. And besides, the drugs were merely passing through Edinburgh; they

102

weren't staying there. Boats would land them on the Fife coast or further north. They would be brought to Edinburgh and from there transferred south. To England. Which meant, in effect, to London. Rebus probed for an Ulster connection, but nobody had anything to tell him.

'So who are the drugs going to in London?'

Again, nobody knew. Or nobody was saying. Rebus sat at his desk, another jigsaw to work on now, but this time in his head – a jigsaw of facts and possibilities. Yes, he should have known from the start. Dismemberment equals gangland. A betrayal, a double-cross. And the penalty for same. Rebus reached for his telephone again and this time put in a call to London.

'Inspector George Flight, please.'

Trust Flight to make it all seem so easy. Rebus gave him the description and an hour later Flight came back with a name. Rebus added some details and Flight went visiting. This time, the phone call came to Rebus's flat. It was late evening and he was lying half-asleep in his chair, the telephone waiting on his lap.

Flight was in good humour. 'I'm glad you told me about the wound,' he said. 'I asked him a few questions, noticed he was a bit stiff. As he stood up to show me out, I slapped him on his right side. I made it seem sort of playful. You know, not malicious like.' He chuckled. 'You should have seen him, John. Doubled over like a bloody pen-knife. It started bleeding again, of course. The silly sod hadn't had it seen to. I wouldn't wonder if it's gone septic or something.'

'When did he get back from Edinburgh?'

'Couple of days ago. Think we can nail him?'

'Maybe. We could do with some evidence though. But I think I can do something about that.'

As Rebus explained to Brian Holmes, it had been more than a 'hunch'. A hunch was, as Dr Curt himself might put it, a stab in the dark. Rebus had a little more light to work by. He told the story as they drove through early-morning Edinburgh towards the Hermitage. The three girls had seen a man appearing from the trees. A wounded man. It seemed clear now that he'd been stabbed in some skirmish nearer to, or by the side of, Braid Hills Road. A switch of drugs from one car to another. An attempted double-cross. He'd been wounded and had fled down the hill into the Hermitage itself, coming into the clearing at the same time as the girls, making himself scarce when he saw them.

Because, of course, he had something to hide: his wound. He had patched himself up, but had stuck around Edinburgh, looking for revenge. Rab Philips had been grabbed, dismembered and his body dumped in the Hermitage as a message to Philips' gang. The message was: you don't mess with London.

Then the wounded villain had finally headed back south. But he was the antithesis of Philips; he wore flashy clothes. 'Probably a white coat,' Rebus had told George Flight. 'White trousers. He's got long hair and a beard.'

Flight had bettered the description. 'It's a white trench-coat,' he'd said. 'And yellow trousers, would you believe. A real old ex-hippy this one.' His name was Shaun McLafferty. 'Everyone on the street knows Shaun,' Flight went on. 'I didn't know he'd started pushing dope though. Mind you, he'd try anything, that one.'

McLafferty. 'He wouldn't,' Rebus asked, 'be Irish by any chance?'

'London Irish,' said Flight. 'I wouldn't be surprised if the IRA was creaming ten per cent off his profits. Maybe more. After all, he either pays up or they take over. It happens.'

Maybe it was as simple as that then. An argument over 'the divide'. An IRA supporter finding himself doing business with a UFF tattoo. The kind of mix old Molotov himself would have appreciated.

'So,' Brian Holmes said, having digested all this, 'Inspector Flight paid a visit to McLafferty?'

Rebus nodded. 'And he was wounded in his right side. Stab wound, according to George.'

'So why,' Holmes said, 'are we here?'

They had parked the car just outside the gates and were now walking into the Hermitage.

'Because,' Rebus said, 'we still lack evidence.'

'What evidence?'

But Rebus wasn't saying; perhaps because he didn't know the answer himself. They were approaching the tree. There was no sign of the once ubiquitous guard, but a familiar figure was kneeling before the tree.

'Morning, Father.'

Father Byrne looked up. 'Good morning, Inspector. You too, Constable.'

Rebus looked around him. 'All alone?'

Byrne nodded. 'Enthusiasm seems to have waned, Inspector. No more megaphones, or coach parties, or cameras.'

'You sound relieved.'

'Believe me, I am.' Father Byrne held out his arms. 'I much prefer it like this, don't you?'

Rebus was obliged to nod his agreement. 'Anyway,' he said, 'we think we can explain what the girls saw.'

Father Byrne merely shrugged.

'No more guard-duties?' Rebus asked.

'The men stopped bothering us.'

Rebus nodded thoughtfully. His eyes were on the tree. 'It wasn't you they were after, Father. It was the tree. But not for the reason you think. Brian, give me a hand, will you?'

A literal hand. Rebus wanted Holmes to form a stirrup from his hands, so that Rebus could place a foot on them and be hoisted up into the tree. Holmes steadied himself against the tree and complied, not without a silent groan. It

105

was feasible that Rebus weighed a good three and a half stones more than him. Still, ours is not to reason why ... and *heave!*

Rebus scrabbled with his hands, finding knot-holes, moss, but nothing else, nothing hidden. He peered upwards, seeking any fissure in the bark, any cranny. Nothing.

'All right, Brian.'

Gratefully, Holmes lowered Rebus groundwards. 'Anything?'

Rebus shook his head. He was gnawing his bottom lip.

'Are you going to tell me what we're looking for?'

'McLafferty had something else to hide from the girls, something on top of the fact that he'd been stabbed. Let's think.' McLafferty had come through the copse, the undergrowth, had rested for a second against the tree, fled back through the copse.

'Chalk!' Rebus thumped the tree with his fist.

'Pardon?'

'Chalk! That morning I came to check on you. When the cadets got up, their knees had white, powdery chalk on them.'

'Yes?'

'Well look!' Rebus led Holmes into the copse. 'There's no white rock here. No bits of chalky stone. That wasn't bloody chalk.' He fell to his knees and began to burrow furiously, raking his hands through the earth.

The girls' parents had messed up the ground, making the white powder inconspicuous. Enough to mark a trouser-knee, but hardly noticeable otherwise. Certainly, nothing a cadet would bother with. And besides, they'd been looking for something *on* the ground, not below it.

'Ah!' He paused, probed a spot with his fingers, then began to dig around it. 'Look,' he said, 'just the one packet and it's burst. That's what it was. Must have burst when

106

McLafferty was burying it. Better call for forensics, Brian. His blood and his prints will be all over it.'

'Right, sir.' Stunned, Brian Holmes sprinted from the clearing, then stopped and turned back. 'Keys,' he explained. Rebus fished his car-keys from his pocket and tossed them to him. Father Byrne, who had been a spectator throughout, came a little closer.

'Heroin, Father. Either that or cocaine. Bigger profits than cannabis, you see. It all comes down to money in the end. They were doing a deal. McLafferty got himself stabbed. He was holding a packet when it happened. Got away somehow, ran down here before he had time to think. He knew he'd better get rid of the stuff, so he buried it. The men who were bothering you, McLafferty's men, it was *this* they were after. Then they got Rab Philips instead and went home satisfied. If it wasn't for your all-night vigil, they'd've had this stuff too.'

Rebus paused, aware that he couldn't be making much sense to the priest. Father Byrne seemed to read his mind and smiled.

'For a minute there, Inspector,' he said, 'I thought you were speaking in tongues.'

Rebus grinned, too, feeling breathless. With McLafferty's prints on the bag, they would have the evidence they needed. 'Sorry you didn't get your miracle,' he said.

Father Byrne's smile broadened. 'Miracles happen every day, Inspector. I don't need to have them invented for me.'

They turned to watch as Holmes came wandering back towards them. But his eyes were concentrating on an area to the left of them. 'They're on their way,' he said, handing Rebus's keys back to him.

'Fine.'

'Who was that by the way?

'Who?'

'The other man.' Holmes looked from Rebus to Byrne back to Rebus again. 'The other man,' he repeated. 'The one who was standing here with you. When I was coming back, he was ...' He was pointing now, back towards the gate, then over towards the left of the tree. But his voice died away.

'No, never mind,' he said. 'I thought ... I just, no never mind. I must be –'

'Seeing things?' Father Byrne suggested, his fingers just touching the wooden cross around his neck.

'That's right, yes. Yes, seeing things.'

Ghosts, thought Rebus. Spirits of the wood. Rab Philips maybe, or the Hermitage Witch. My God, those two would have a lot to talk about, wouldn't they?

A Good Hanging

I

It was quite some time since a scaffold had been seen in Parliament Square. Quite some time since Edinburgh had witnessed a hanging, too, though digging deeper into history the sight might have been common enough. Detective Inspector John Rebus recalled hearing some saloon-bar story of how criminals, sentenced to hang, would be given the chance to run the distance of the Royal Mile from Parliament Square to Holyrood, a baying crowd hot on their heels. If the criminal reached the Royal Park before he was caught, he would be allowed to remain there, wandering in safety so long as he did not step outside the boundary of the park itself. True or not, the tale conjured up the wonderful image of rogues and vagabonds trapped within the confines of Arthur's Seat, Salisbury Crags and Whinny Hill. Frankly, Rebus would have preferred the noose.

'It's got to be a prank gone wrong, hasn't it?'

A prank. Edinburgh was full of pranks at this time of year. It was Festival time, when young people, theatrical people, flooded into the city with their enthusiasm and their energy. You couldn't walk ten paces without someone pressing a handbill upon you or begging you to visit their production. These were the 'Fringe lunatics' as Rebus had not very originally, but to his own satisfaction, termed them. They came for two or three or four weeks, mostly from London and they squeezed into damp sleeping-bags on bedsit floors throughout the city, going home much paler, much more tired and almost always the poorer. It

109

was not unusual for the unlucky Fringe shows, those given a venue on the outskirts, those with no review to boast of, starved of publicity and inspiration, for those unfortunate shows to play to single-figure audiences, if not to an audience of a single figure.

Rebus didn't like Festival time. The streets became clogged, there seemed a despair about all the artistic fervour and, of course, the crime rate rose. Pickpockets loved the festival. Burglars found easy pickings in the overpopulated, underprotected bedsits. And, finding their local pub taken over by the 'Sassenachs', the natives were inclined to throw the occasional punch or bottle or chair. Which was why Rebus avoided the city centre during the Festival, skirting around it in his car, using alleyways and half-forgotten routes. Which was why he was so annoyed at having been called here today, to Parliament Square, the heart of the Fringe, to witness a hanging.

'Got to be a prank,' he repeated to Detective Constable Brian Holmes. The two men were standing in front of a scaffold, upon which hung the gently swaying body of a young man. The body swayed due to the fresh breeze which was sweeping up the Royal Mile from the direction of Holyrood Park. Rebus thought of the ghosts of the royal park's inmates. Was the wind of their making? 'A publicity stunt gone wrong,' he mused.

'Apparently not, sir,' Holmes said. He'd been having a few words with the workmen who were trying to erect a curtain of sorts around the spectacle so as to hide it from the view of the hundreds of inquisitive tourists who had gathered noisily outside the police cordon. Holmes now consulted his notebook, while Rebus, hands in pockets, strolled around the scaffold. It was of fairly ramshackle construction, which hadn't stopped it doing its job.

'The body was discovered at four-fifty this morning. We don't think it had been here long. A patrol car passed this way at around four and they didn't see anything.'

'That doesn't mean much,' Rebus interrupted in a mutter.

Holmes ignored the remark. 'The deceased belonged to a Fringe group called Ample Reading Time. They come from the University of Reading, thus the name.'

'It also makes the acronym ART,' Rebus commented.

'Yes, sir,' said Holmes. His tone told the senior officer that Holmes had already worked this out for himself. Rebus wriggled a little, as though trying to keep warm. In fact, he had a summer cold.

'How did we discover his identity?' They were in front of the hanging man now, standing only four or so feet below him. Early twenties, Rebus surmised. A shock of black curly hair.

'The scaffold has a venue number pinned to it,' Holmes was saying. 'A student hall of residence just up the road.'

'And that's where the ART show's playing?'

'Yes, sir.' Holmes consulted the bulky Fringe programme which he had been holding behind his notebook. 'It's a play of sorts called "Scenes from a Hanging".' The two men exchanged a look at this. 'The blurb,' Holmes continued, consulting the company's entry near the front of the programme, 'promises "thrills, spills and a live hanging on stage".'

'A live hanging, eh? Well, you can't say they didn't deliver. So, he takes the scaffold from the venue, wheels it out here – I notice it's on wheels, presumably to make it easier to trundle on and off the stage – and in the middle of the night he hangs himself, without anyone hearing anything or seeing anything.' Rebus sounded sceptical.

'Well,' said Holmes, 'be honest, sir.' He was pointing towards and beyond the crowd of onlookers. 'Does anything look suspicious in Edinburgh at this time of year?'

Rebus followed the direction of the finger and saw that a twelve-foot-high man was enjoying a grandstand view of the spectacle, while somewhere to his right someone was

111

juggling three saucepans high into the air. The stilt-man walked towards the pans, grabbed one from mid-air and set it on his head, waving down to the crowd before moving off. Rebus sighed.

'I suppose you're right, Brian. Just this once you may be right.'

A young DC approached, holding a folded piece of paper towards them. 'We found this in his trousers back-pocket.'

'Ah,' said Rebus, 'the suicide note.' He plucked the sheet from the DC's outstretched hand and read it aloud.

' "Pity it wasn't *Twelfth Night*".'

Holmes peered at the line of type. 'Is that it?'

'Short but sweet,' said Rebus. '*Twelfth Night*. A play by Shakespeare and the end of the Christmas season. I wonder which one he means?' Rebus refolded the note and slipped it into his pocket. 'But is it a suicide note or not? It could just be a bog-standard note, a reminder or whatever, couldn't it? I still think this is a stunt gone wrong.' He paused to cough. He was standing beside the cobblestone inset of the Heart of Midlothian, and like many a Scot before him, he spat for luck into the centre of the heart-shaped stones. Holmes looked away and found himself gazing into the dead man's dulled eyes. He turned back as Rebus was fumbling with a handkerchief.

'Maybe,' Rebus was saying between blows, 'we should have a word with the rest of the cast. I don't suppose they'll have much to keep them occupied.' He gestured towards the scaffold. 'Not until they get back their prop. Besides, we've got a job to do, haven't we?'

II

'Well, I say we keep going!' the voice yelled. 'We've got an important piece of work here, a play people should *see*. If anything, David's death will bring audiences *in*. We

shouldn't be pushing them away. We shouldn't be packing
our bags and crawling back south.'

'You sick bastard.'

Rebus and Holmes entered the makeshift auditorium as
the speaker of these last three words threw himself forwards
and landed a solid punch against the side of the speech-
maker's face. His glasses flew from his nose and slid along
the floor, stopping an inch or two short of Rebus's scuffed
leather shoes. He stooped, picked up the spectacles and
moved forward.

The room was of a size, and had an atmosphere, that
would have suited a monastery's dining-hall. It was long
and narrow, with a stage constructed along its narrow face
and short rows of chairs extending back into the gloom.
What windows there were had been blacked-out and the
hall's only natural light came from the open door through
which Rebus had just stepped, to the front left of the stage
itself.

There were five of them in the room, four men and a
woman. All looked to be in their mid- to late-twenties.
Rebus handed over the glasses.

'Not a bad right-hook that,' he said to the attacker, who
was looking with some amazement at his own hand, as
though hardly believing it capable of such an action. 'I'm
Inspector Rebus, this is Detective Sergeant Holmes. And
you are?'

They introduced themselves in turn. Sitting on the stage
was Pam, who acted. Beside her was Peter Collins, who also
acted. On a chair in front of the stage, legs and arms
crossed and having obviously enjoyed tremendously the
one-sided bout he had just witnessed, sat Marty Jones.

'I don't act,' he said loudly. 'I just design the set, build
the bloody thing, make all the props and work the lights
and the music during the play.'

'So it's your scaffold then?' commented Rebus. Marty
Jones looked less confident.

'Yes,' he said. 'I made it a bit too bloody well, didn't I?'

'We could just as easily blame the rope manufacturer, Mr Jones,' Rebus said quietly. His eyes moved to the man with the spectacles, who was nursing a bruised jaw.

'Charles Collins,' the man said sulkily. He looked towards where Peter Collins sat on the stage. 'No relation. I'm the director. I also wrote "Scenes from a Hanging".'

Rebus nodded. 'How have the reviews been?'

Marty Jones snorted.

'Not great,' Charles Collins admitted. 'We've only had four,' he went on, knowing if he didn't say it someone else would. 'They weren't exactly complimentary.'

Marty Jones snorted again. Stiffening his chin, as though to take another punch, Collins ignored him.

'And the audiences?' Rebus asked, interested.

'Lousy.' This from Pam, swinging her legs in front of her as though such news was not only quite acceptable, but somehow humorous as well.

'Average, I'd say,' Charles Collins corrected. 'Going by what other companies have been telling me.'

'That's the problem with staging a new play, isn't it?' Rebus said knowledgeably, while Holmes stared at him. Rebus was standing in the midst of the group now, as though giving them a pre-production pep talk. 'Trying to get audiences to watch new work is always a problem. They prefer the classics.'

'That's right,' Charles Collins agreed enthusiastically. 'That's what I've been telling –' with a general nod in everyone's direction, 'them. The classics are "safe". That's why we need to challenge people.'

'To excite them,' Rebus continued, 'to shock them even. Isn't that right, Mr Collins? To give them a spectacle?'

Charles Collins seemed to see where Rebus's line, devious though it was, was leading. He shook his head.

'Well, they got a spectacle all right,' Rebus went on, all enthusiasm gone from his voice. 'Thanks to Mr Jones's scaffold, the people got a shock. Someone was hanged. I think his name's David, isn't it?'

'That's right.' This from the attacker. 'David Caulfield.' He looked towards the writer/director. 'Supposedly a friend of ours. Someone we've known for three years. Someone we never thought could ...'

'And you are?' Rebus was brisk. He didn't want anyone breaking down just yet, not while there were still questions that needed answers.

'Hugh Clay.' The young man smiled bitterly. 'David always said it sounded like "ukulele".'

'And you're an actor?'

Hugh Clay nodded.

'And so was David Caulfield?'

Another nod. 'I mean, we're not really professionals. We're students. That's all. Students with pretensions.'

Something about Hugh Clay's voice, its tone and its slow rhythms, had made the room darken, so that everyone seemed less animated, more reflective, remembering at last that David Caulfield was truly dead.

'And what do you think happened to him, Hugh? I mean, how do you think he died?'

Clay seemed puzzled by the question. 'He killed himself, didn't he?'

'Did he?' Rebus shrugged. 'We don't know for certain. The pathologist's report may give us a better idea.' Rebus turned to Marty Jones, who was looking less confident all the time. 'Mr Jones, could David have operated the scaffold by himself?'

'That's the way I designed it,' Jones replied. 'I mean, David worked it himself every night. During the hanging scene.'

Rebus pondered this. 'And could someone else have worked the mechanism?'

Jones nodded. 'No problem. The neck noose we used was a dummy. The real noose was attached around David's chest, under his arms. He held a cord behind him and at the right moment he pulled the cord, the trapdoor opened and he fell about a yard. It looked pretty bloody realistic. He had to wear padding under his arms to stop bruising.' He glanced at Charles Collins. 'It was the best bit of the show.'

'But,' said Rebus, 'the scaffold could easily be rejigged to work properly?'

Jones nodded. 'All you'd need is a bit of rope. There's plenty lying around backstage.'

'And then you could hang yourself? Really hang yourself?'

Jones nodded again.

'Or someone could hang you,' said Pam, her eyes wide, voice soft with horror.

Rebus smiled towards her, but seemed to be thinking about something else. In fact, he wasn't thinking of anything in particular: he was letting them stew in the silence, letting their minds and imaginations work in whatever way they would.

At last, he turned to Charles Collins. 'Do you think David killed himself?'

Collins shrugged. 'What else?'

'Any particular reason why he would commit suicide?'

'Well,' Collins looked towards the rest of the company. 'The show,' he said. 'The reviews weren't very complimentary about David's performance.'

'Tell me a little about the play.'

Collins tried not to sound keen as he spoke. Tried, Rebus noticed, but failed. 'It took me most of this year to write,' he said. 'What we have is a prisoner in a South American country, tried and found guilty, sentenced to death. The play opens with him standing on the scaffold, the noose around his neck. Scenes from his life are played out around him, while his own scenes are made up of soliloquies dealing with the larger questions. What I'm asking the audience to do is to ask themselves the same questions he's asking himself on the scaffold. Only the answers are perhaps more urgent, more important for him, because they're the last things he'll ever know.'

Rebus broke in. The whole thing sounded dreadful. 'And David would be on stage the entire time?' Collins nodded. 'And how long was that?'

'Anywhere between two hours and two and a half –' with a glance towards the stage, 'depending on the cast.'

'Meaning?'

'Sometimes lines were forgotten, or a scene went missing.' (Peter and Pam smiled in shared complicity.) 'Or the pace just went.'

' "Never have I prayed so ardently for a death to take place", as one of the reviews put it,' Hugh Clay supplied. 'It was a problem of the play. It didn't have anything to do with David.'

Charles Collins looked ready to protest. Rebus stepped in. 'But David's mentions weren't exactly kind?' he hinted.

'No,' Clay admitted. 'They said he lacked the necessary *gravitas* whatever that means.'

' "Too big a part for too small an actor",' interrupted Marty Jones, quoting again.

'Bad notices then,' said Rebus. 'And David Caulfield took them to heart?'

'David took everything to heart,' explained Hugh Clay. 'That was part of the problem.'

'The other part being that the notices were true,' sniped Charles Collins. But Clay seemed prepared for this.

' "Overwritten and messily directed by Charles Collins",' he quoted. Another fight seemed to be on the cards. Rebus blew his nose noisily.

'So,' he said. 'Notices were bad, audiences were poor. And you didn't decide to remedy this situation by staging a little publicity stunt? A stunt that just happened – nobody's fault necessarily – to go wrong?'

There were shakes of the head, eyes looked to other eyes, seemingly innocent of any such plans.

'Besides,' said Marty Jones, 'you couldn't hang yourself accidentally on that scaffold. You either had to mean to do it yourself, or else someone had to do it for you.'

More silence. An impasse seemed to have been reached. Rebus collapsed noisily into a chair. 'All things considered,' he said with a sigh, 'you might have been better off sticking to *Twelfth Night*.'

'That's funny,' Pam said.

'What is?'

'That's the play we did last year,' she explained. 'It went down very well, didn't it?' She had turned to Peter Collins, who nodded agreement.

'We got some good reviews for that,' he said. 'David was a brilliant Malvolio. He kept the cuttings pinned to his bedroom wall, didn't he, Hugh?'

Hugh Clay nodded. Rebus had the distinct feeling that Peter Collins was trying to imply something, perhaps that Hugh Clay had seen more of David Caulfield's bedroom walls than was strictly necessary.

He fumbled in his pocket, extracting the note from below the handkerchief. Brian Holmes, he noticed, was staying very much in the wings, like the minor character in a minor scene. 'We found a note in David's pocket,' Rebus said without preamble. 'Maybe your success last year explains it.' He read it out to them. Charles Collins nodded.

'Yes, that sounds like David all right. Harking back to past glories.'

'You think that's what it means?' Rebus asked conversationally.

Collins nodded. 'You should know, Inspector, that actors are conceited. The greater the actor, the greater the ego. And David was, I admit, on occasion a very gifted actor.'

He was speechifying again, but Rebus let him go on. Perhaps it was the only way a director could communicate with his cast.

'It would be just like David to get depressed, suicidal even, by bad notices, and just like him to decide to stage as showy an exit as he could, something to hit the headlines. I happen to think he succeeded splendidly.'

No one seemed about to contradict him on this, not even David Caulfield's stalwart defender, Hugh Clay. It was Pam who spoke, tears in her eyes at last.

'I only feel sorry for Marie,' she said.

Charles Collins nodded. 'Yes, Marie's come into her own in "Scenes from a Hanging".'

'She means,' Hugh Clay said through gritted teeth, 'she feels sorry for Marie because Marie's lost David, not because Marie can no longer act in your bloody awful play.'

Rebus felt momentary bemusement, but tried not to show it. Marty Jones, however, had seen all.

'The other member of ART,' he explained to Rebus. 'She's back at the flat. She wanted to be left on her own for a bit.'

'She's pretty upset,' Peter Collins agreed.

Rebus nodded slowly. 'She and David were ...?'

'Engaged,' Pam said, the tears falling now, Peter Collins' arm snaking around her shoulders. 'They were going to be married after the Fringe was finished.'

Rebus stole a glance towards Holmes, who raised his eyebrows in reply. Just like every good melodrama, the raised eyebrows said. A twist at the end of every bloody act.

III

The flat the group had rented, at what seemed to Rebus considerable expense, was a dowdy but spacious second-floor affair on Morrison Street, just off Lothian Road.

Rebus had been to the block before, during the investiga-
tion of a housebreaking. That had been years ago, but the
only difference in the tenement seemed to be the installation of a communal intercom at the main door. Rebus
ignored the entry-phone and pushed at the heavy outside
door. As he had guessed, it was unlocked anyway.

'Bloody students,' had been one of Rebus's few voiced
comments during the short, curving drive down the back of
the Castle towards the Usher Hall and Lothian Road. But
then Holmes, driving, had been a student, too, hadn't he?
So Rebus had not expanded on his theme. Now they
climbed the steep winding stairwell until they arrived at the
second floor. Marty Jones had told them that the name on
the door was BLACK. Having robbed the students of an
unreasonable rent (though no doubt the going rate), Mr
and Mrs Black had departed for a month-long holiday on
the proceeds. Rebus had borrowed a key from Jones and
used it to let Holmes and himself in. The hall was long,
narrow and darker than the stairwell. Off it were three
bedrooms, a bathroom, a kitchen and the living-room. A
young woman, not quite out of her teens, came out of the
kitchen carrying a mug of coffee. She was wearing a long
baggy T-shirt and nothing else, and there was a sleepy,
tousled look to her, accompanying the red streakiness of her
eyes.

'Oh,' she said, startled. Rebus was quick to respond.

'Inspector Rebus, miss. This is Detective Constable
Holmes. One of your friends lent us a key. Could we have a
word?'

'About David?' Her eyes were huge, doe-like, her face
small and round. Her hair was short and fair, the body
slender and brittle. Even in grief – perhaps especially in
grief – she was mightily attractive, and Holmes raised his
eyebrows again as she led them into the living-room.

Two sleeping bags lay on the floor, along with paperback
books, an alarm clock, mugs of tea. Off the living-room was

a box-room, a large walk-in cupboard. These were often used by students to make an extra room in a temporary flat and light coming from the half-open door told Rebus that this was still its function. Marie went into the room and switched off the light, before joining the two policemen.

'It's Pam's room,' she explained. 'She said I could lie down there. I didn't want to sleep in our ... in my room.'

'Of course,' Rebus said, all understanding and sympathy.

'Of course,' Holmes repeated. She signalled for them to sit, so they did, sinking into a sofa the consistency of marshmallow. Rebus feared he wouldn't be able to rise again without help and struggled to keep himself upright. Marie meantime had settled, legs beneath her, with enviable poise on the room's only chair. She placed her mug on the floor, then had a thought.

'Would you like ...?'

A shake of the head from both men. It struck Rebus that there was something about her voice. Holmes beat him to it.

'Are you French?'

She smiled a pale smile, then nodded towards the Detective Constable. 'From Bordeaux. Do you know it?'

'Only by the reputation of its wine.'

Rebus blew his nose again, though pulling the hankie from his pocket had been a struggle. Holmes took the hint and closed his mouth. 'Now then, Miss ...?' Rebus began.

'Hivert, Marie Hivert.'

Rebus nodded slowly, playing with the hankie rather than trying to replace it in his pocket. 'We're told that you were engaged to Mr Caulfield.'

Her voice was almost a whisper. 'Yes. Not officially, you understand. But there was – a promise.'

'I see. And when was this promise made?'

'Oh, I'm not sure exactly. March, April. Yes, early April I think. Springtime.'

'And how were things between David and yourself?' She seemed not quite to understand. 'I mean,' said Rebus, 'how did David seem to you?'

She shrugged. 'David was David. He could be –' she raised her eyes to the ceiling, seeking words, 'impossible, nervous, exciting, foul-tempered.' She smiled. 'But mostly exciting.'

'Not suicidal?'

She gave this serious thought. 'Oh yes, I suppose,' she admitted. 'Suicidal, just as actors can be. He took criticism to heart. He was a perfectionist.'

'How long had you known him?'

'Two years. I met him through the theatre group.'

'And you fell in love?'

She smiled again. 'Not at first. There was a certain ... competitiveness between us, you might say. It helped our acting. I'm not sure it helped our relationship altogether. But we survived.' Realising what she had said, she grew silent, her eyes dimming. A hand went to her forehead as, head bowed, she tried to collect herself.

'I'm sorry,' she said, collapsing into sobs. Holmes raised his eyebrows: someone should be here with her. Rebus shrugged back: she can handle it on her own. Holmes' eyebrows remained raised: can she? Rebus looked back at the tiny figure, engulfed by the armchair. Could actors always tell the real world from the illusory?

We survived. It was an interesting phrase to have used. But then she was an interesting young woman.

She went to the bathroom to splash water on her face and while she was gone Rebus took the opportunity to rise awkwardly to his feet. He looked back at the sofa.

'Bloody thing,' he said. Holmes just smiled.

When she returned, composed once more, Rebus asked if David Caulfield might have left a note somewhere. She shrugged. He asked if she minded them having a quick look round. She shook her head. So, never men to refuse a gift,

Rebus and Holmes began looking.

The set-up was fairly straightforward. Pam slept in the box-room, while Marty Jones and Hugh Clay had sleeping-bags on the living-room floor. Marie and David Caulfield had shared the largest of the three bedrooms, with Charles and Peter Collins having a single room each. Charles Collins' room was obsessively tidy, its narrow single bed made up for the night and on the quilt an acting-copy of 'Scenes from a Hanging', covered in marginalia and with several long speeches, all Caulfield's, seemingly excised. A pencil lay on the typescript, evidence that Charles Collins was taking the critics' view to heart himself and attempting to shorten the play as best he could.

Peter Collins' room was much more to Rebus's personal taste, though Holmes wrinkled his nose at the used underwear underfoot, the contents of the hastily unpacked rucksack scattered over every surface. Beside the unmade bed, next to an overflowing ashtray, lay another copy of the play. Rebus flipped through it. Closing it, his attention was caught by some doodlings on the inside cover. Crude heart shapes had been constructed around the words 'I love Edinburgh'. His smile was quickly erased when Holmes held the ashtray towards him.

'Not exactly Silk Cut,' Holmes was saying. Rebus looked. The butts in the ashtrays were made up of cigarette papers wrapped around curled strips of cardboard. They were called 'roaches' by those who smoked dope, though he couldn't remember why. He made a tutting sound.

'And what were we doing in here when we found these?' he asked. Holmes nodded, knowing the truth: they probably couldn't charge Peter Collins even if they'd wanted to, since there was no reason for their being in his room. *We were looking for someone else's suicide note* probably wouldn't impress a latter-day jury.

The double room shared by Marie Hivert and David Caulfield was messiest of all. Marie helped them sift through a few of Caulfield's things. His diary proved a dead end, since he had started it faithfully on 1st January but the entries ceased on 8th January. Rebus, having tried keeping a diary himself, knew the feeling.

But in the back of the diary were newspaper clippings, detailing Caulfield's triumph in the previous year's *Twelfth Night*. Marie, too, had come in for some praise as Viola, but the glory had been Malvolio's. She wept again a little as she read through the reviews. Holmes said that he'd make another cup of coffee. Did he want her to fetch Pam from the theatre? She shook her head. She'd be all right. She promised she would.

While Marie sat on the bed and Holmes filled the kettle, Rebus wandered back into the living-room. He peered into the box-room, but saw little there to interest him. Finally, he came back to the sleeping-bags on the floor. Marie was coming back into the room as he bent to pick up the paperback book from beside one sleeping-bag. It was Tom Wolfe's *Bonfire of the Vanities*. Rebus had a hardback copy at home, still unopened. Something fell from the back of the book, a piece of card. Rebus retrieved it from the floor. It was a photograph of Marie, standing on the Castle ramparts with the Scott Monument behind her. The wind blew her hair fiercely against her face and she was attempting to sweep the hair out of her eyes as she grinned towards the camera. Rebus handed the picture to her.

'Your hair was longer then,' he said.

She smiled and nodded, her eyes till moist. 'Yes,' she said. 'That was in June. We came to look at the venue.'

He waved the book at her. 'Who's the Tom Wolfe fan?'

'Oh,' she said, 'it's doing the rounds. I think Marty's reading it just now.' Rebus flipped through the book again, his eyes lingering a moment on the inside cover. 'Tom Wolfe's had quite a career,' he said before placing the book, face down as it had been, beside the sleeping-bag. He pointed towards the photograph. 'Shall I put it back?' But she shook her head.

'It was David's,' she said. 'I think I'd like to keep it.'

Rebus smiled an avuncular smile. 'Of course,' he said. Then he remembered something. 'David's parents. Have you been in touch at all?'

She shook her head, horror growing within her. 'Oh God,' she said, 'they'll be devastated. David was very close to his mother and father.'

'Well,' said Rebus, 'give me the details and I'll phone them when I get back to the station.'

She frowned. 'But I don't ... No, sorry,' she said, 'all I know is that they live in Croydon.'

'Well, never mind,' said Rebus, knowing, in fact, that the parents had already been notified, but interested that Caulfield's apparent fiancée should know their address only vaguely. If David Caulfield had been so close to his mother and father, wouldn't they have been told of the engagement? And once told, wouldn't they have wanted to meet Marie? Rebus's knowledge of English geography wasn't exactly Mastermind material, but he was fairly sure that Reading and Croydon weren't at what you would call opposite ends of the country.

Interesting, all very interesting. Holmes came in carrying three mugs of coffee, but Rebus shook his head, suddenly the brisk senior officer.

'No time for that, Holmes,' he said. 'There's plenty of work waiting for us back at the station.' Then, to Marie: 'Take care of yourself, Miss Hivert. If there's anything we can do, don't hesitate.'

Her smile was winning. 'Thank you, Inspector.' She turned to Holmes, taking a mug from him. 'And thank you, too, constable,' she said. The look on Holmes' face kept Rebus grinning all the way back to the station.

IV

There the grin promptly vanished. There was a message

marked URGENT from the police pathologist asking Rebus to call him. Rebus pressed the seven digits on his new-fangled telephone. The thing had a twenty-number memory and somewhere in that memory was the single-digit number that would connect him with the pathologist, but Rebus could never remember which number was which and he kept losing the sheet of paper with all the memory numbers on it.

'It's four,' Holmes reminded him, just as he'd come to the end of dialling. He was throwing Holmes a kind of half-scowl when the pathologist himself answered.

'Oh, yes, Rebus. Hello there. It's about this hanging victim of yours. I've had a look at him. Manual strangulation, I'd say.'

'Yes?' Rebus, his thoughts on Marie Hivert, was waiting for some punch-line.

'I don't think you understand me, Inspector. *Manual* strangulation. From the Latin *manus*, meaning the hand. From the deep body temperature, I'd say he died between midnight and two in the morning. He was strung up on that contraption some time thereafter. Bruising around the throat is definitely consistent with thumb-pressure especially.'

'You mean someone strangled him?' Rebus said, really for Holmes' benefit.

'I *think* that's what I've been telling you, yes. If I find out anything more, I'll let you know.'

'Are the forensics people with you?'

'I've contacted the lab. They're sending someone over with some bags, but to be honest, we started off on this one thinking it was simple suicide. We may have inadvertently destroyed the tinier scraps of evidence.'

'Not to worry,' Rebus said, a father-confessor now, easing guilt. 'Just get what you can.'

He put down the receiver and stared at his Detective

Constable. Or, rather, stared *through* him. Holmes knew that there were times for talking and times for silence, and that this fell into the latter category. It took Rebus a full minute to snap out of his reverie.

'Well I'll be buggered,' he said. 'We've been talking with a murderer this morning, Brian. A cold-blooded one at that. And we didn't even know it. I wonder whatever happened to the famous police "nose" for a villain. Any idea?'

Holmes frowned. 'About what happened to the famous police "nose"?'

'No,' cried Rebus, exasperated. 'I mean, any idea who did it?'

Holmes shrugged, then brought the Fringe programme back out from where it had been rolled up in his jacket pocket. He started turning pages. 'I think,' he said, 'there's an Agatha Christie playing somewhere. Maybe we could get a few ideas?'

Rebus's eyes lit up. He snatched the programme from Holmes' hands. 'Never mind Agatha Christie,' he said, starting through the programme himself. 'What we want is Shakespeare.'

'What, *Macbeth*? *Hamlet*? *King Lear*?'

'No, not a tragedy, a good comedy, something to cheer the soul. Ah, here we go.' He stabbed the open page with his finger. '*Twelfth Night*. That's the play for us, Brian. That's the very play for us.'

The problem, really, in the end was: which *Twelfth Night*? There were three on offer, plus another at the Festival proper. One of the Fringe versions offered an update to gangster Chicago, another played with an all-female cast and the third boasted futuristic stage-design. But Rebus wanted traditional fare, and so opted for the Festival performance. There was just one hitch: it was a complete sell-out.

Not that Rebus considered this a hitch. He waited while Holmes called his girlfriend, Nell Stapleton, and apologised to her about some evening engagement he was breaking, then the two men drove to the Lyceum, tucked in behind the Usher Hall so as to be almost invisible to the naked eye.

'There's a five o'clock performance,' Rebus explained. 'We should just make it.' They did. There was a slight hold-up while Rebus explained to the house manager that this really was police business and not some last-minute culture beano, and a place was found for them in a dusty corner to the rear of the stalls. The lights were dimming as they entered.

'I haven't been to a play in years,' Rebus said to Holmes, excited at the prospect. Holmes, bemused, smiled back, but his superior's eyes were already on the stage, where the curtain was rising, a guitar was playing and a man in pale pink tights lay across an ornate bench, looking as cheesed off with life as Holmes himself felt. Why did Rebus always have to work from instinct, and always alone, never letting anyone in on whatever he knew or thought he knew? Was it because he was afraid of failure? Holmes suspected it was. If you kept your ideas to yourself, you couldn't be proved wrong. Well, Holmes had his own ideas about this case, though he was damned if he'd let Rebus in on them.

'If music be the food of love ...' came the voice from the stage. And that was another thing – Holmes was starving. It was odds-on the back few rows would soon find his growling stomach competition for the noises from the stage.

'Will you go hunt, my lord?'

'What, Curio?'

'The hart.'

'Why, so I do, the noblest that I have ...'

Holmes sneaked a glance towards Rebus. To say the older man's attention was rapt would have been understating the case. He'd give it until the end of Act One, then sneak out to the nearest chip shop. Leave Rebus to his

Shakespeare; Holmes was a nationalist when it came to literature. A pity Hugh MacDiarmid had never written a play.

In fact, Holmes went for a wander, up and down Lothian Road as far as the Caledonian Hotel to the north and Tollcross to the south. Lothian Road was Edinburgh's fast-food centre and the variety on offer brought with it indecision. Pizza, burgers, kebabs, Chinese, baked potatoes, more burgers, more pizza and the once-ubiquitous fish and chip shop (more often now an offshoot of a kebab or burger restaurant). Undecided, he grew hungrier, and stopped for a pint of lager in a noisy barn of a pub before finally settling for a fish supper, naming himself a nationalist in cuisine as well as in writing.

By the time he returned to the theatre, the players were coming out to take their applause. Rebus was clapping as loudly as anyone, enjoyment evident on his face. But when the curtain came down, he turned and dragged Holmes from the auditorium, back into the foyer and out onto the street.

'Fish and chips, eh?' he said. 'Now there's an idea.'

'How did you know?'

'I can smell the vinegar coming off your hands. Where's the chippie?'

Holmes nodded in the direction of Tollcross. They started walking. 'So did you learn anything?' Holmes asked. 'From the play, I mean?'

Rebus smiled. 'More than I'd hoped for, Brian. If you'd been paying attention, you'd have noticed it, too. The only speech that mattered was way back in Act One. A speech made by the Fool, whose name is Feste. I wonder who played Feste in ART's production last year? Actually, I think I can guess. Come on then, where's this chip shop? A man could starve to death on Lothian Road looking for something even remotely edible.'

129

'It's just off Tollcross. It's nothing very special.'

'So long as it fills me up, Brian. We've got a long evening ahead of us.'

'Oh?'

Rebus nodded vigorously. 'Hunting the heart, Brian.' He winked towards the younger man. 'Hunting the heart.'

V

The door of the Morrison Street flat was opened by Peter Collins. He looked surprised to see them.

'Don't worry, Peter,' Rebus said, pushing past him into the hall. 'We're not here to put the cuffs on you for possession.' He sniffed the air in the hall, then tutted. 'Already? At this rate you'll be stoned before *News at Ten*.'

Peter blushed.

'All right if we come in?' Rebus asked, already sauntering down the hall towards the living-room. Holmes followed him indoors, smiling an apology. Peter closed the door behind them.

'They're mostly out,' Peter called.

'So I see,' said Rebus, in the living-room now. 'Hello, Marie, how are you feeling?'

'Hello again, Inspector. I'm a little better.' She was dressed, and seated primly on the .chair, hands resting on her knees. Rebus looked towards the sofa, but thought better of sitting down. Instead he rested himself on the sofa's fairly rigid arm. 'I see you're all getting ready to go.' He nodded towards the two rucksacks parked against the living-room wall. The sleeping-bags from the floor had been folded away, as had books and alarm clocks.

'Why bother to stay?' Peter said. He flopped onto the sofa and pushed a hand through his hair. 'We thought we'd drive down through the night. Be back in Reading by dawn with any luck.'

Rebus nodded at this. 'So the show does *not* go on?'

'It'd be a bit bloody heartless, don't you think?' This from Peter Collins, with a glance towards Marie.

'Of course,' Rebus agreed. Holmes had stationed himself between the living-room door and the rucksacks. 'So where is everyone?'

Marie answered. 'Pam and Marty have gone for a last walk around.'

'And Charles is almost certainly off getting drunk somewhere,' added Collins. 'Rueing his failed show.'

'And Hugh?' asked Rebus. Collins shrugged.

'I think,' Marie said, 'Hugh went off to get drunk, too.'

'But for different reasons, no doubt,' Rebus speculated.

'He was David's best friend,' she answered quietly.

Rebus nodded thoughtfully. 'Actually, we just bumped into him – literally.'

'Who?' asked Peter.

'Mr Clay. He seems to be in the middle of a pub crawl the length of Lothian Road. We were coming out of a chip shop and came across him weaving his way to the next watering-hole.'

'Oh?' Collins didn't sound particularly interested.

'I told him where the best pubs in this neighbourhood are. He didn't seem to know.'

'That was good of you,' Collins said, voice heavy with irony.

'Nice of them all to leave you alone, isn't it though?'

The question hung in the air. At last, Marie spoke. 'What do you mean?'

But Rebus shifted on his perch and left the comment at that. 'No,' he said instead, 'only I thought Mr Clay might have had a better idea of the pubs, seeing how he was here last year, and then again in June to look at the venue. But of course, as he was good enough to explain, he *wasn't* here in June. There were exams. Some people had to study harder than others. Only three of you came to Edinburgh in June.' Rebus raised a finger shiny with chip-fat. 'Pam, who has what I'd call a definite crush on you, Peter.' Collins smiled at this, but weakly. Rebus raised a second and then third finger. 'And you two. Just the three of you. That, I presume, is where it started.'

'What?' The blood had drained from Marie's face, making her somehow more beautiful than ever. Rebus shifted again, seeming to ignore her question.

'It doesn't really matter who took that photo of you, the one I found in *Bonfire of the Vanities*.' He was staring at her quite evenly now. 'What matters is that it was there. And on the inside cover someone had drawn a couple of hearts, very similar to some I happened to see on Peter's copy of the play. It matters that on his copy of the play, Peter has also written the words "I love Edinburgh".' Peter Collins was ready to protest, but Rebus studiously ignored him, keeping his eyes on Marie's, fixing her, so that there might only have been the two of them in the room.

'You told me,' he continued, 'that you'd come to Edinburgh to check on the venue. I took that "you" to mean all of you, but Hugh Clay has put me right on that. You came without David, who was too busy studying to make the trip. And you told me something else earlier. You said your relationship with him had "survived". Survived what? I asked myself afterwards. The answer seems pretty straightforward. Survived a brief fling, a fling that started in Edinburgh and lasted the summer.'

Now, only now, did he turn to Peter Collins. 'Isn't that right, Peter?'

Collins, his face mottled with anger, made to rise.

'Sit down,' Rebus ordered, standing himself. He walked towards the fireplace, turned and faced Collins, who looked to be disappearing into the sofa, reducing in size with the passing moments. 'You love Edinburgh,' he went on, 'because that's where your little fling with Marie started. Fair enough, these things are never anyone's fault, are they? You managed to keep it fairly secret. The Tom Wolfe book belongs to you, though, and that photo you'd kept in it –

maybe forgetting it was there – that photo might have been a giveaway, but then again it could all be very innocent, couldn't it?

'But it's hard to keep something like that so secret when you're part of a very small group. There were sixteen of you in ART last year; that might have made it manageable. But not when there were only seven of you. I'm not sure who else knows about it. But I am sure that David Caulfield found out.' Rebus didn't need to turn round to know that Marie was sobbing again. He kept staring at Peter Collins. 'He found out, and last night, late and backstage, perhaps drunk, the two of you had a fight. Quite dramatic in its way, isn't it? Fighting over the heroine and all that. But during the fight you just happened to strangle the life out of David Caulfield.' He paused, waiting for a denial which didn't come.

'Perhaps,' he continued, 'Marie wanted to go to the police. I don't know. But if she did, you persuaded her not to. Instead, you came up with something more dramatic. You'd make it look like suicide. And by God, what a suicide, the kind that David himself might just have attempted.' Rebus had been moving forward without seeming to, so that now he stood directly over Peter Collins.

'Yes,' he went on, 'very dramatic. But the note was a mistake. It was a bit too clever, you see. You thought everyone would take it as a reference to David's success in last year's production, but you knew yourself that there was a double meaning in it. I've just been to see *Twelfth Night*. Bloody good it was, too. You played Feste last year, didn't you, Peter? There's one speech of his ... how does it go?' Rebus seemed to be trying to remember. 'Ah yes: "Many a good hanging prevents a bad marriage." Yes, that's it. And that's when I knew for sure.'

Peter Collins was smiling thinly. He gazed past Rebus towards Marie, his eyes full and liquid. His voice when he spoke was tender. ' "Many a good hanging prevents a bad marriage; and for turning away, let summer bear it out." '

'That's right,' Rebus said, nodding eagerly. 'Summer bore it out, all right. A summer fling. That's all. Not worth killing someone for, was it, Peter? But that didn't stop you. And the hanging was so apt, so neat. When you recalled the Fool's quote, you couldn't resist putting that note in David's pocket.' Rebus was shaking his head. 'More fool you, Mr Collins. More fool you.'

Brian Holmes went home from the police station that night in sombre mood. The traffic was slow, too, with theatre-goers threading in and out between the near-stationary cars. He rolled down the driver's-side window, trying to make the interior less stuffy, less choked, and instead let in exhaust fumes and balmy late-evening air. Why did Rebus have to be such a clever bugger so much of the time? He seemed always to go into a case at an odd angle, like someone cutting a paper shape which, apparently random, could then be folded to make an origami sculpture, intricate and recognisable.

'Too clever for his own good,' he said to himself. But what he meant was that his superior was too clever for Holmes' own good. How was he expected to shine, to be noticed, to push forwards towards promotion, when it was always Rebus who, two steps ahead, came up with the answers? He remembered a boy at school who had always beaten Holmes in every subject save History. Yet Holmes had gone to university; the boy to work on his father's farm. Things could change, couldn't they? Though all he seemed to be learning from Rebus was how to keep your thoughts to yourself, how to be devious, how to, well, how to *act*. Though all this were true, he would still be the best understudy he possibly could be. One day, Rebus wouldn't be there to come up with the answers, or — occasion even more to be relished — would be unable to find the answers.

And when that time came, Holmes would be ready to take the stage. He felt ready right now, but then he supposed every understudy must feel that way.

A flybill was thrown through his window by a smiling teenage girl. He heard her pass down the line of cars, yelling 'Come and see our show!' as she went. The small yellow sheet of paper fluttered onto the passenger seat and stayed there, face up, to haunt Holmes all the way back to Nell. Growing sombre again, it occurred to him how different things might have been if only Priestley had called the play *A Detective Constable Calls* instead.

Tit for Tat

Before he'd arrived in Edinburgh in 1970, Inspector John Rebus had fixed in his mind an image of tenement life. Tenements were things out of the Gorbals in the early years of the century, places of poverty and despair, safe havens for vermin and disease. They were the enforced homes of the poorest of the working class, a class almost without a class, a sub-class. Though tenements rose high into the air, they might as well have been dug deep into the ground. They were society's replacement for the cave.

Of course, in the 1960s the planners had come up with something even more outrageous – the tower-block. Even cities with plenty of spare land started to construct these space-saving horrors. Perhaps the moral rehabilitation of the tenement had something to do with this new contender. Nowadays, a tenement might contain the whole of society in microcosm – the genteel spinster on the ground floor, the bachelor accountant one floor above, then the bar-keeper, and above the barkeeper, always it seemed right at the top of the house, the students. This mix was feasible only because the top two floors contained flats rented out by absentee landlords. Some of these landlords might own upwards of one hundred separate flats – as was spectacularly the case in Glasgow, where the figure was even rumoured, in one or two particulars, to rise into four figures.

But in Edinburgh, things were different. In Edinburgh, the New Town planners of the nineteenth century had come up with streets of fashionable houses, all of them, to

Rebus's latter-day eyes, looking like tenements. Some prosperous areas of the city, such as Marchmont where Rebus himself lived, boasted almost nothing *but* tenements. And with the price of housing what it was, even the meaner streets were seeing a kind of renaissance, stone-blasted clean by new owner-occupiers who kept the cooking-range in the living-room as an 'original feature'.

The streets around Easter Road were as good an example as any. The knock-on effect had reached Easter Road late. People had to decide first that they couldn't afford Stockbridge, then that they couldn't quite afford any of the New Town or its immediate surroundings, and at last they might arrive in Easter Road, not by chance but somehow through fate. Soon, an enterprising soul saw his or her opportunity and opened a delicatessen or a slightly upmarket cafe, much to the bemusement of the 'locals'. These were quiet, accepting people for the most part, people who liked to see the tenement buildings being restored even if they couldn't understand why anyone would pay good money for bottled French water. (After all, you were always told to steer clear of the water on foreign holidays, weren't you?)

Despite this, the occasional Alfa Romeo or Golf GTi might find itself scratched maliciously, as might a too-clean 2CV or a coveted Morris Minor. But arson? Attempted murder? Well, that was a bit more serious. That was a very serious turn of events indeed. The trick was one perfected by racists in mixed areas. You poured petrol through the letter-box of a flat, then you set light to a rag and dropped it through the letter-box, igniting the hall carpet and ensuring that escape from the resulting fire was made difficult if not impossible. Of course, the noise, the smell of petrol meant that usually someone inside the flat was alerted early on, and mostly these fires did not spread. But sometimes ... sometimes.

'His name's John Brodie, sir,' the police constable

informed Rebus as they stood in the hospital corridor. 'Age thirty-four. Works for an insurance company in their accounts department.'

None of which came as news to Rebus. He had been to the second-floor flat, just off Easter Road, reeking of soot and water now; an unpleasant clean-up ahead. The fire had spread quickly along the hall. Some jackets and coats hanging from a coat-stand had caught light and sent the flames licking along the walls and ceiling. Brodie, asleep in bed (it all happened around one in the morning) had been wakened by the fire. He'd dialled 999, then had tried putting the fire out himself, with a fair degree of success. A rug from the living-room had proved useful in snuffing out the progress of the fire along the hall and some pans of water had dampened things down. But there was a price to pay — burns to his arms and hands and face, and smoke inhalation. Neighbours, alerted by the smoke, had broken down the door just as the fire engine was arriving. CID, brought to the scene by a police constable's suspicions, had spoken with some of the neighbours. A quiet man, Mr Brodie, they said. A decent man. He'd only moved in a few months before. Worked for an insurance company. Nobody thought he smoked, but they seemed to assume he'd left a cigarette burning somewhere.

'Careless that. Even supposing we *do* live in Auld Reekie.' And the first-floor occupier had chuckled to himself, until his wife yelped from their flat that there was water coming in through the ceiling. The man looked helpless and furious.

'Insurance should cover it,' Rebus commented, pouring oil on troubled ... no, not the best image that. The husband went off to investigate further and the other tenement dwellers began slouching off to bed, leaving Rebus to head into the burnt-out hallway itself.

But even without the Fire Officer, the cause of the fire

had been plain to Rebus. Chillingly plain. The smell of
petrol was everywhere.

He took a look round the rest of the flat. The kitchen was
tiny, but boasted a large sash-window looking down onto
back gardens and across to the back of the tenement over
the way. The bathroom was smaller still, but kept very
neat. No ring of grime around the bath, no strewn towels or
underpants, nothing steeping in the sink. A very tidy
bachelor was Mr Brodie. The living-room, too, was
uncluttered. A series of framed prints more or less covered
one wall. Detailed paintings of birds. Rebus glanced at one
or two: willow warbler, bearded tit. The rooms would need
to be redecorated, of course, otherwise the charred smell
would always be there. Insurance would probably cover it.
Brodie was an insurance man, wasn't he? He'd know.
Maybe he'd even squeeze a cheque out of the company
without too much haggling.

Finally, Rebus went into the bedroom. Messier here,
mostly as a result of the hurriedly flung-back bedclothes.
Pyjama bottoms lying crumpled on the bed itself. Slippers
and a used mug sitting on the floor beside the bed, and in
one corner, next to the small wardrobe, a tripod atop which
was fixed a good make of SLR camera. On the floor against
the wall was a large-format book, *Better Zoom Pictures*, with
a photograph of an osprey on the front. Probably one of the
Loch Garten ospreys, thought Rebus. He'd taken his
daughter there a couple of times in the past. Tourists,
plenty of them, he had seen, but ospreys were there none.

If anyone had asked him what he thought most odd
about the flat, he would have answered: there's no
television set. What did Mr Brodie do for company then of
an evening?

For no real reason, Rebus bent down and peered beneath
the bed itself, and was rewarded with a pile of magazines.
He pulled one out. Soft porn, a 'readers' wives' special. He
pushed it back into place. The tidy bachelor's required

bedtime companion. And, partly, an answer to his earlier question.

He left the flat and sought out one or two of the still wakeful neighbours. No one had seen or heard anything. Access to the tenement itself was easy; you just pushed open the communal front door, the lock of which had broken recently and was waiting to be fixed.

'Any reason,' Rebus asked, 'why anyone would bear Mr Brodie a grudge?'

That gave them pause. No smouldering cigarette then, but arson. But there were shakes of rumpled heads. No reason. A very quiet man. Kept himself to himself. Worked in insurance. Always stopped for a chat if you met him on the stairs. Always cleaned the stairs promptly when his turn came, not like some they could mention. Probably paid his rent promptly, too. Tea was being provided in the kitchen of one of the first-floor flats, where the 'Auld Reekie' wag was being consoled.

'I only painted that ceiling three months back. Do you know how much textured paint costs?'

Soon enough everyone found the answer. The man's wife looked bored. She smiled towards the tea-party's hostess.

'Wasn't that first fireman dishy?' she said.

'Which one?'

'The one with the blue eyes. The one who told us not to worry. He could give me a fireman's lift anytime.'

The hostess snorted into her tea. Rebus made his excuses and left.

Rebus had dealt with racist arson attacks before. He'd even come across 'anti-yuppie' attacks, usually in the form of graffiti on cars or the outside walls of property. A warehouse conversion in Leith had been sprayed with the slogan HOUSES FOR THE NEEDY, NOT THE GREEDY. The attack on Brodie seemed more personal, but it was worth considering all the possible motives. He was crossing things off from a list in his mind as he drove to the hospital. Once there, he talked to the police constable in the corridor and, after nodding his head a few times, he entered the ward where John Brodie had been 'made comfortable'. Despite the hour, Brodie was far from asleep. He was propped up against a pillow, his arms lying out in front of him on top of the sheets. Thick creamy white cotton pads and delicate-looking bandages predominated. Part of his hair had been shaved away, so that burns to the scalp could be treated. He had no eyebrows, and only remnants of eyelashes. His face was round and shiny; easy to imagine it breaking into a chuckle, but probably not tonight.

Rebus picked a chair out from a pile against the far wall and sat down, only then introducing himself.

Brodie's voice was shaky. 'I know who did it.'

'Oh?' Rebus kept his voice low, in deference to the sleeping bodies around him. This was not quite how he'd expected the conversation to begin.

Brodie swallowed. 'I know who did it and I know *why* she did it. But I don't want to press charges.'

Rebus wasn't about to say that this decision was not up to Brodie himself. He didn't want the man clamming up. He wanted jaw-jaw. He nodded as if in agreement. 'Is there anything I can get you?' he said, inviting further confessions, as though from one friend to another.

'She must be a bit cracked,' Brodie went on, as though Rebus hadn't spoken at all. 'I told the police that at the time. She's doolally, I said. Must be. Well, this proves it, doesn't it?'

'You think she needs help?'

'Maybe. Probably.' He seemed deep in thought for a moment. 'Yes, almost certainly. I mean, it's going a bit far, isn't it? Even if you think you've got grounds. But she didn't have grounds. The police *told* her that.'

'But they didn't manage to convince her.'

'That's right.'

Rebus thought he was playing this fairly well. Obviously, Brodie was in shock. Maybe he was even babbling a bit, but as long as he was kept talking, Rebus would be able to piece together whatever the story was that he was trying to tell. There was a wheezy, dry laugh from the bed.

Brodie's eyes twinkled. 'You don't know what I'm talking about, do you?' Rebus was obliged to shake his head. 'Of course you don't. Well, I'll have a sip of water and then I'll tell you.'

And he did.

The morning was bright but grey: 'sunshine and showers', the weatherman would term it. It wasn't quite autumn yet. The too-short summer might yet have some surprises. Rebus waited in his room – his desk located not too far from the radiator – until the two police constables could be found. They were uneasy when they came in, until he reassured them. Yes, as requested, they had brought their notebooks with them. And yes, they remembered the incident very well indeed.

'It started with anonymous phone calls,' one of them began. 'They seemed to be genuine enough. Miss Hooper told us about one of them in particular. Her phone rings. Man on the other end identifies himself as a police inspector and tells her there's an anonymous caller who's going through the Edinburgh directory trying number after number. He says her number might come up soon, but the police have put a trace on her line. So can she keep the man talking for as long as possible.'

'Oh yes.' Really, Rebus didn't need to hear the rest. But he listened patiently to the constable's story.

'Later on that day, a man did ring. He asked her some very personal questions and she kept him talking. After-wards, she rang the police station to see if they'd caught him. Only, of course, the name the so-called inspector had given wasn't known to the station. It was the anonymous caller himself, setting her up.'

Rebus shook his head slowly. It was old, but clever. 'So she complained about anonymous calls?'

'Yes, sir. But then the calls stopped. So that didn't seem too bad. No need for an operator to intercept or a change of number or anything.'

'How did Miss Hooper seem at the time?'

The constable shrugged and turned to his colleague, who now spoke. 'A bit nervy, sir. But that was understandable, wasn't it? A very nice lady, I'd say. Not married. I don't think she even had a boyfriend.' He turned his head towards his colleague. 'Didn't she say something like that, Jim?'

'I think so, yes.'

'So then what happened?' asked Rebus.

'A few weeks later, this would be just over a week ago, we had another call from Miss Hooper. She said a man in the tenement across the back from her was a peeping tom. She'd seen him at a window, aiming his binoculars towards her building. More particularly, she thought, towards her own flat. We investigated and spoke to Mr Brodie. He appeared quite concerned about the allegations. He showed us the binoculars and admitted using them to watch from his kitchen window. But he assured us that he was bird-watching.' The other constable smiled at this. ' "Bird-watching," he said.'

'Ornithology,' said Rebus.

'That's right, sir. He said he was very interested in birds, a bird-fancier sort of thing.' Another smile. They were obviously hoping Rebus would come to enjoy the joke with them. They were wrong, though they didn't seem to sense this just yet.

'Go on,' he said simply.

'Well, sir, there did seem to be a lot of pictures of birds in his flat.'

'You mean the prints in the living-room?'

'That's right, sir, pictures of an ornithological nature.'

Now the other constable interrupted. 'You won't believe it, sir. He said he was watching the tenement and the garden because he'd seen some ...' pause for effect ... 'bearded tits.'

Now both the young constables were grinning.

'I'm glad you find your job so amusing,' Rebus said. 'Because I don't think frightening phone calls, peeping toms and arson attacks are material for jokes!'

The grins disappeared.

'Get on with it,' Rebus demanded. The constables looked at one another.

'Not much more to tell, sir,' said the one called Jim. 'The gentleman, Mr Brodie, seemed genuine enough. But he promised to be a bit more careful in future. Like I say, he seemed genuinely concerned. We informed Miss Hooper of our findings. She didn't seem entirely convinced.'

'Obviously not,' said Rebus, but he did not go on to clarify. Instead, he dismissed the two officers and sat back in his chair. Brodie suspected Hooper of the arson attack, not, it would appear, without reason. What was more, Brodie had said he couldn't think of any other enemies he might have made. Either that or he wasn't about to tell Rebus about them. Rebus leaned back in his chair and rested his arm along the radiator, enjoying its warmth. The next person to speak to, naturally, was Miss Hooper herself. Another day, another tenement.

'Bearded tits,' Rebus said to himself. This time, he allowed himself a smile.

'It's your lucky day,' Miss Hooper told him. 'Normally I don't come home for lunch, but today I just felt like it.'

Lucky indeed. Rebus had knocked on the door of Miss

145

Hooper's first-floor flat but received no answer. Eventually, another door on the landing had opened, revealing a woman in her late forties, stern of face and form.

'She's not in,' the woman had stated, unnecessarily.

'Any idea when she'll be back?'

'Who are you then?'

'Police.'

The woman pursed her lips. The nameplate above her doorbell, to the left of the door itself, read McKAY. 'She works till four o'clock. She's a schoolteacher. You'll catch her at school if you want her.'

'Thank you. Mrs McKay, is it?'

'It is.'

'Could I have a word?'

'What about?'

By now, Rebus was standing at Mrs McKay's front door. Past her, he caught sight of a dark entrance hall strewn with bits and pieces of machinery, enough to make up most, but not quite all, of a motorbike.

'About Miss Hooper,' he said.

'What about her?'

No, she was not about to let him in. He could hear her television blaring. Lunchtime game-show applause. The resonant voice of the questionmaster. Master of the question.

'Have you known her long?'

'Ever since she moved in. Three, four years. Aye, four years.' She had folded her arms now, and was resting one shoulder against the door-jamb. 'What's the problem?'

'I suppose you must know her quite well, living on the same landing?'

'Well enough. She comes in for a cuppa now and again.' She paused, making it quite clear to Rebus that this was not an honour *he* was about to receive.

'Have you heard about the fire?'

'Fire?'

146

'Across the back.' Rebus gestured in some vague direction with his head.

'Oh aye. The fire engine woke me right enough. Nobody hurt though, was there?'

'What makes you say that?'

She shuffled now, unfolding her arms so one hand could rub at another. 'Just ... what I heard.'

'A man was injured, quite seriously. He's in hospital.'

'Oh.'

And then the main door opened and closed. Sound of feet on stone echoing upwards.

'Oh, here's Miss Hooper now,' said Mrs McKay. Said with relief, Rebus thought to himself. Said with relief ...

Miss Hooper let him in and immediately switched on the kettle. She hoped he wouldn't mind if she made herself a sandwich? And would he care for one himself? Cheese and pickle or peanut butter and apple? No, on second thoughts, she'd make some of both, and he could choose for himself.

A teacher? Rebus could believe it. There was something in her tone, in the way she seemed to have to utter all of her thoughts aloud, and in the way she asked questions and then answered them herself. He could see her standing in her classroom, asking her questions and surrounded by silence.

Alison Hooper was in her early thirties. Small and slim, almost schoolboyish. Short straight brown hair. Tiny earrings hooked into tiny ears. She taught in a primary school only ten minutes' walk from her flat. The flat itself was scattered with books and magazines, from many of which had been cut illustrations, clearly intended to find their way into her classroom. Mobiles hung from her living-room ceiling: some flying pigs, an alphabet, teddy bears waving from aeroplanes. There were colourful rugs on her walls, but no rugs at all on the stripped floor. She had a breathy, nervous way with her and an endearing twitch to her nose. Rebus followed her into the kitchen and watched her open a loaf of brown sliced bread.

'I usually take a packed lunch with me, but I slept in this morning and didn't have time to make it. I could have eaten in the canteen, of course, but I just felt like coming home. Your lucky day, Inspector.'

'You had trouble sleeping last night then?'

'Well, yes. There was a fire in the tenement across the back.' She pointed through her window with a buttery knife. 'Over there. I heard sirens and the fire-engine's motor kept rumbling away, so I couldn't for the life of me get back to sleep.'

Rebus went across to the window and looked out. John Brodie's tenement stared back at him. It could have been any tenement anywhere in the city. Same configuration of windows and drainpipes, same railing-enclosed drying-green. He angled his head further to look into the back garden of Alison Hooper's tenement. Movement there. What was it? A teenager working on his motorbike. The motorbike standing on the drying-green, and all the tools and bits and pieces lying on a piece of plastic which had been spread out for the purpose. The nearby garden shed stood with its door propped open by a wooden stretcher. Through the doorway Rebus could see yet more motorbike spares and some oil cans.

'The fire last night,' he said, 'it was in a flat occupied by Mr John Brodie.'

'Oh!' she said, her knife-hand pausing above the bread. 'The peeping tom?' Then she swallowed, not slow on the uptake. 'That's why you're here then.'

'Yes. Mr Brodie gave us your name, Miss Hooper. He thought perhaps –'

'Well, he's right.'

'Oh?'

'I mean, I do have a grudge. I do think he's a pervert. Not that I seem able to convince the police of that.' Her voice was growing shriller. She stared at the slices of bread in a fixed, unblinking way. 'No, the police don't seem to think there's a problem. But I know. I've talked to the other residents. We *all* know.' Then she relaxed, smiled at the bread. She slapped some peanut butter onto one slice. Her voice was calm. 'I do have a grudge, Inspector, but I did not set fire to that man's flat. I'm even pleased that he wasn't injured.'

'Who says he wasn't?'

'What?'

'He's in hospital.'

'Is he? I thought someone said there'd been no —'

'Who said?'

She shrugged. 'I don't know. One of the other teachers. Maybe they'd heard something on the radio. I don't know. Tea or coffee?'

'Whatever you're having.'

She made two mugs of decaffeinated instant. 'Let's go through to the living-room,' she said.

There, she gave him the story of the phone calls, and the story of the man with the binoculars.

'Bird-watching my eye,' she said. 'He was looking into people's windows.'

'Hard to tell, surely.'

She twitched her nose. 'Looking into people's windows,' she repeated.

'Did anyone else see him?'

'He stopped after I complained. But who knows? I mean, it's easy enough to see someone during the day. But at night, in that room of his with the lights turned off. He could sit there all night watching us. Who would know?'

'You say you spoke to the other residents?'

'Yes.'

'All of them?'

'One or two. That's enough, word gets round.'

I'll bet, thought Rebus. And he had another thought,

which really was just a word: tenementality. He ate the spicy sandwich and the sickly sandwich quickly, drained his mug and said he'd leave her to finish her lunch in peace. ('Finish your piece in peace,' he'd nearly said, but hadn't, just in case she didn't get the joke.) He walked downstairs, but instead of making along the passage to the front door, turned right and headed towards the tenement's back door.

Outside, the biker was fitting a bulb to his brake-light. He took the new bulb from a plastic box and tossed the empty box onto the sheet of plastic.

'Mind if I take that?' asked Rebus. The youth looked round at him, saw where he was pointing, then shrugged and returned to his work. There was a small cassette recorder playing on the grass beside him. Heavy Metal. The batteries were low and the sound was tortuous.

'Can if you like,' he said.

'Thanks.' Rebus lifted the box by its edges and slipped it into his jacket pocket. 'I use them to keep my flies in.'

The biker turned and grinned.

'Fishing flies,' Rebus explained, smiling himself. 'It's just perfect for keeping my fishing flies in.'

'No flies on you, eh?' said the youth.

Rebus laughed. 'Are you Mrs McKay's son?' he asked.

'That's right.' The bulb was fitted, the casing was being screwed back into place.

'I'd test that before you put the casing on. Just in case it's a dud. You'd only have to take it apart again.'

The boy looked round again. 'No flies on you,' he repeated. He took the casing off again.

'I've just been up seeing your mum.'

'Oh aye?' The tone told Rebus that the boy's parents were either separated, or else the father was dead. You're her latest, are you? the tone implied. Mum's latest fancy-man.

'She was telling me about the fire.'

The boy examined the casing closely. 'Fire?'

'Last night. Have you noticed any of your petrol-cans disappearing? Or maybe one's got less in than you thought?'

Now, the red see-through casing might have been a gem under a microscope. But the boy was saying nothing.

'My name's Rebus, by the way, Inspector Rebus.'

Rebus had a little courtroom conversation with himself on the way back to the station.

And did the suspect drop anything when you revealed your identity to him?

Yes, he dropped his jaw.

Dropped his jaw?

That's right. He looked like a hairless ape with a bad case of acne. And he lost his nut.

Lost his nut?

A nut he'd been holding. It fell into the grass. He was still looking for it when I left.

What about the plastic box, Inspector, the one in which the new brake-light bulb had been residing? Did he ask for it back?

I didn't give him the chance. It's my intention *never* to give a sucker an even chance.

Back at the station, comfortable in his chair, the desk solid and reliable in front of him, the heater solid and reliable behind, Rebus thought about fire, the easy assassin. You didn't need to get your hands on a gun. Didn't even need to buy a knife. Acid, poison, again, difficult to find. But fire ... fire was everywhere. A disposable lighter, a box of matches. Strike a match and you had fire. Warming, nourishing, dangerous fire. Rebus lit a cigarette, the better to help him think. There wouldn't be any news from the lab for some time yet. Some time. Something was niggling. Something he'd heard. What was it? A saying came to mind: prompt payment will be appreciated. You used to get that on the bottom of invoices. Prompt payment.

Probably pays his rent promptly, too.

Well, well. Now there was a thing. Owner-occupier. Not every owner *did* occupy, and not every occupier was an owner. Rebus recalled that Detective Sergeant Hendry of Dunfermline CID was a keen bird-watcher. Once or twice, on courses or at conferences, he'd collared Rebus and bored him with tales of the latest sighting of the Duddingston bittern or the Kilconquhar red-head smew. Like all hobbyists, Hendry was keen to have others share his enthusiasm. Like all anti-hobbyists, Rebus would yawn with more irony than was necessary.

Still, it was worth a phone-call.

'I'll have to call you back, John,' said a busy DS Hendry. 'It's not the sort of thing I could tell you offhand. Give me your number at home and I'll ring you tonight. I didn't know you were interested.'

'I'm not, believe me.'

But his words went unheeded. 'I saw siskins and twite earlier in the year.'

'Really?' said Rebus. 'I've never been one for country and western music. Siskins and Twite, eh? They've been around for years.'

By the following morning, he had everything he needed. He arrived as Mrs McKay and her son were eating a late breakfast. The television was on, providing the noise necessary to their lives. Rebus had come accompanied by two other officers, so that there could be no doubting he meant business. Gerry McKay's jaw dropped again as Rebus began to speak. The tale itself was quickly told. John Brodie's front door had been examined, the metal letterbox checked for fingerprints. Some good, if oily, prints had been found, and these matched those found on the plastic box Rebus had taken from Gerry McKay. There could be no doubting that Gerry McKay had pushed open John Brodie's letterbox. If Gerry would accompany the officers to the station.

'Mum!' McKay was on his feet, yelling, panicky. 'Mum, tell them! Tell them!'

Mrs McKay had a face as dark as ketchup. Rebus was glad he had brought the other officers. Her voice trembled when she spoke. 'It wasn't Gerry's idea,' she said. 'It was mine. If there's anyone you want to talk to about it, it should be me. It was my idea. Only, I knew Gerry'd be faster getting in and out of the stairwell. That's all. He's got nothing to do with it.' She paused, her face turning even nastier. 'Besides, that wee shite deserved all he got. Dirty, evil little runt of a man. You didn't see the state Alison was in. Such a nice wee girl, wouldn't say boo to a goose, and to be got into a state like that. I couldn't let him get away with it, hell. And if it were up to you lot, he'd have gotten off scot-free, wouldn't he? It's nothing to do with Gerry.'

'It'll be taken into account at the trial,' Rebus said quietly.

John Brodie looked not to have moved since Rebus had left him. His arms still lay on the top of the bed-cover, and he was still propped up against a pillow.

'Inspector Rebus,' he said. 'Back again.'

'Back again,' said Rebus, placing a chair by the bed and seating himself. 'The doctor says you're doing fine.'

'Yes,' said Brodie.

'Anything I can get you?' Brodie shook his head. 'No? Juice? A bit of fruit maybe? How about something to read? I notice you like girlie mags. I saw one in your flat. I could get you a few of those if you like.' Rebus winked. 'Readers' wives, eh? Amateurs. That's your style. All those blurry Polaroid shots, heads cut off. That's what you like, eh, John?'

But John Brodie was saying nothing. He was looking at

153

his arms. Rebus drew the chair closer to the bed. Brodie flinched, but could not move.

'*Panurus biarmicus*,' Rebus hissed. Now Brodie looked blankly at him. Rebus repeated the words. Still Brodie looked blank. 'Go on,' Rebus chided, 'take a guess.'

'I don't know what you're talking about.'

'No?' Rebus was wide-eyed. 'Curious that. Sounds like the name of a disease, doesn't it? Maybe you know it better as the bearded tit.'

'Oh.' Brodie smiled shyly, and nodded. 'Yes, the bearded tit.'

Rebus smiled too, but coldly. 'You didn't know, you didn't have a clue. Shall I tell you something about the bearded tit? No, better yet, Mr Brodie, you tell *me* something about it.' He sat back and folded his arms expectantly.

'What?'

'Go on.'

'Look, what's all this about?'

'It's quite simple, you see.' Rebus sat forward again. 'The bearded tit isn't commonly found in Scotland. I got that from an expert. Not commonly found, that's what he said. More than that, its habitat – and I'm quoting here – is "extensive and secluded reed-beds". Do you see what I'm getting at? You'd hardly call Easter Road a reed-bed, would you?'

Brodie raised his head a little, his thin lips very straight and wide. He was thinking, but he wasn't talking.

'You see what I'm getting at, don't you? You told those two constables that you were watching bearded tits from your window. But that's just not true. It couldn't possibly be true. You said the name of the first bird that came into your head, and it came into your head because there was a drawing on your living-room wall. I saw it myself. But it's not you that's the bird-watcher, John. It's your landlord and landlady. You rented the place furnished and you haven't changed anything. It's their drawings on the wall. They got in touch about the insurance, you see. Wondering whether the fire was accidental. They saw a bit about it in the newspaper. They could appreciate that they hadn't heard from you, what with you being in hospital and all, but they wanted to sort out the insurance. So I was able to ask them about the birds on the wall. *Their* birds, John, not yours. It was quick thinking of you to come up with the story. It even fooled those two PCs. It might have fooled me. That book about zoom photography, even that had a picture of birds on the front.' He paused. 'But you're a peeper, John, that's all. That's what you are, a nasty little voyeur. Miss Hooper was right all the time.'

'Was it her who –?'

'You'll find out soon enough.'

'It's all lies, you know. Hearsay, circumstantial. You've no proof.'

'What about the photos?'

'What photos?'

Rebus sighed. 'Come on, John. All that gear in your bedroom. Tripod, camera, zoom lenses. Photographing birds, were you? I'd be interested to see the results. Because it wasn't just binoculars, was it? You took piccies, too. In your wardrobe, are they?' Rebus checked his watch. 'With luck I'll have the search warrant inside the hour. Then I intend to take a good look round your flat, John. I intend taking a *very* good look.'

'There's nothing there.' He was shaking now, his arms moving painfully in their gauze bandages. 'Nothing. You've no right. Someone tried to kill ... No right. They tried to kill me.'

Rebus was willing to concede a point. 'Certainly they tried to scare you. We'll see what the courts decide.' He rose to his feet. Brodie was still twittering on. Twit, twit, twit. It would be a while before he'd be able to use a camera again.

'Do you want to know something else, John?' Rebus said, unable to resist one of his parting shots. 'Something about the bearded tit? It's classified as a *babbler*.' He smiled a smile of warm sunshine. 'A babbler!' he repeated. 'Looks to me like you're a bit of a babbler yourself. Well,' he picked up the chair and pretended to be considering something, 'at any rate, I'd certainly classify you as a tit.'

He returned that evening to his own tenement and his roaring gas fire. But there was a surprise awaiting him on the doorhandle of his flat. A reminder from Mrs Cochrane downstairs. A reminder that it was his week for washing the stairs and that he hadn't done it yet and it was nearly the end of the week and when was he going to do it? Rebus sent a roar into the stairwell before slamming shut the door behind him. It was only a moment before other doors started to open, faces peering out, and another Edinburgh tenement conversation began, multi-storeyed, undertone and echoing.

Not Provan

How badly did Detective Inspector John Rebus want to nail Willie Provan? Oh, badly, very badly indeed. Rebus visualised it as a full-scale crucifixion, each nail going in slowly, the way Willie liked to put the boot and the fist slowly, methodically, into the victims of his violence.

Rebus had first encountered Willie Provan five years before, as a schoolkid spiralling out of control. Both parents dead, Willie had been left in the charge of a dotty and near-deaf aunt. He had taken charge of her house, had held wild parties there, parties to which the police were eventually, habitually called by neighbours at the end of their tether.

Entering the house had been like stepping into an amateur production of *Caligula*: naked, under-aged couples so drunk or drugged they could not complete the act which so interested them; emptied tins of solvent, polythene bags encrusted with the dregs of the stuff. A whiff of something animal, something less-than-human in the air. And, in a small back room upstairs, the aunt, locked in and sitting up in her bed, a cold cup of tea and a half-eaten sandwich on the table beside her.

By the time he left school, Willie was already a legend. Four years on the dole had benefited him little. But he had learned cunning, and so far the police had been unable to put him away. He remained a thorn in Rebus's side. Today, Rebus felt someone might just come along and pluck that thorn out.

He sat in the public gallery and watched the court proceedings. Near him were a few of Willie Provan's friends, members of his gang. They called themselves the Tiny Alice, or T-Alice. No one knew why. Rebus glanced over towards them. Sleeves rolled up, sporting tattoos and unshaven grins. They were the city's sons, the product of an Edinburgh upbringing, but they seemed to belong to another culture, another civilisation entirely, reared on Schwarzenegger videos and bummed cigarettes. Rebus shivered, feeling he understood them better than he liked to admit.

The case against Provan was solid and satisfying. On a cup-tie evening several months ago, a football fan had been heading towards the Heart of Midlothian ground. He was late, his train from Fife having been behind time. He was an away supporter and he was on his own in Gorgie.

An arm snaked around his neck, yanked him into a tenement stairwell, and there Willie Provan had kicked and punched him into hospitalisation. For what reason? Rebus could guess. It had nothing to do with football, nothing with football hooliganism. Provan pretended a love of Hearts, but had never, to Rebus's knowledge, attended a game. Nor could he name more than two or three players in the current team's line-up.

Nevertheless, Gorgie was his patch, his territory. He had spotted an invader and had summarily executed him, in his own terms. But his luck had run out. A woman had heard some sounds from the stairwell and had opened her door to investigate. Provan saw her and ran off. But she had given the police a good description and had later identified Provan as the attacker. Moreover, a little while after the attack, a constable, off duty and happening to pass Tynecastle Park, had spotted a young man, apparently disorientated. He had approached the man and asked him if he was all right, but at that point some members of T-Alice had appeared from their local pub, directly opposite the Hearts ground and had taken the man inside.

The constable thought little of it, until he heard about

the assault and was given a description of the attacker. The description matched that of the disorientated man, and that man turned out to be Willie Provan. With Provan's previous record, this time he would go down, Rebus was sure of that. So he sat and he watched and he listened.

He watched the jurors, too. They winced, perceptibly as they were told of the injuries to the victim, injuries which still, several months on, kept him in hospital, unable to walk and with respiratory difficulties to boot. To boot. Ha! Rebus let a short-lived smile wrinkle his face. Yes, the jury would convict. But Rebus was most interested in one juror in particular, an intense young man who was taking copious notes, sending intelligent written questions to the judge, studying photographs and diagrams with enthusiasm. The model juror, ready to see that justice was done and all was fair and proper. At one point, the young man looked up and caught Rebus watching him. After that, he gave Rebus some of his attention, but still scribbled his notes and checked and rechecked what he had written.

The other jurors were solemn, looked bored even. Passive spectators at a one-horse race. Guilty. Probably by the end of the day. Rebus would sit it out. The prosecution had finished its case, and the defence case had already begun. The usual stuff when an obviously guilty party pleaded not guilty: trying to catch out prosecution witnesses, instilling mistrust, trying to persuade the jury that things were not as cut and dried as they seemed, that there was probable cause for doubt. Rebus sat back and let it wash over him. Provan would go down.

Then came the iceberg, ripping open the bow of Rebus's confidence.

The defence counsel had called the off-duty constable, the one who had spotted Provan outside the Hearts ground. The constable was young, with a bad case of post-juvenile acne. He tried to stand to attention as the questions were put to him, but when flustered would raise a hand towards his scarred cheeks. Rebus remembered his own first time on the witness stand. A Glasgow music-hall stage could not have been more terrifying.

'And what time do you say it was when you first saw the accused?' The defence counsel had a slight Irish brogue, and his eyes were dark from want of sleep. His cheap ballpoint pen had burst, leaving black stains across his hands. Rebus felt a little sorry for him.

'I'm not sure, sir.'

'You're not sure?' The words came slowly. The inference was: this copper is a bit thick, isn't he? How can you the jury trust him? For the counsel was staring at the jury as he spoke and this seemed to unnerve the constable further. A hand rubbed against a cheek.

'Roughly then,' continued the defence counsel. 'Roughly what time was it?'

'Sometime between seven-thirty and eight, sir.'

The counsel nodded, flipping through a sheaf of notes. 'And what did you say to the accused?' As the constable was about to reply, the counsel interrupted, still with his face towards the jury. 'I say "the accused" because there's no disagreement that the person the constable saw outside the football ground was my client.' He paused. 'So constable, what did you say?'

' "Are you all right?" Something like that.'

Rebus glanced towards where Provan sat in the dock. Provan was looking terribly confident. His clear blue eyes were sparkling and he sat forwards in his chair, keen to catch the dialogue going on before him. For the first time, Rebus felt an uneasy stab: the thorn again, niggling him. What was going on?

'You asked him if he was all right.' It was a statement. The counsel paused again. Now the prosecution counsel was frowning: he too was puzzled by this line of questioning. Rebus felt his hands forming into fists.

'You asked him if he was all right, and he replied? What exactly *did* he reply?'

'I couldn't really make it out, sir.'

'Why was that? Were his words slurred perhaps?'

The constable shrugged. 'A little, maybe.'

'A little? Mmm.' The counsel looked at his notes again. 'What about the noise from the stadium?'

'Sir?'

'You were directly outside the ground. There was a cup-tie being played in front of thousands of spectators. It was noisy, wasn't it?'

'Yes, sir,' agreed the constable.

'In fact, it was *very* noisy, wasn't it, Constable Davidson? It was *extraordinarily* noisy. That was why you couldn't hear my client's reply. Isn't that the case?'

The constable shrugged again, not sure where any of this was leading, happy enough to agree with the defence. 'Yes, sir,' he said.

'In fact, as you approached my client, you may remember that there was a sudden upsurge in the noise from the ground.'

The constable nodded, seeming to remember. 'That's right, yes. I think a goal had just been scored.'

'Indeed, a goal had been scored. Just after you had first spotted my client, as you were walking towards him. A goal was scored, the noise was terrific. You shouted your question to my client, and he replied, but his words were drowned out by the noise from the ground. His friends saw him from the Goatfell public house and came to his aid, leading him inside. The noise was still very great, even then. They were shouting to you to let you know they would take care of him. Isn't that right?'

Now, the counsel turned to the constable, fixing him with his dark eyes.

'Yes, sir.'

The counsel nodded, seeming satisfied. Willie Provan,

too, looked satisfied. Rebus's nerves were jangling. He was reminded of a song lyric: *there's something happening here, but you don't know what it is.* Something was most definitely happening here, and Rebus didn't like it. The defence counsel spoke again.

'Do you know what the score was that night?'

'No, sir.'

'It was one-nil. The home team won by a single goal, the single goal you heard from outside the ground. A single goal scored –' picking up the notes for effect, turning again to face the jury, 'in the fifteenth minute of the game, a game that kicked off ... when? Do you happen to recall?'

The constable knew now, knew where this was leading. His voice when he spoke had lost a little of its life. 'It was a seven–thirty kick-off.'

'That's right, it was. So you see, Police Constable Davidson, it was seven forty-five when you saw my client outside the ground. I don't think you would contest that now, would you? And yet we heard Mrs McClintock say that it was twenty to eight when she heard a noise on her stairwell and went to her door. She was quite specific because she looked at her clock before she went to the door. Her call to the police was timed at seven forty-two, just two minutes later.'

Rebus didn't need to hear any more, tried to shut his ears to it. The tenement where the assault had taken place was over a mile from Tynecastle Park and the Goatfell pub. To have been where he was when the constable had approached him, Provan would have had to run, in effect, a four-minute mile. Rebus doubted he was capable of it, doubted everything now. But looking at Provan he could *see* the little prick was guilty. He was as guilty as hell and he was about to get away scot bloody free. Rebus's knuckles were white, his teeth were gritted. Provan looked up at him and smiled. The thorn was in Rebus's side again, working away relentlessly, bleeding the policeman to death.

* * *

It couldn't be true. It just couldn't. The trial wasn't over yet. Things had been strung out over the afternoon, the prosecution clearly flustered and playing for time, wondering what tactic to try next, what question to ask. He had lasted the afternoon and court had been adjourned after the summings up. It was all to do with time, as the defence counsel contended. The prosecution tried to negate the time factor and rely instead on the one and only witness. He asked: can we be certain a goal had been scored at that precise moment when PC Davidson approached the accused? Is it not better to trust the identification of the witness, Mrs McClintock, who had actually disturbed the attacker in the course of the assault? And so on. But Rebus knew the case was doomed. There was too much doubt now, way too much. Not guilty, or maybe that Scots get-out clause of 'not proven', whatever. If only the victim had caught a glimpse of Provan, if only. If, if, if. The jury would assemble again tomorrow at ten-thirty, retire to their room and emerge before lunch with a decision which would make Provan a free man. Rebus shook his head.

He was sitting in his car, not up to driving. Just sitting there, the key in the ignition, trying to think things through. But going around in circles, no clear direction, his mind filled with Provan's smile, a smile he would happily tear from that face. Illegal thoughts coursed through his head, ways of fixing Provan, ways of putting him inside. But no: it had to be clean, it had to be *right*. Justification was only part of the process; justice demanded more.

At last, he gave an audible growl, the sound of a caged animal, and turned the ignition, starting the car, heading nowhere in particular. At home he would only brood. A pub might be an idea. There were a few pubs, their clientele almost silent, where a man might drink in solitude and quiet. A kind of a wake for The Law. Damn it, no, he knew where he was headed. Tried not to know, but knew all the same. He was driving towards Gorgie, driving deep into Willie Provan's territory, into the gangland ruled by Tiny Alice. He was heading into the Wild West End of Edinburgh.

The streets were narrow, tenements rising on either side. A cold October wind was blowing, forcing people to angle their walk into the wind, giving them the jack-knife look of a Lowry painting. They were all coming home from work. It was dark, the headlamps of cars and buses like torches in a cave. Gorgie always seemed dark. Even on a summer's day it seemed dark. It had something to do with the narrowness of the streets and the height of the tenements; they seemed like trees in the Amazon, blocking out the light to the pallid vegetation beneath.

Rebus found Cooper Road and parked on the opposite side of the street from number 42. He switched off his engine and wondered what to do now. He was treading dangerously: not the physical danger of the T-Alice, but the more enveloping danger of involvement in a case. If he spoke with Mrs McClintock and the defence counsel were to learn of it, Rebus might be in serious trouble. He wasn't even sure he should be in the vicinity of the crime. Should he turn back? No. Provan was going to get off anyway, whether because of an unconvinced jury or a procedural technicality. Besides, Rebus wasn't getting involved. He was just in the area, that was all.

He was about to get out of the car when he saw a man dressed in duffel coat and jeans shuffle towards the door of number 42 and stop there, studying it. The man pushed at the door and it opened. He looked around before entering the stairwell, and Rebus recognised with a start the intent face of the keen juror from Provan's trial.

Now *this* might be trouble. This might be very bad indeed. What the hell was the juror doing here anyway? The answer seemed simple enough: he was becoming involved, the same as Rebus. Because he, too, could not believe Provan's luck. But what was he doing at number

42? Was he going to talk to Mrs McClintock? If so, he faced certain disqualification from the jury. Indeed, it was Rebus's duty as a police officer, having seen the juror enter that stairwell, to report this fact to the court officials.

Rebus gnawed at his bottom lip. He could go in and warn the juror, of course, but then he, a policeman, would be guilty of approaching a juror on the very evening prior to a judgment. That could mean more than a slapped wrist and a few choice words from the Chief Super. That could mean the end of his career.

Suddenly, Rebus's mind was made up for him. The door of the tenement was heaved open and out ran the juror, an eye on his watch as he turned left and sprinted towards Gorgie Road. Rebus smiled with relief and shook his head. 'You little bugger,' he murmured in appreciation. The juror was timing the whole thing. It was all a matter of time, so the defence had said, and the juror wanted to time things for himself. Rebus started the car and drove off, following behind the juror until the young man discovered a short cut and headed off down an alleyway. Unable to follow, Rebus fed into the traffic on the main road and found himself in the rush hour jams, heading west out of town. It didn't matter: he knew the juror's destination.

Turning down a sidestreet, Rebus rounded a bend and came immediately upon Tynecastle Park. The Goatfell was ahead of him on the other side of the street. Rebus stopped the car on some double yellow lines by the stadium side of the road. Opposite the Goatfell, the juror was doubled over on the pavement, hands pressing into his sides, exhausted after the run and trying to regain his breath. Rebus examined his watch. Eight minutes since the juror had started off from the tenement. The only witness placed the attack at seven-forty, absolutely certain in her mind that this had been the time. The goal had been scored at seven forty-five. Perhaps Mrs McClintock's clock had been wrong? It could be that simple, couldn't it? But they'd have a hell of a job proving it in court, and no jury would convict on the possibility of a dodgy clock.

Besides, her call to the police had been logged, hadn't it? There was no room for manoeuvre on the time, unless ... Rebus tapped his fingers against the steering wheel. The juror had recovered some of his equilibrium, and was now staring at the Goatfell. *Don't do it, son*, Rebus intoned mentally. *Don't*.

The juror looked both ways as he crossed the road and, once across, he looked both ways again before pushing open the door of the Goatfell and letting it rattle shut behind him. Rebus groaned and screwed shut his eyes.

'Stupid little ...' He pulled the keys from the ignition, and leaned across the passenger seat to lock the passenger side door. You couldn't be too careful around these parts. He stared at his radio. He could call for back-up, *should* call for back-up, but that would involve explanations. No, he was in this one alone.

He opened his own door and swivelled out of his seat, closing the door after him. Pausing to lock the door, he hesitated. After all, you never knew when a quick getaway might be needed. He left the door unlocked. Then, having taken three steps in the direction of the Goatfell, he stopped again and returned to the car, this time unlocking the passenger-side door, too.

You can't afford to get involved, John, he told himself. But his feet kept moving forwards. The front of the Goatfell was uninviting, its bottom half a composition of large purple and black tiles, some missing, the others cracked and chipped and covered in graffiti. The top half was constructed from glass panels, some frosted, some bottle glass. From the fact that there seemed no rhyme or reason to the pattern of these different panels, Rebus guessed that many a fight or thrown stone had seen most of the original panels replaced over time with whatever was available and cheap. He stopped for a moment at the solid wooden door, considering his madness, his folly. Then he pushed open the door and went inside.

The interior was, if anything, less prepossessing than the exterior. Red stubbled linoleum, plastic chairs and long wooden benches, a pool table, its green baize torn in several places. The lone gaming machine coughed up a few coins for an unshaven man who looked as though he had spent most of his adult life battling with it. At one small table sat three thick-set men and a dozing greyhound. Behind the pool table, three more men, younger, shuffling, were arguing over selections from the jukebox. And at the bar stood a solitary figure – the juror – being served with a half pint of lager by the raw-faced barman.

Rebus went to the far end of the bar, as far from the juror as he could get and, keeping his face towards the optics, waited to be served.

'What'll it be?' The barman's question was not unfriendly.

'Half of special and a Bell's,' replied Rebus. This was his gambit in any potentially rough pub. He could think of no good reason why; somehow it just seemed like the right order. He remembered the roughest drinking den he'd ever encountered, deep in a Niddrie housing scheme. He'd given his order and the barman asked, in all seriousness, whether he wanted the two drinks in the same glass. That had shaken Rebus, and he hadn't lingered.

Served with two glasses this evening, one foaming, the other a generous measure of amber, he thanked the barman with a nod and the exact money. But the barman was already turning away, walking back to the conversation he had been having at the other end of the bar before Rebus had walked in, the conversation he'd been having with the juror.

'Aye, that was some game all right. Pity you missed it.'

'Well,' explained the juror, 'what with being away for so long. I've kind of lost touch with their fortunes.'

'Fortune had nothing to do with that night. Cracker of a goal. I must've seen it on the telly a dozen times. Should have been goal of the season.'

The juror sighed. 'Wish I'd been here to see it.'

'Where did you say you'd been again?'

'Europe mostly. Working. I'm only back for a few weeks, then I'm off again.'

Rebus had to admit that the juror made a convincing actor. Of course, there might be a grain of truth in his story, but Rebus doubted it. All the same, good actor or no, he was digging too deep too soon into the barman's memory of that night.

'When did you say the goal was scored?'

'Eh?' The barman seemed puzzled.

'How far into the game,' explained the juror.

'I don't know. Fifteen, twenty minutes, something like that. What difference does it make?'

'Oh, nothing, no, no difference. I was just wondering.'

But the barman was frowning, suspicious now. Rebus felt his grip on the whisky glass tightening.

There's no need for this, son. I know the answer now. It was you that led me to it, but I know now. Just drink your drink and let's get out of here.

Then, as the question and answer session between the juror and barman began again, Rebus glanced into a mirror and his heart dipped fast. The three young men had turned from the wall-mounted jukebox and were now in the process of starting a game of pool. Rebus recognised one of them from the public gallery. Tattoos. Tattoos had sat in the public gallery most of the morning and a little of the afternoon. He seemed not to have recognised Rebus. More to the point, he had not yet recognised the juror – but he would. Rebus had no doubt in his mind about that. Tattoos had spent a long portion of the day staring at fifteen faces, fifteen individuals who, collectively, could put his good friend Willie Provan away for a stretch. Tattoos would

168

recognise the juror, and God alone could tell what would happen then.

God was in a funny mood. Tattoos, standing back while one of the other two T-Alice members played a thunderous break-shot, glanced towards the bar and saw the juror. Perhaps because Rebus was much further away, and partly hidden from view by the juror, Tattoos gave him no heed. But his eyes narrowed as he spotted the juror and Rebus could feel the young man trying to remember where he'd seen the drinker at the bar before. Where and when. Not too long ago. But not to speak to; just a face, a face in a crowd. On a bus? No. In a shop? No. But just a short time ago.

A grunt from one of the other players told Tattoos it was his turn. He lifted a cue from against the wall and bent low over the table, potting an easy ball. Meantime, Rebus had missed the low-voiced conversation between the juror and the barman. From the look on the juror's face, however, it was clear he had discovered something of import: the same 'something' Rebus had deduced while sitting in his car. Keen to leave now that he had his answer, the juror finished his drink.

Tattoos was walking around the table to his next shot. He looked again towards the bar, then towards the table. Then towards the bar again. Rebus, watching this in the wall mirror, saw Tattoos' jaw visibly drop open. Damn him, he had finally placed the juror. He placed his cue on the table and started slowly towards the bar. Rebus felt the tide rising around him. Here he was, where he shouldn't be, following a jury member on the eve of a retiral for verdict and now said juror was about to be approached by a friend of the accused.

For 'approached' read 'nobbled', or at the very least 'scared off'.

There was nothing for it. Rebus finished off the whisky and pushed the half pint away.

Tattoos had reached his quarry, who was just turning to go. Tattoos pointed an unnecessary finger.

'It's you, isn't it? You're on my pal's case. One of the jury. Christ, it *is* you.' Tattoos sounded as though he would have been less surprised to have encountered the entire Celtic team supping in his local. He grabbed hold of the juror's shoulder. 'Come on, I want a wee word.'

The juror's face, once red from running, had drained of all colour. Tattoos was hauling him towards the pub door.

'Easy, Dobbs!' called the barman.

'Not your concern, shite-face!' Tattoos, aka Dobbs, growled, tugging the door open and propelling the juror through it, out onto the street.

The bar fell quiet again. The dog, who had awakened at the noise, rested its head back on its paws. The pool game continued. A record came on the jukebox.

'Turn it up a bit!' yelled one of the pool players. 'I can hardly hear it!'

Rebus nodded to the barman in a gesture of farewell. Then he, too, made for the door.

Outside, he knew he must act quickly. At any sign of trouble, members of T-Alice would crawl out of the woodwork like so many termites. Tattoos had pinned the juror to a shop-front window between the Goatfell and Rebus's car. Rebus's attention was drawn from the conflict to the car itself. Its doors were open! He could see two kids playing inside it, crawling over its interior, pretending they were at the wheel of a racing car. Rebus hissed and moved forwards. He was almost passing Tattoos and the juror when he yelled:

'Get out of my bloody car!'

Even Tattoos turned at this and as he did so Rebus hammered a clenched fist into his nose. It had to be fast: Rebus didn't want Tattoos to be able ever to identify him. The sound of the nose flattening was dull and unmistakable. Tattoos let go of the juror and held his hands to his

face. Rebus hit him again, this time in proper boxing
fashion, knuckles against the side of the jaw. Tattoos fell
against the glass shop-front and sank to the pavement.

It was Rebus's turn to grab the juror's shoulder,
marching him towards the car with no words of explanation. The juror went quietly, glancing back just the once
towards the prone body.

Seeing Rebus approach, brimstone in his eyes, the two
boys ran from the car. Rebus watched them go, committing
their faces to memory. Future Willie Provans.

'Get in,' he said to the juror, shoving him towards the
passenger side. They both shut the car doors after them.
Rebus's police radio was missing, and wires protruded from
beneath the dashboard, evidence of an attempted hot-
wiring. Rebus was relieved the attempt hadn't worked.
Otherwise he would be trapped in Gorgie, surrounded by
hostile natives. It didn't bear thinking about.

The car started first time and Rebus revved it hard as he
drove off, never looking back.

'I know you,' said the juror. 'You were in the public
gallery, too.'

'That's right.'

The juror grew quiet. 'You're not one of ...?'

'I want to see Willie Provan behind bars. That's all you
need to know, and I don't want to know anything about
you. I just want you to go home, go back to court
tomorrow, and do your duty.'

'But I know how he –'

'So do I.' Rebus stopped at a red traffic light and
checked in the mirror. No one was following. He turned to
the juror. 'It was a cup-tie, a big crowd,' he said. 'And ever
since Hillsborough, the football bosses and the police have
been careful about big crowds.'

'That's right.' The juror was bursting to come out with
it first. 'So they held up the game for ten minutes to let
everybody in. The barman told me.'

Rebus nodded. The game had been a seven-thirty kick-off all right, but that intended kick-off time had been delayed. The goal, scored fifteen minutes into the game, had been scored at seven fifty-five, *not* seven forty-five, giving Provan plenty of time to make the one-mile trip from Cooper Road to the Goatfell. The truth would have come out eventually, but it might have taken a little time. The situation, however, was still dangerous. The light turned green, and Rebus moved off.

'So you think Provan is guilty?' he asked the juror.

'I know he is. It's obvious.'

Rebus nodded. 'He could still get away with it.'

'How?'

'If,' Rebus explained carefully, 'it comes to light that you and I have been doing a little snooping. You'll be thrown off the jury. It could go to a retrial, or some technicality might arise which would see Provan go free. We can't let that happen, can we?'

Rebus heard his own words. They sounded calm. Yet inside him the adrenalin was racing and his fist was pleasantly sore from use.

'No,' answered the juror, as Rebus had hoped he would.

'So,' continued Rebus, 'what I propose is that I have a quiet word with the prosecution counsel. Let's let him stand up in court and come out with the solution. That way no problems or technicalities arise. You just stay quiet and let the process work through.'

The juror seemed disheartened. This was his feat, after all, his sleuthing had turned things around. And for what?

'There's no glory in it, I'm afraid,' said Rebus. 'But at least you'll have the satisfaction of knowing Provan is inside, not out there, waiting to pick off another victim.' Rebus nodded through the windscreen and the juror stared at the city streets, thinking it over.

'Okay,' he said at last. 'Yes, you're right.'

'So we keep it quiet?'

'We keep it quiet,' the juror agreed. Rebus nodded slowly. This might shape up all right after all. The whisky was warming his veins. A quiet word to the prosecution, maybe by way of a typed and anonymous note, something that would keep Rebus out of the case. It was a pity he couldn't be in court tomorrow for the revelation. But the last thing he wanted was to encounter a broken-nosed Tattoos. A pity though; he wanted to see Provan's face and he wanted to catch Provan's eyes and he wanted to give him a great big pitiless smile.

'You can stop here,' said the juror, waking Rebus from his reverie. They were approaching Princes Street. 'I just live down Queens –'

'Don't tell me,' Rebus said abruptly. The juror looked at him.

'Technicalities?' he ventured. Rebus smiled and nodded. He pulled the car over to the side of the road. The juror opened his door, got out, but then bent down into the car again.

'I don't even know who you are,' he said.

'That's right,' said Rebus, reaching across and pulling shut the door. 'You don't.'

He drove off into the Edinburgh evening. No thorn jabbed him now. By tomorrow there would be another. And then he'd have to report the theft of his radio. There would be smiles at that, smiles and, behind his back if not to his face, laughter.

John Rebus could laugh, too.

Sunday

Where was that light coming from? Bright, hot light. Knives in the night. Last night, was it? No, the night before. Just another Friday in Edinburgh. A drug haul at a dance hall. A few of the dealers trying to run for it. Rebus cornering one. The man, sweating, teeth bared, turning before Rebus's eyes into an animal, something wild, predatory, scared. And cornered. The glint of a knife ...

But that was Friday, the night before last. So this was Sunday. Yes! Sunday morning. (Afternoon, maybe.) Rebus opened his eyes and squinted into the sunshine, streaming through his uncurtained window. No, not sunshine. His bedside lamp. Must have been on all night. He had come to bed drunk last night, drunk and tired. Had forgotten to close the curtains. And now warming light, birds resting on the window-ledge. He stared into a small black eye, then checked his watch. Ten past eight. Morning then, not afternoon. Early morning.

His head was the consistency of syrup, his limbs stiff. He'd been fit as a young man; not fitness daft, but fit all the same. But one day he had just stopped caring. He dressed quickly, then checked and found that he was running out of clean shirts, clean pants, clean socks. Today's chore then: doing the laundry. Ever since his wife had left him, he had taken his dirty washing to a public laundrette at the top of Marchmont Road, where a service wash cost very little and the manageress always used to fold his clean clothes away very neatly, a smile on her scrupulous lips. But in a fit of madness one Saturday afternoon, he had walked calmly into an electrical shop and purchased a washer/dryer for the flat.

He pressed the dirty bundle into the machine and found he was down to one last half-scoop of washing powder. What the hell, it would have to do. There were various buttons and controls on the machine's fascia, but he only ever used one programme: Number 5 (40 Degrees), full load, with ten minutes' tumble dry at the end. The results were satisfactory, if never perfect. He switched the machine on, donned his shoes and left the flat, double-locking the door behind him.

His car, parked directly outside the main entrance to the tenement, scowled at him. *I need a wash, pal.* It was true, but Rebus shook his head. Not today, today was his day off, the only day this week. Some other time, some other free time. Who was he kidding? He'd drive into a car wash one afternoon between calls. His car could like it or lump it.

The corner shop was open. Rebus had seldom seen it closed. He bought ground coffee, rolls, milk, margarine, a packet of bacon. The bacon, through its plastic wrapping, had an oily, multi-coloured look to it, but its sell-by date seemed reasonable. Pigs: very intelligent creatures. How could one intelligent creature eat another? Guilty conscience, John? It must be Sunday. Presbyterian guilt, Calvinist guilt. Mea culpa, he thought to himself, taking the bacon to the check-out till. Then he turned back and bought some washing powder, too.

Back in the flat, the washing machine was churning away. He put Coleman Hawkins on the hi-fi (not too loud; it was only quarter to nine). Soon the church bells would start ringing, calling the faithful. Rebus would not answer. He had given up church-going. Any day but Sunday he might have gone. But Sunday, Sunday was the only day off he had. He remembered his mother, taking him with her to church every Sunday while his father stayed at home in bed with tea and the paper. Then one Sunday, when he was twelve or thirteen, his mother had said he could choose: go with her or stay with his father. He stayed and saw his little brother's jealous eyes glance at him, desperate to be of an age where he would be given the same choice.

Ah me, John, Sunday morning. Rubbedy-rrub of the washing machine, the coffee's aroma wafting up from the filter. (Getting short on filters, but no panic: he only used them on Sunday.) He went into the bathroom. Suddenly, staring at the bath itself, he felt an overwhelming urge to steep himself in hot water. Wednesdays and Saturdays: those were his usual days for a bath. Go on, break the rules. He turned on the hot tap, but it was a mere trickle. Damn! the washing machine was being fed all the flat's hot water. Oh well. Bath later. Coffee now.

At five past nine, the Sunday papers thudded through the letterbox. *Sunday Post*, *Mail*, and *Scotland on Sunday*. He seldom read them, but they helped the day pass. Not that he got bored on a Sunday. It was the day of rest, so he rested. A nice lazy day. He refilled his coffee mug, went back into the bathroom and walked over to the toilet to examine a roughly circular patch on the wall beside it, a couple of feet up from floor level. The patch was slightly discoloured and he touched it with the palm of his hand. Yes, it was damp. He had first noticed the patch a week ago. Damp, slightly damp. He couldn't think why. There was no dampness anywhere else, no apparent source of the damp. Curious, he had peeled away the paper from the patch, had scratched at the plaster wall. But no answer had emerged. He shook his head. That would irritate him for the rest of the day. As before, he went to the bedroom and returned with an electric hair-drier and an extension flex. He plugged the hair-drier into the flex, and rested the drier on the toilet seat, aimed towards the patch, then switched on the hair-drier and tested that it was hitting the spot. That would dry things out a bit, but he knew the patch would return.

177

Washing machine rumbling. Hair-drier whirring. Coleman Hawkins in the living-room. He went into the living-room. Could do with a tidy, couldn't it? Hoover, dust. Car sitting outside waiting to be washed. Everything could wait. There were the papers to be read. There they were on the table, just next to his briefcase. The briefcase full of documents for his attention, half-completed case-notes, reminders of appointments, all the rubbish he hadn't found time for during the week at the station. All the so-important paperwork, without which his life would be milk and honey. Some toast perhaps? Yes, he would eat some toast.

He checked his watch: ten past eleven. He had switched off the hairdrier, but left it sitting on the toilet, the extension lead snaking across the floor to the wall-socket in the hall. The washing machine was silent, spent. One more cup of coffee left in the pot. He had flicked through the papers, looking for the interesting, the unusual. Same old stories: court cases, weekend crime, sport. There was even a paragraph on Friday night's action. He skipped that, but remembered all the same. Bright knife's flat edge, caught in the lamplight. Sour damp smell in the alleyway. Feet standing in something soft. Don't look down, look at him, look straight at him, the cornered animal. Look at him, talk to him with your eyes, try to calm him, or quell him.

There were birds on the window sill, chirping, wanting some crumbled up crusts of bread, but he had no bread worth the name left in the flat; just fresh rolls, too soft to be thrown out. Ach, he'd never eat six rolls though, would he? One or two would go stale and then he'd give them to the birds. So why not give them some in advance, while the rolls are soft and sweet?

In the kitchen he prepared the broken pieces of bread on a plate, then took it to the birds on the window-ledge. Hell: what about lunch? Sunday afternoon lunch. In the freezer compartment, he found a steak. How long would it take to defrost? Damn! he meant to pick up the microwave during the week. The shop had called him to say they'd fixed the fault. He was supposed to have collected it on Friday, but he'd been too busy. So: defrost in a low oven. And wine. Yes, open a bottle. He could always drink just one or two glasses, then keep the rest of the bottle for some other occasion. Last Christmas, a friend had given him a vacuum-tube. It was supposed to keep wine fresh after opening. Where had he put it? In the cupboard beside the wine: that would make sense. But there was no gadget to be found.

He chose a not-bad bottle, bought from a reliable wine merchant in Marchmont and stood it on the table in the living-room. Beside his briefcase. Let the sediment settle. That's what Sunday was all about, wasn't it? Maybe he could try one of the crosswords. It was ages since he'd done a crossword. A glass of wine and a crossword while he waited for the meat to thaw. Sediment wouldn't be settled yet, but what the hell. He opened the bottle and poured an inch into his glass. Glanced at his watch again. It was half past eleven. A bit early to be drinking. Cheers.

You could break the rules on a Sunday, couldn't you? Christ, what a week it had been at work. Everything from a senile rapist to a runaway blind boy. A shotgun robbery at a bookmaker's shop and an apparently accidental drowning at the docks. Drunk, the victim had been. Dead drunk. Fished about a bottle of whisky and a recently dismembered kebab from his stomach. Annual crime figures for the Lothians were released: murder slightly up on the previous year, sexual assaults well up, burglaries up, street crime down a little, motoring offences significantly reduced. The clear-up rate for housebreakings in some parts of Edinburgh was standing at less than five per cent. Rebus was not exactly a fascist, not quite a totalitarian, but he knew that given wider powers of entry and search, that final figure could be higher. There were high-rise blocks where a flat on the twelfth floor would be broken into time after time. Was someone climbing twelve flights to break in? Of course not: someone in the block was responsible, but without the powers of immediate and indiscriminate search, they'd never find the culprit.

And that was the tip of the whole polluted iceberg. Maniacs were put back on the streets by institutions unable or unwilling to cope. Rebus had never seen so many beggars in Edinburgh as in this past year. Teenagers (and younger) up to grandparents, dossing, cadging the occasional quid or cigarette. Christ, it depressed him to think of it almost as much as it did to pretend he could ignore it. He stalked through to the kitchen and felt the steak. It was still solid at its core. He lifted the nearly dry clothes out of the machine and draped them over the cold radiators throughout the flat. More music on the hi-fi. Art Pepper this time, a little louder, the hour being respectable. Not that the neighbours ever complained. Sometimes he could see in their eyes that they wanted to complain – complain about his noise, his irregular comings and goings, the way he revved his car or coughed his way up the stairwell. They wanted to complain, but they daren't, for fear that he would somehow 'stitch them up' or would prove not to be amenable to some favour they might ask one day. They all watched the TV police dramas and thought they must know their neighbour pretty well. Rebus shook his head and poured more wine: two inches deep in the glass this time. They knew nothing about him. Nothing. He didn't have a TV, hated all the game shows and the cop shows and the news programmes. Not having a TV had set him apart from his colleagues at the station: he found he had little to discuss with them of a morning. His mornings were quieter and saner for it.

He checked the damp patch in the bathroom again, letting his hand rest against it for half a minute. Mmm: it still wasn't completely dry. But then maybe his hands were damp from the washing he had been carrying. What the hell. Back in the bedroom, he picked up some books from the floor and stacked them against a wall, beside other columns of paperbacks and hardbacks, read and unread. One day he would get time to read them. They were like contraband: he couldn't stop himself buying them, but then he never really did anything with them once he'd bought them. The buying was the thing, that sense of ownership. Perhaps somewhere in Britain someone had exactly the same collection of books as him, but he doubted it. The range was too eclectic, everything from secondhand rugby yearbooks to dense philosophical works. Meaningless, really; without pattern. So much of his working life was spent to a pattern, a modus operandi. A series of rules for the possible (not probable) solving of crimes. One of the rules would have it that he get through the briefcase full of work before Monday morning and, preferably, while still sober.

Bell. Bell?

Bell. Someone at his front door. Jesus, on a *Sunday*? Not on a Sunday, please, God. The wrong door: they'd got the wrong door. Give them a minute and they would realise their mistake. Bell again. Bloody hell's bells. Right then, he would answer it.

He pulled the door open slowly, peering around it. Detective Constable Brian Holmes was standing on the tenement landing.

'Brian?'

'Hello, sir. Hope you don't mind. I was in the neighbourhood and thought I'd ... you know.'

Rebus held open the door. 'Come in.'

He led Holmes through the hall, stepping over the electric flex. Holmes stared at the flex, an alarmed look on his face.

'Don't worry,' said Rebus, pausing at the threshold of

the living-room. 'I'm not going to jump in the bath with an electric fire. Just drying out a damp patch.'

'Oh.' Holmes sounded unconvinced. 'Right.'

'Sit down,' said Rebus. 'I've just opened a bottle of wine. Would you like some?'

'Bit early for me,' Holmes said, glancing towards Rebus's glass.

'Well, coffee then. I think there's still some in the pot.'

'No thanks, I'm fine.'

They were both seated, Rebus in his usual chair, Holmes perched on the edge of the sofa. Rebus knew why the younger officer was here, but he was damned if he would make it easy for him.

'In the neighbourhood you say?'

'That's right. I was at a party last night in Mayfield. Afterwards, I stopped the night.'

'Oh?'

Holmes smiled. 'No such luck, I slept on the sofa.'

'It's still off with Nell then?'

'I don't know. Sometimes she ... let's change the subject.'

He flipped one of the newspapers over so that he could study the back page. 'Did you see the boxing last night?'

'I don't have a television.'

Holmes looked around the room, then smiled again. 'Neither you do. I hadn't noticed.'

'I'll bear that in mind when you come up for promotion, Constable.' Rebus took a large gulp of wine, watching Holmes over the rim of the glass. Holmes was looking less comfortable by the second.

'Any plans for the day?'

'Such as?'

Holmes shrugged. 'I don't know. I thought maybe you had a Sunday routine. You know: clean the car, that sort of thing.'

Rebus nodded towards the briefcase on the table. 'Paperwork. That'll keep me busy most of the day.'

Holmes nodded, flicking through the paper until he came, as Rebus knew he would, to the piece about the nightclub bust.

'It's at the bottom of the page,' Rebus said. 'But then you know that, don't you? You've already seen it.' He rose from his chair sharply and walked to the hi-fi, turning the record over. Alto sax bloomed from the speakers. Holmes still hadn't said anything. He was pretending to read the paper, but his eyes weren't moving. Rebus returned to his seat.

'Was there really a party, Brian?'

'Yes.' Holmes paused. 'No.'

'And you weren't just passing?'

'No. I wanted to see how you were.'

'And how am I?'

'You look fine.'

'That's because I *am* fine.'

'Are you sure?'

'Perfectly.'

Holmes sighed and threw aside the paper. 'I'm glad to hear it. I was worried, John. We were all a bit shaken up.'

'I've killed someone before, Brian. It wasn't the first time.'

'Yes, but Christ, I mean ...' Holmes got up and walked to the window, looking down on the street. A nice quiet street in a quiet part of town. Net curtains and trim front gardens, the gardens of professional people, lawful people, people who smiled at you in shops or chatted in a bus queue.

But Rebus's mind flashed again to the dark alleyway, a distant streetlamp, the cornered drug dealer. He had thrown packets from his pockets onto the ground as he had run. Like sowing seed. Small polythene bags of drugs soft and hard. Sowing them in the soft mud, every year a new crop.

Then the blinding light. The flat steel of a knife. Not a
huge knife, but how big did a knife need to be? An inch of
blade would be enough. Anything more was excess. It was a
very excessive knife indeed, curved, serrated edge, a
commando special. The kind you could buy from a
camping shop. The kind *anybody* could buy from a
camping shop. A serious knife for outdoor pursuits. Rebus
had the idea they called them 'survival' knives.

The man – not much more than a boy in reality, eighteen
or nineteen – had not hesitated. He slid the knife out from
the waistband of his trousers. He lunged, one swipe, two
swipes. Rebus wasn't fit, but his reactions were fast. On the
third swipe, he snapped out a hand and caught the wrist,
twisting it all the way. The knife fell to the ground. The
dealer cried out in pain and dropped to one knee. No words
had passed between the two men. There was no real need
for words.

But then Rebus had realised that his opponent was not
on his knees as a sign of defeat. He was scrabbling around
for the knife and found it with his free hand. Rebus let go
of the dead wrist and pinned the man's left arm to his body,
but the arm was strong and the blade sheared through
Rebus's trousers, cutting a red line up across his thigh.
Rebus brought his knee up hard into his adversary's crotch
and felt the body go limp. He repeated the action, but the
dealer wasn't giving up. The knife was rising again. Rebus
grabbed the wrist with one hand, the other going for the
man's throat. Then he felt himself being spun and pushed
hard up against the wall of the alley. The wall was damp,
smelling of mould. He pressed a thumb deep into the
dealer's larynx, still wrestling with the knife. His knee
thudded into the man's groin again. And then, as the
strength in the knife-arm eased momentarily, Rebus yanked
the wrist and pushed.

Pushed hard, driving the dealer across the alley and
against the other wall. Where the man gasped, gurgled, eyes

bulging. Rebus stood back and released his grasp on the wrist, the wrist which held the knife, buried up to the hilt in the young man's stomach.

'Oh shit,' he whispered. 'Oh shit, oh shit, oh shit.'

The dealer was staring in surprise at the handle of the knife. His hand fell away from it, but the knife itself stayed put. He shuffled forward, walking past Rebus, who could only stand and watch, making for the entrance to the alleyway. The tip of the knife was protruding through the back of the dealer's jacket. He made it to the mouth of the alley before falling to his knees.

'Sir?'

'Mmm?' Rebus looked up and saw that Holmes was studying him from the window. 'What is it, Brian?'

'Are you okay?'

'I told you, I'm fine.' Rebus tipped the last of the wine down his throat and placed the glass on the floor, trying to control the trembling in his hand.

'It's just that ... well, I've never –'

'You've never killed anyone.'

'That's right,' Holmes came back to the sofa. 'I haven't.' He sat down, hands pressed between his knees, leaning slightly forwards as he spoke. 'What does it feel like?'

'Feel like?' Rebus smiled with half his mouth. 'It doesn't feel like anything. I don't even think about it. That's the best way.'

Holmes nodded slowly. Rebus was thinking: *get to the point.* And then Holmes came to the point.

'Did you mean to do it?' he asked.

Rebus had no hesitation. 'It was an accident. I didn't know it had happened until it did happen. We got into a clinch and somehow the knife ended up where it ended up. That's all. That's what I told them back at the station and that's what I'll tell any inquiry they shove at me. It was an accident.'

'Yes,' said Holmes quietly, nodding. 'That's what I thought.'

Accidents will happen, won't they?

Like burning the steak. Like finishing the bottle when you'd meant to have just a couple of glasses. Like punching a dent in the bathroom wall. Accidents happened and most of them happened in the home.

Holmes refused the offer of lunch and left. Rebus sat in the chair for a while, just listening to jazz, forgetting all about the steak. He only remembered it when he went to open another bottle of wine. The corkscrew had found its way back into the cutlery drawer, and he plucked out a knife by mistake. A small sharp-bladed knife with a wooden handle. He kept this knife for steaks especially.

It was good of Holmes to look in, no matter what the motive. And it was good of him not to stay, too. Rebus needed to be alone, needed time and space enough to think. He had told Holmes he never thought about it, never thought about death. That was a lie; he thought about it all the time. This weekend he was replaying Friday night, going over the scene time and time again in his head. Trying to answer the question Holmes himself had asked: was it an accident? But every time Rebus went through it, the answer became more and more vague. The hand was holding the knife, and then Rebus was angling that hand away from himself, propelling the hand and the body behind it backward into the wall of the alley. Angling the hand ... That was the vital moment. When he grabbed the wrist so that the knife was pointing towards the dealer, what had been going through his mind then? The thought that he was saving himself? Or that he was about to kill the dealer?

Rebus shook his head. It was no clearer now than it had been at the time. The media had chalked it up yesterday as self-defence and the internal inquiry would come to the same conclusion. Could he have disarmed the young man? Probably. Would the man have killed Rebus, given the chance? Certainly. Had he lived, would he have become Prime Minister, or fascist dictator, or Messiah? Would he have seen the error of his ways, or would he have gone on dispensing the only thing he had to sell? What about his parents, his family, his friends who had known him at school, who had known him as a child: what would they be thinking now? Were the photograph albums and the paper hankies out? Pictures of the dealer as a boy, dressed up as a cowboy on his birthday, pictures of him splashing in the bath as a baby. Memories of someone John Rebus had never known.

He shook his head again. Thinking about it would do no good, but it was the only way to deal with it. And yes, he felt guilty. He felt soiled and defeated and bad. But he would stop feeling bad, and then eventually he would stop feeling anything at all. He had killed before; it might be he would kill again. You never knew until the moment itself.

And sometimes even then, you still didn't know, and would continue not to know. Holmes mentioned Mayfield. Rebus knew of a church in Mayfield with an evening service on a Sunday. A church with a restrained congregation and a minister not overly keen on prying into one's affairs. Maybe he would go there later. Meantime, he felt like a walk. He would walk through The Meadows and back across Bruntsfield Links, with a diversion towards the ice-cream shop near Tollcross. Maybe he'd bump into his friend Frank.

For this was Sunday, his day off, and he could do whatever he liked, couldn't he? After all, Sunday was a day for breaking the rules. It was the only day he could afford.

Auld Lang Syne

Places Detective Inspector John Rebus did not want to be at midnight on Hogmanay: number one, the Tron in Edinburgh.

Which was perhaps, Rebus decided, why he found himself at five minutes to midnight pushing his way through the crowds which thronged the area of the Royal Mile outside the Tron Kirk. It was a bitter night, a night filled with the fumes of beer and whisky, of foam licking into the sky as another can was opened, of badly sung songs and arms around necks and stooped, drunken proclamations of undying love, proclamations which would be forgotten by morning.

Rebus had been here before, of course. He had been here the previous Hogmanay, ready to root out the eventual troublemakers, to break up fights and crunch across the shattered glass covering the setts. The best and worst of the Scots came out as another New Year approached: the togetherness, the sharpness, the hugging of life, the inability to know when to stop, so that the hug became a smothering stranglehold. These people were drowning in a sea of sentiment and sham. *Flower of Scotland* was struck up by a lone voice for the thousandth time, and for the thousandth time a few more voices joined in, all falling away at the end of the first chorus.

'Gawn yirsel there, big man.'

Rebus looked around him. The usual contingent of uniformed officers was going through the annual ritual of having hands shaken by a public suddenly keen to make friends. It was the WPCs Rebus felt sorry for, as another slobbering kiss slapped into the cheek of a young female officer. The police of Edinburgh knew their duty: they always offered one sacrificial lamb to appease the multitude. There was actually an orderly queue standing in front of the WPC waiting to kiss her. She smiled and blushed. Rebus shivered and turned away. Four minutes to midnight. His nerves were like struck chords. He hated crowds. Hated drunken crowds more. Hated the fact that another year was coming to an end. He began to push through the crowd with a little more force than was necessary.

People Detective Inspector John Rebus would rather not be with at midnight on Hogmanay: number one, detectives from Glasgow CID.

He smiled and nodded towards one of them. The man was standing just inside a bus shelter, removed from the general scrum of the road itself. On top of the shelter, a Mohican in black leather did a tribal dance, a bottle of strong lager gripped in one hand. A police constable shouted for the youth to climb down from the shelter. The punk took no notice. The man in the bus shelter smiled back at John Rebus. He's not waiting for a bus, Rebus thought to himself, he's waiting for a bust.

Things Detective Inspector John Rebus would rather not be doing at midnight on Hogmanay: number one, working.

So he found himself working, and as the crowd swept him up again, he thought of Dante's *Inferno*. Three minutes to midnight. Three minutes away from hell. The Scots, pagan at their core, had always celebrated New Year rather than Christmas. Back when Rebus was a boy, Christmases were muted. New Year was the time for celebration, for first-footing, black bun, madeira cake, coal wrapped in silver foil, stovies during the night and steak pie the following afternoon. Ritual after ritual. Now he found himself observing another ritual, another set of procedures. A meeting was about to take place. An exchange would be made: a bag filled with money for a parcel full of dope. A consignment of heroin had entered Scotland via a west coast fishing village. The CID in Glasgow had been tipped off, but failed to intercept the package. The trail had gone cold for several days, until an informant came up with the vital information. The dope was in Edinburgh. It was about to be handed on to an east coast dealer. The dealer was known to Edinburgh CID, but they'd never been able to pin a major possession charge on him. They wanted him badly. So did the west coast CID.

'It's to be a joint operation,' Rebus's boss had informed him, with no trace of irony on his humourless face. So now here he was, mingling with the crowds, just as another dozen or so undercover officers were doing. The men about to make the exchange did not trust one another. One of them had decided upon the Tron as a public enough place to make the deal. With so many people around, a double-cross was less likely to occur. The Tron at midnight on Hogmanay: a place of delirium and riot. No one would notice a discreet switch of cases, money for dope, dope for money. It was perfect.

Rebus, pushing against the crowd again, saw the money-man for the very first time. He recognised him from photographs. Alan Lyons, 'Nal' to his friends. He was twenty-seven years old, drove a Porsche 911 and lived in a detached house on the riverside just outside Haddington. He had been one of Rab Philips' men until Philips' demise. Now he was out on his own. He listed his occupation as 'entrepreneur'. He was sewerage.

Lyons was resting his back against a shop window. He smoked a cigarette and gave the passers-by a look that said he was not in the mood for handshakes and conversation. A glance told Rebus that two of the Glasgow crew were keeping a close watch on Lyons, so he did not linger. His interest now was in the missing link, the man with the package. Where was he? A countdown was being chanted all around him. A few people reckoned the New Year was less than ten seconds away; others, checking their watches, said there was a minute left. By Rebus's own watch, they were already into the New Year by a good thirty seconds. Then, without warning, the clock chimes rang and a great cheer went up. People were shaking hands, hugging, kissing. Rebus could do nothing but join in.

'Happy New Year.'

'Happy New Year, pal.'

'Best of luck, eh?'

'Happy New Year.'

'All the best.'

'Happy New Year.'

Rebus shook a Masonic hand, and looked up into a face he recognised. He returned the compliment – 'Happy New Year' – and the man smiled and moved on, hand already outstretched to another well-wisher, another stranger. But this man had been no stranger to Rebus. Where the hell did he know him from? The crowd had rearranged itself, shielding the man from view. Rebus concentrated on the memory of the face. He had known it younger, less jowly, but with darker eyes. He could hear the voice: a thick Fife accent. The hands were like shovels, miner's hands. But this man was no miner.

He had his radio with him, but trapped as he was in the midst of noise there was no point trying to contact the others on the surveillance. He wanted to tell them something. He wanted to tell them he was going to follow the mystery man. Always supposing, that was, he could find him again in the crowd.

And then he remembered: Jackie Crawford. Dear God, it was Jackie Crawford!

People Rebus did not want to shake hands with as the old year became the new: number one, Jackie 'Trigger' Crawford.

Rebus had put Crawford behind bars four years ago for

armed robbery and wounding. The sentence imposed by the judge had been a generous stretch of ten years. Crawford had headed north from court in a well-guarded van. He had not gained the nickname 'Trigger' for his quiet and homely outlook on life. The man was a headcase of the first order, gun happy and trigger happy. He'd taken part in a series of bank and building society robberies; short, violent visits to High Streets across the Lowlands. That nobody had been killed owed more to strengthened glass and luck than to Crawford's philanthropy. He'd been sent away for ten, he was out after four. What was going on? Surely, the man could not be out and walking the streets *legally*? He had to have broken out, or at the very least cut loose from some day-release scheme. And wasn't it a coincidence that he should bump into Rebus, that he should be here in the Tron at a time when the police were waiting for some mysterious drug pedaller?

Rebus believed in coincidence, but this was stretching things a bit too far. Jackie Crawford was somewhere in this crowd, somewhere shaking hands with people whom, a scant four years before, he might have been terrorising with a sawn-off shotgun. Rebus had to do something, whether Crawford was the 'other man' or not. He began squeezing through the crowd again, this time ignoring proffered hands and greetings. He moved on his toes, craning his head over the heads of the revellers, seeking the square-jawed, wiry-haired head of his prey. He was trying to recall whether there was some tradition in Scotland that ghosts from your past came to haunt you at midnight on Hogmanay. He thought not. Besides, Crawford was no ghost. His hands had been meaty and warm, his thumb pressing speculatively against Rebus's knuckles. The eyes which had glanced momentarily into Rebus's eyes had been clear and blue, but uninterested.

Had Crawford recognised his old adversary? Rebus couldn't be sure. There had been no sign of recognition, no raising of eyebrows or opening of the mouth. Just three mumbled words before moving on to the next hand. Was Crawford drunk? Most probably: few sane and sober individuals visited the Tron on this night of all nights. Good: a drunken Crawford would have been unlikely to recognise him. Yet the voice had been quiet and unslurred, the eyes focussed. Crawford had not seemed drunk, had not acted drunk. Sober as a judge, in fact. This, too, worried Rebus.

But then, *everything* worried him this evening. He couldn't afford any slip-ups from the operation's Edinburgh contingent. It would give too much ammo to the Glasgow faction: there was a certain competitive spirit between the two forces. For 'competitive spirit' read 'loathing'. Each would want to claim any arrest as *its* victory; and each would blame any foul-up on the other.

This had been explained to him very clearly by Chief Inspector Lauderdale.

'But surely, sir,' Rebus had replied, 'catching these men is what's most important.'

'Rubbish, John,' Lauderdale had replied. 'What's important is that we don't look like arseholes in front of McLeish and his men.'

Which, of course, Rebus had already known: he just liked winding his superior up a little the better to watch him perform. Superintendent Michael McLeish was an outspoken and devout Catholic, and Rebus's chief did not like Catholics. But Rebus hated bigots, and so he wound up Lauderdale whenever he could and had a name for him behind his back: the Clockwork Orangeman.

The crowd was thinning out as Rebus headed away from the Tron and uphill towards the castle. He was, he knew, moving away from the surveillance and should inform his fellow officers of the fact, but if his hunch was right, he was also following the man behind the whole deal. Suddenly he caught sight of Crawford, who seemed to be moving purposefully out of the crowd, heading onto the pavement and giving a half-turn of his head, knowing he was being followed.

So he had recognised Rebus, and now had seen him hurrying after him. The policeman exhaled noisily and pushed his way through the outer ring of the celebrations. His arms ached, as though he had been swimming against a strong current, but now that he was safely out of the water, he saw that Crawford had vanished. He looked along the row of shops, separated each from the other by narrow, darkened closes. Up those closes were the entrances to flats, courtyards surrounded by university halls of residence, and many steep and worn steps leading from the High Street down to Cockburn Street. Rebus had to choose one of them. If he hesitated, or chose wrongly, Crawford would make good his escape. He ran to the first alley and, glancing down it, listening for footsteps, decided to move on. At the second close, he chose not to waste any more time and ran in, passing dimly-lit doorways festooned with graffiti, dank walls and frozen cobbles. Until, launching himself down a flight of steps into almost absolute darkness, he stumbled. He flailed for a hand-rail to stop him from falling, and found his arm grabbed by a powerful hand, saving him.

Crawford was standing against the side of the alley, on a platform between flights of steps. Rebus sucked in air, trying to calm himself. There was a sound in his ears like the aftermath of an explosion.

'Thanks,' he spluttered.

'You were following me.' The voice was effortlessly calm.

'Was I?' It was a lame retort and Crawford knew it. He chuckled.

'Yes, Mr Rebus, you were. You must have gotten a bit of a shock.'

Rebus nodded. 'A bit, yes, after all these years, Jackie.'

'I'm surprised you recognised me. People tell me I've changed.'

'Not that much.' Rebus glanced down at his arm, which was still in Crawford's vice-like grip. The grip relaxed and fell away.

'Sorry.'

Rebus was surprised at the apology, but tried not to let it show. He was busy covertly studying Crawford's body, looking for any bulge big enough to be a package or a gun.

'So what were you doing back there?' he asked, not particularly interested in the answer, but certainly interested in the time it might buy him.

Crawford seemed amused. 'Bringing in the New Year, of course. What else would I be doing?'

It was a fair question, but Rebus chose not to answer it. 'When did you get out?'

'A month back.' Crawford could sense Rebus's suspicion. 'It's legit. Honest to God, Sergeant, as He is my witness. I haven't done a runner or anything.'

'You ran from *me*. And it's Inspector now, by the way.'

Crawford smiled again. 'Congratulations.'

'Why did you run?'

'Was I running?'

'You know you were.'

'The reason I was running was because the last person I wanted to see tonight of all nights was you, Inspector Rebus. You spoilt it for me.'

Rebus frowned. He was *looking* at Trigger Crawford, but felt he was talking to somebody else, someone calmer and less dangerous, someone, well, *ordinary*. He was confused, but still suspicious. 'Spoilt what exactly?'

'My New Year resolution. I came here to make peace with the world.'

It was Rebus's turn to smile, though not kindly. 'Make peace, eh?'

'That's right.'

'No more guns? No more armed robberies?'

Crawford was shaking his head slowly. Then he held open his coat. 'No more shooters, Inspector. That's a promise. You see, I've made my own peace.'

Peace or piece? Rebus couldn't be sure. He was reaching into his own jacket pocket, from which he produced a police radio. Crawford looked on the level. He even sounded on the level, but facts had to be verified. So he called in and asked for a check to be made on John Crawford, nickname 'Trigger'. Crawford smiled shyly at the mention of that name. Rebus held onto the radio, waiting for the computer to do its stuff, waiting for the station to respond.

'It's been a long time since anyone called me Trigger,' Crawford said. 'Quite some time.'

'How come they released you after four?'

'A bit less than four, actually,' corrected Crawford. 'They released me because I was no longer a threat to society. You'll find that hard to believe. In fact, you'll find it *impossible* to believe. That's not my fault, it's yours. You think men like me can never go straight. But we can. You see, something happened to me in prison. I found Jesus Christ.'

Rebus knew the look on his face was a picture, and it caused Crawford to smile again, still shyly. He looked down at the tips of his shoes.

'That's right, Inspector. I became a Christian. It wasn't any kind of blinding light. It took a while. I got bored inside and I started reading books. One day I picked up the Bible and just opened it at random. What I read there seemed to make sense. It was the Good News Bible, written in plain English. I read bits and pieces, just flicked through it. Then I went to one of the Sunday services, mainly because there were a few things I couldn't understand and I wanted to ask the minister about them. And he helped me a bit. That's how it started. It changed my life.'

Rebus could think of nothing to say. He thought of himself as a Christian, too, a sceptical Christian, a little like Crawford himself perhaps. Full of questions that needed answering. No, this couldn't be right. He was *nothing* like Crawford. Nothing at all like him. Crawford was an animal; his kind never changed. Did they? Just because he had never met a 'changed man', did that mean such a thing did not exist? After all, he'd never met the Queen or the Prime Minister either. The radio crackled to life in his hand.

'Rebus here,' he said, and then listened.

It was all true. The details from Crawford's file were being read to him. Model prisoner. Bible class. Recommended for early release. Personal tragedy.

'Personal tragedy?' Rebus looked at Crawford.

'Ach, my son died. He was only in his twenties.'

Rebus, having heard enough, had already switched off the radio. 'I'm sorry,' he said. Crawford just shrugged, shrugged shoulders beneath which were tucked no hidden shotguns, and slipped his hands into his pockets, pockets where no pistols lurked. But Rebus held out a hand towards him.

'Happy New Year,' he said.

Crawford stared at the hand, then brought out his own right hand. The two men shook warmly, their grips firm.

'Happy New Year,' said Crawford. Then he glanced back up the close. 'Look, Inspector, if it's all right with you I think I'll go back up the Tron. It was daft of me to run away in the first place. There are plenty of hands up there I've not shaken yet.'

Rebus nodded slowly. He understood now. For Crawford, the New Year was something special, a new start in more ways than one. Not everyone was given that chance.

'Aye,' he said. 'On you go.'

Crawford had climbed three steps before he paused. 'Incidentally,' he called, 'what were *you* doing at the Tron?'

'What else would I be doing there on New Year?' replied Rebus. 'I was working.'

'No rest for the wicked, eh?' said Crawford, climbing the slope back up to the High Street.

Rebus watched until Crawford disappeared into the gloom. He knew he should follow him. After all, he *was* still working. He was sure now that Crawford had been speaking the truth, that he had nothing to do with the drug deal. Their meeting had been coincidence, nothing more. But who would have believed it? Trigger Crawford a 'model prisoner'. And they said mankind no longer lived in an age of miracles.

Rebus climbed slowly. There seemed more people than ever on the High Street. He guessed things would be at their busiest around half past midnight, with the streets emptying quickly after that. If the deal was going to go through, it would take place before that time. He recognised one of the Glasgow detectives heading towards him. As he spotted Rebus, the detective half-raised his arms.

'Where have you been? We thought you'd buggered off home.'

'Nothing happening then?'

The detective sighed. 'No, nothing at all. Lyons looks a bit impatient. I don't think he's going to give it much longer himself.'

'I thought your informant was air-tight?'

'As a rule. Maybe this will be the exception.' The detective smiled, seemingly used to such disappointments in his life. Rebus had noticed earlier that the young man possessed badly chewed fingernails and even the skin around the nails was torn and raw-looking. A stressed young man. In a few years he would be overweight and then would become heart attack material. Rebus knew that he himself was heart attack material: h.a.m., they called it back at the station. You were lean (meaning fit) or you were ham. Rebus was decidedly the latter.

'So anyway, where were you?'

'I bumped into an old friend. Well, to be precise an old adversary. Jackie Crawford.'

'Jackie Crawford? You mean Trigger Crawford?' The young detective was rifling through his memory files. 'Oh yes, I heard he was out.'

'Did you? Nobody bothered to tell me.'

'Yes, something about his son dying. Drug overdose. All the fire went out of Crawford after that. Turned into a Bible basher.'

They were walking back towards the crowd. Back towards where Alan Lyons waited for a suitcase full of heroin. Rebus stopped dead in his tracks.

'Drugs? Did you say his son died from drugs?'

The detective nodded. 'The big H. It wasn't too far from my patch. Somewhere in Partick.'

'Did Crawford's son live in Glasgow then?'

'No, he was just visiting. He stayed here in Edinburgh.' The detective was not as slow as some. He knew what Rebus was thinking. 'Christ, you don't mean ...?'

And then they were both running, pushing their way through the crowd, and the detective from Glasgow was shouting into his radio, but there was noise all around him, yelling and cheering and singing, smothering his words. Their progress was becoming slower. It was like moving through water chest-high. Rebus's legs felt useless and sore and there was a line of sweat trickling down his spine. Crawford's son had died from heroin, heroin purchased most probably in Edinburgh, and the man behind most of the heroin deals in Edinburgh was waiting somewhere up ahead. Coincidence? He had never really believed in coincidences, not really. They were convenient excuses for shrugging off the unthinkable.

What had Crawford said? Something about coming here tonight to make peace. Well, there were ways and ways of making peace, weren't there? 'If any mischief should follow, then thou shalt give life for life.' That was from Exodus. A dangerous book, the Bible. It could be made to say anything, its meaning in the mind of the beholder.

What was going through Jackie Crawford's mind? Rebus dreaded to think. There was a commotion up ahead, the crowd forming itself into a tight semi-circle around a shop-front. Rebus squeezed his way to the front.

'Police,' he shouted. 'Let me through, please.'

Grudgingly, the mass of bodies parted just enough for him to make progress. Finally he found himself at the front, staring at the slumped body of Alan Lyons. A long smear ran down the shop window to where he lay and his chest was stained dark red. One of the Glasgow officers was trying unsuccessfully to stem the flow of blood, using his own rolled-up coat, now sopping wet. Other officers were keeping back the crowd. Rebus caught snatches of what they were saying.

'Looked like he was going to shake hands.'

'Looked like he was hugging him.'

'Then the knife ...'

'Pulled out a knife.'

'Stabbed him twice before we could do anything.'

'Couldn't do anything.'

A siren had started nearby, inching closer. There were always ambulances on standby near the Tron on Hogmanay. Beside Lyons, still gripped in his left hand, was the bag containing the money for the deal.

'Will he be all right?' Rebus said to nobody in particular, which was just as well since nobody answered. He was remembering back a month to another dealer, another knife ... Then he saw Crawford. He was being restrained on the edge of the crowd by two more plainclothes men. One held his arms behind him while the other frisked him for weapons. On the pavement between where Crawford stood and Alan Lyons lay dying or dead there was a fairly ordinary looking knife, small enough to conceal in a sock or a waistband, but enough for the job required. More than an inch of blade was excess. The other detective was beside Rebus.

'Aw, Christ,' he said. But Rebus was staring at Crawford and Crawford was staring back, and in that moment they understood one another well enough. 'I don't suppose,' the detective was saying, 'we'll be seeing the party with the merchandise. Always supposing he was going to turn up in any event.'

'I'm not so sure about that,' answered Rebus, turning his gaze from Crawford. 'Ask yourself this: how did Crawford know Lyons would be in the High Street tonight?' The detective did not answer. Behind them, the crowd was pressing closer for a look at the body and then making noises of revulsion before opening another can of lager or half-bottle of vodka. The ambulance was still a good fifty yards away. Rebus nodded towards Crawford.

'He knows where the stuff is, but he's probably dumped it somewhere. Somewhere nobody can ever touch it. It was just bait, that's all. Just bait.'

And as bait it had worked. Hook, line and bloody sinker. Lyons had swallowed it, while Rebus, equally fooled, had swallowed something else. He felt it sticking in his throat like something cancerous, something no amount of coughing would dislodge. He glanced towards the prone body again and smiled involuntarily. A headline had come to mind, one that would never be used.

LYONS FED TO THE CHRISTIAN.

Someone was being noisily sick somewhere behind him. A bottle shattered against a wall. The loudest voices in the crowd were growing irritable and hard-edged. In fifteen minutes or so, they would cease to be revellers and would be transformed into trouble-makers. A woman shrieked from one of the many darkened closes. The look on Jackie Crawford's face was one of calm and righteous triumph. He offered no resistance to the officers. He had known they were watching Lyons, had known he might kill Lyons but he would never get away. And still he had driven home the knife. What else was he to do with his freedom?'

The night was young and so was the year. Rebus held out his hand towards the detective.

'Happy New Year,' he said. 'And many more of them.'

The young man stared at him blankly. 'Don't think you're blaming us for this,' he said. 'This was your fault. You let Crawford go. It's Edinburgh's balls-up, not ours.'

Rebus shrugged and let his arm fall to his side. Then he started to walk along the pavement, moving further and further from the scene. The ambulance moved past him. Someone slapped him on the back and offered a hand. From a distance, the young detective was watching him retreat.

'Away to hell,' said Rebus quietly, not sure for whom the message was intended.

The Gentlemen's Club

It was the most elegant of all Edinburgh's elegant Georgian circuses, a perfect circle in design and construction, the houses themselves as yet untouched by the private contractors who might one day renovate and remove, producing a dozen tiny flats from each.

A perfect circle surrounding some private gardens, the gardens a wash of colour despite the January chill: violet, pink, red, green and orange. A tasteful display, though. No flower was allowed to be too vibrant, too bright, too inelegant.

The gate to the gardens was locked, of course. The keyholders paid a substantial fee each year for the privilege of that lock. Everyone else could look, could peer through the railings as he was doing now, but entrance was forbidden. Well, that was Edinburgh for you, a closed circle within a closed circle.

He stood there, enjoying the subtle smells in the air now that the flurry of snowflakes had stopped. Then he shifted his attention to the houses, huge three- and four-storey statements of the architect's confidence. He found himself staring at one particular house, the one outside which the white police Sierra was parked. It was too ripe a day to be spoiled, but duty was duty. Taking a final deep breath, he turned from the garden railings and walked towards number 16, with its heavy closed curtains but its front door ajar.

Once inside, having introduced himself, John Rebus had to

climb three large flights of stairs to 'the children's floor', as his guide termed it. She was slender and middle-aged and dressed from head to toe in grey. The house was quiet, only one or two shafts of sunlight penetrating its gloom. The woman walked near-silently and quickly, while Rebus tugged on the bannister, breathing hard. It wasn't that he was unfit, but somehow all the oxygen seemed to have been pumped out of the house.

Arriving at last at the third floor, the woman passed three firmly closed doors before stopping at a fourth. This one was open, and inside Rebus could make out the gleaming tiles of a large bathroom and the shuffling, insect-like figures of Detective Constable Brian Holmes and the police pathologist, not the lugubrious Dr Curt but the one everybody called – though not to his face, never to his face – Doctor Crippen. He turned to his guide.

'Thank you, Mrs McKenzie.' But she had already averted her eyes and was making back for the safety of the stairs. She was a brave one though, to bring him all the way up here in the first place. And now there was nothing for it but to enter the room. 'Hello, Doctor.'

'Inspector Rebus, good morning. Not a pretty sight, is it?'

Rebus forced himself to look. There was not much water in the bath, and what water there was had been dyed a rich ruby colour by the girl's blood. She was undressed and as white as a statue. She had been very young, sixteen or seventeen, her body not yet quite fully formed. A late developer.

Her arms lay peacefully by her sides, wrists turned upwards to reveal the clean incisions. Holmes used a pair of tweezers to hold up a single razor blade for Rebus's inspection. Rebus winced and shook his head.

'What a waste,' he said. He had a daughter himself, not much older than this girl. His wife had taken their daughter with her when she left him. Years ago now. He'd lost touch, the way you do sometimes with family, though you keep in contact with friends.

He was moving around the bath, committing the scene to memory. The air seemed to glow, but the glow was already fading.

'Yes,' said Holmes. 'It's a sin.'

'Suicide, of course,' Rebus commented after a silence. The pathologist nodded, but did not speak. They were not usually so awkward around a corpse, these three men. Each thought he had seen the worst, the most brutal, the most callous. Each had anecdotes to relate which would make strangers shudder and screw shut their eyes. But this, this was different. Something had been taken quietly, deliberately and ruinously from the world.

'The question,' Rebus said, for the sake of filling the void, 'is why.'

Why indeed. Here he was, standing in a bathroom bigger than his own living-room, surrounded by powders and scents, thick towels, soaps and sponges. But here was this gruesome and unnecessary death. There had to be a reason for it. Silly, stupid child. What had she been playing at? Mute anger turned to frustration, and he almost staggered as he made his way out to the landing.

There had to be a reason. And he was just in the mood now to track it down.

'I've told you already,' said Thomas McKenzie irritably, 'she was the happiest girl in Christendom. No, we didn't spoil her, and no, we never forbade her seeing anyone. There is no reason in the world, Inspector, why Suzanne should have done what she did. It just doesn't make sense.'

McKenzie broke down again, burying his face in his hands. Rebus loathed himself, yet the questions had to be asked.

'Did she,' he began, 'did she have a boyfriend, Mr McKenzie?'

McKenzie got up from his chair, walked to the sideboard and poured himself another whisky. He motioned to Rebus who, still cradling a crystal inch of the stuff, shook his head. Mrs McKenzie was upstairs resting. She had been given a sedative by her doctor, an old friend of the family who had seemed in need of similar treatment himself.

But Thomas McKenzie had not needed anything. He was sticking to the old remedies, sloshing a fresh measure of malt into his glass.

'No,' he said, 'no boyfriends. They've never really been Suzanne's style.'

Though he would not be travelling to his office today, McKenzie had still dressed himself in a dark blue suit and tie. The drawing-room in which Rebus sat had about it the air of a commercial office, not at all homely or lived-in. He couldn't imagine growing up in such a place.

'What about school?' he asked.

'What do you mean?'

'I mean, was she happy there?'

'Very.' McKenzie sat down with his drink. 'She gets good reports, good grades. She ... she *was* going to the University in October.'

Rebus watched him gulp at the whisky. Thomas McKenzie was a tough man, tough enough to make his million young and then canny enough not to lose it. He was forty-four now, but looked younger. Rebus had no idea how many shops McKenzie now owned, how many company directorships he held along with all his other holdings and interests. He was new money trying to look like old money, making his home in Stockbridge, convenient for Princes Street, rather than further out in bungalow land.

'What was she going to study?' Rebus stared past McKenzie towards where a family portrait sat on a long, polished sideboard. No family snapshot, but posed, a sitting for a professional photographer. Daughter gleaming in the centre, sandwiched by grinning parents. A mock-up cloudscape behind them, the clouds pearl-coloured, the sky blue.

'Law,' said McKenzie. 'She had a head on her shoulders.'

Yes, a head of mousy-brown hair. And her father had found her early in the morning, already cold. McKenzie hadn't panicked. He'd made the phone calls before waking his wife and telling her. He always rose first, always went straight to the bathroom. He had remained calm, most probably from shock. But there was a stiffness to McKenzie, too, Rebus noticed. He wondered what it would take really to rouse the man.

Something niggled. Suzanne had gone to the bathroom, run some water into the bath, lain down in it, and slashed her wrists. Fine, Rebus could accept that. Maybe she had expected to be found and rescued. Most failed suicides were cries for help, weren't they? If you *really* wanted to kill yourself, you went somewhere quiet and secret, where you couldn't possibly be found in time. Suzanne hadn't done that. She had almost certainly expected her father to find her in time. Her timing had been a little awry.

Moreover, she must have known her father always rose before her mother, and therefore that he would be the first to find her. This notion interested Rebus, though no one around him seemed curious about it.

'What about friends at school,' Rebus went on. 'Did Suzanne have many friends?'

'Oh yes, lots.'

'Anyone in particular?'

McKenzie was about to answer when the door opened and his wife walked in, pale from her drugged sleep.

'What time is it?' she asked, shuffling forwards.

'It's eleven, Shona,' her husband said, rising to meet her. 'You've only been asleep half an hour.' They embraced one another, her arms tight around his body. Rebus felt like an intruder on their grief, but the questions still had to be asked.

'You were about to tell me about Suzanne's friends, Mr McKenzie.'

Husband and wife sat down together on the sofa, hands clasped.

'Well,' said McKenzie, 'there were lots of them, weren't there, Shona?'

'Yes,' said his wife. She really was an attractive woman. Her face had the same smooth sheen as her daughter's. She was the sort of woman men would instinctively feel protective towards, whether protection was needed or not. 'But I always liked Hazel best,' she went on.

McKenzie turned to Rebus and explained. 'Hazel Frazer, daughter of Sir Jimmy Frazer, the banker. A peach of a girl. A real peach.' He paused, staring at his wife, and then began, softly, with dignity, to cry. She rested his head against her shoulder and stroked his hair, talking softly to him. Rebus averted his eyes and drank his whisky. Then bit his bottom lip, deep in thought. In matters of suicide, just who was the victim, who the culprit?

Suzanne's room was a cold and comfortless affair. No posters on the walls, no teenage clutter or signs of an independent mind. There was a writing-pad on the dressing table, but it was blank. A crumpled ball of paper sat in the bottom of an otherwise empty bin beside the wardrobe. Rebus carefully unfolded the sheet. Written on it, in a fairly steady hand, was a message: 'Told you I would.'

Rebus studied the sentence. Told whom? Her parents seemed to have no inkling their daughter was suicidal, yet the note had been meant for someone. And having written it, why had she discarded it? He turned it over. The other side, though blank was slightly tacky. Rebus sniffed the paper, but could find no smell to identify the stickiness. He carefully folded the paper and slipped it into his pocket.

In the top drawer of the dressing-table was a leather-bound diary. But Suzanne had been no diarist. Instead of the expected teenage outpourings, Rebus found only one-line reminders, every Tuesday for the past six months or so, 'The Gentlemen's Club – 4.00'. Curiouser and curiouser. The last entry was for the previous week, with nothing in the rest of the diary save blank pages.

The Gentlemen's Club – what on earth could she have meant? Rebus knew of several clubs in Edinburgh, dowdy remnants of a former age, but none was called simply The Gentlemen's Club. The diary went into his pocket along with the note.

Thomas McKenzie saw him to the door. The tie around his neck was hanging loosely now and his voice was sweet with whisky.

'Just two last questions before I go,' Rebus said.

'Yes?' said McKenzie, sighing.

'Do you belong to a club?'

McKenzie seemed taken aback, but shrugged. 'Several, actually. The Strathspey Health Club. The Forth Golf Club. And Finlay's as was.'

'Finlay's Gentlemen's Club?'

'Yes, that's right. But it's called Thomson's now.'

Rebus nodded. 'Final question,' he said. 'What did Suzanne do on Tuesdays at four?'

'Nothing special. I think she had some drama group at school.'

'Thank you, Mr McKenzie. Sorry to have troubled you. Goodbye.'

'Goodbye, Inspector.'

Rebus stood on the top step, breathing in lungfuls of fresh air. Too much of a good thing could be stifling. He wondered if Suzanne McKenzie had felt stifled. He still wondered why she had died. And, knowing her father would be the first to find her, why had she lain down *naked* in the bath? Rebus had seen suicides before – lots of them – but whether they chose the bathroom or the bedroom, they were always clothed.

'Naked I came,' he thought to himself, remembering the passage from the Book of Job, 'and naked shall return.'

On his way to Hawthornden School for Girls, Rebus received a message from Detective Constable Holmes, who had returned to the station.

'Go ahead,' said Rebus. The radio crackled. The sky overhead was the colour of a bruise, the static in the air playing havoc with the radio's reception.

'I've just run McKenzie's name through the computer,' said Holmes, 'and come up with something you might be interested in.'

Rebus smiled. Holmes was as thorough as any airport sniffer dog. 'Well?' he said. 'Are you going to tell me, or do I have to buy the paperback?'

There was a hurt pause before Holmes began to speak and Rebus remembered how sensitive to criticism the younger man could be. 'It seems,' Holmes said at last, 'that Mr McKenzie was arrested several months back for loitering outside a school.'

'Oh? Which school?'

'Murrayfield Comprehensive. He wasn't charged, but it's on record that he was taken to Murrayfield police station and questioned.'

'That *is* interesting. I'll talk to you later.' Rebus terminated the call. The rain had started to fall in heavy drops. He picked up the radio again and asked to be put through to Murrayfield police station. His luck was in. A colleague there remembered the whole incident.

'We kept it quiet, of course,' the Inspector told Rebus. 'And McKenzie swore he'd just stopped there to call into his office. But the teachers at the school were adamant he'd parked there before, during the lunch-break. It's not the most refined area of town after all, is it? A Daimler does tend to stand out from the crowd around there, especially when there isn't a bride in the back of it.'

'I take your point,' said Rebus, smiling. 'Anything else?'

'Yes, one of the kids told a teacher he'd seen someone get into McKenzie's Daimler once, but we couldn't find any evidence of that.'

'Vivid imaginations, these kids,' Rebus agreed. This was all his colleague could tell him, but it was enough to muddy the water. Had Suzanne discovered her father's secret and, ashamed, killed herself? Or perhaps her schoolfriends had found out and teased her about it? If McKenzie liked kids, there might even be a tang of incest about the whole thing. That would at least go some way towards explaining Suzanne's nudity: she wasn't putting on show anything her father hadn't seen before. But what about The Gentlemen's Club? Where did it fit in? At Hawthornden School, Rebus hoped he might find some answers.

It was the sort of school fathers sent their daughters to so that they might learn the arts of femininity and ruthlessness. The headmistress, as imposing a character as the school building itself, fed Rebus on cakes and tea before leading him to Suzanne's form mistress, a Miss Selkirk, who had prepared more tea for him in her little private room.

Yes, she told him, Suzanne had been a very popular girl and news of her death came as quite a shock. She had run around with Hazel Frazer, the banker's daughter. A very vivacious girl, Hazel, head of school this year, though Suzanne hadn't been far behind in the running. A competitive pair, their marks for maths, English, languages almost identical. Suzanne the better at sciences; Hazel the better at economics and accounts. Splendid girls, the pair of them.

Biting into his fourth or fifth cake, Rebus nodded again.

These women were all so commanding that he had begun to feel like a schoolboy himself. He sat with knees primly together, smiling, asking his questions almost apologetically.

'I don't suppose,' he said, 'the name The Gentlemen's Club means anything to you?'

Miss Selkirk thought hard. 'Is it,' she said at last, 'the name of a discotheque?'

Rebus smiled. 'I don't think so. Why do you ask?'

'Well, it's just that I do seem to recall having heard it before from one of the girls, quite recently, but only in passing.'

Rebus looked disappointed.

'I am sorry, Inspector.' She tapped her skull. 'This old head of mine isn't what it used to be.'

'That's quite all right,' said Rebus quietly. 'One last thing, do you happen to know who takes the school's drama classes?'

'Ah,' said Miss Selkirk, 'that's young Miss Phillips, the English teacher.'

Miss Phillips, who insisted that Rebus call her Jilly, was not only young but also very attractive. Waves of long auburn hair fell over her shoulders and down her back. Her eyes were dark and moist with recently shed tears. Rebus felt more awkward than ever.

'I believe,' he said, 'that you run the school's drama group.'

'That's right.' Her voice was fragile as porcelain.

'And Suzanne was in the group?'

'Yes. She was due to play Celia in our production of *As You Like It*.'

'Oh?'

'That's Shakespeare, you know.'

'Yes,' said Rebus, 'I do know.'

They were talking in the corridor, just outside her classroom, and through the panes of glass in the door,

Rebus could see a class of fairly mature girls, healthy and from well-ordered homes, whispering together and giggling. Odd that, considering they'd just lost a friend.

'Celia,' he said, 'is Duke Frederick's daughter, isn't she?'

'I'm impressed, Inspector.'

'It's not my favourite Shakespeare play,' Rebus explained, 'but I remember seeing it at the Festival a few years back. Celia has a friend, doesn't she?'

'That's right, Rosalind.'

'So who was going to play Rosalind?'

'Hazel Frazer.'

Rebus nodded slowly at this. It made sense. 'Is Hazel in your classroom at the moment?'

'Yes, she's the one with the long black hair. Do you see her?'

Oh yes, Rebus could see her. She sat, calm and imperturbable, at the still centre of a sea of admirers. The other girls giggled and whispered around her, hoping to catch her attention or a few words of praise, while she sat oblivious to it all.

'Yes,' he said, 'I see her.'

'Would you care to speak with her, Inspector?'

He knew Hazel was aware of him, even though she averted her eyes from the door. Indeed, he knew precisely *because* she refused to look, while the other girls glanced towards the corridor from time to time, interested in this interruption to their classwork. Interested and curious. Hazel pretended to be neither, which in itself interested Rebus.

'No,' he said to Jilly Phillips, 'not just now. She's probably upset, and it wouldn't do much good for me to go asking her questions under the circumstances. There was one thing, though.'

'Yes, Inspector?'

'This after-school drama group of yours, the one that

215

meets on Tuesdays, it doesn't happen to have a nickname, does it?'

'Not that I know of.' Jilly Phillips furrowed her brow. 'But, Inspector?'

'Yes?'

'You're under some kind of misapprehension. The drama group meets on Fridays, not Tuesdays. And we meet before lunch.'

Rebus drove out of the school grounds and parked by the side of the busy main road. The drama group met during school hours, so what had Suzanne done on Tuesdays after school, while her parents thought she was there? At least, McKenzie had said he'd thought that's what she'd done on Tuesdays. Suppose he'd been lying? Then what?

A maroon-coloured bus roared past Rebus's car. A 135, on its way to Princes Street. He started up the car again and followed it along its route, all the time thinking through the details of Suzanne's suicide. Until suddenly, with blinding clarity, he saw the truth of the thing, and bit his bottom lip fiercely, wondering just what on earth he could – should – do about it.

Well, the longer he thought about doing something, the harder it would become to do it. So he called Holmes and asked him for a large favour, before driving over to the house owned by Sir Jimmy Frazer.

Frazer was not just part of the Edinburgh establishment – in many ways he *was* that establishment. Born and educated in the city, he had won hard-earned respect, friendship and awe on his way to the top. The nineteenth-century walled house in which his family made its home was part of his story. It had been about to be bought by a company, an English company, and knocked down to make way for a new apartment block. There were public protests about this act of vandalism and in had stepped Sir Jimmy Frazer, purchasing the house and making it his own.

That had been years ago, but it was a story still heard told by hard men to other hard men in watering holes throughout the city. Rebus examined the house as he drove in through the open gates. It was an ugly near-Gothic invention, mock turrets and spires, hard, cold and uninviting. A maid answered the door. Rebus introduced himself and was ushered into a large drawing-room, where Sir Jimmy's wife, tall and dark haired like her daughter, waited.

'I'm sorry to trouble you, Lady –' Rebus was cut short by an imperious hand, but an open smile.

'Just Deborah, please.' And she motioned for Rebus to sit.

'Thank you,' he said. 'I'm sorry to trouble you, but –'

'Yes, your call *was* intriguing, Inspector. Of course, I'll do what I can. It's a tragedy, poor Suzanne.'

'You knew her then?'

'Of course. Whyever shouldn't we know her? She visited practically every Tuesday.'

'Oh?' Rebus had suspected as much, but was keen to learn more.

'After school,' Lady Deborah continued. 'Hazel and Suzanne and a few other chums would come back here. They didn't stay late.'

'But what exactly did they do?'

She laughed. 'I've no idea. What do girls of that age do? Play records? Talk about boys? Try to defer growing up?' She gave a wry smile, perhaps thinking of her own past. Rebus checked his wristwatch casually. Five to four. He had a few minutes yet.

'Did they,' he asked, 'confine themselves to your daughter's room?'

'More or less. Not her bedroom, of course. There's an old playroom upstairs. Hazel uses that as a kind of den.'

Rebus nodded. 'May I see it?'

217

Lady Deborah seemed puzzled. 'I suppose so, though I can't see —'

'It would help,' Rebus interrupted, 'to give me an overall picture of Suzanne. I'm trying to work out the kind of girl she was.'

'Of course,' said Lady Deborah, though she sounded unconvinced.

Rebus was shown to a small, cluttered room at the end of a long corridor. Inside, the curtains were closed. Lady Deborah switched on the lights.

'Hazel won't allow the maid in here,' Lady Deborah explained, apologising for the untidiness. '*Secrets*, I suppose,' she whispered.

Rebus did not doubt it. There were two small sofas, piles of pop and teenage magazines scattered on the floor, an ashtray full of dog-ends (which Lady Deborah pointedly chose to ignore), a stereo against one wall and a desk against another, on which sat a personal computer, its screen switched on but blank.

'She always forgets to turn that thing off,' said Lady Deborah. Rebus could hear the telephone ringing downstairs. The maid answered it and then called up to Lady Deborah.

'Oh dear. Please excuse me, Inspector.'

Rebus smiled and bowed slightly as she left. His watch said four o'clock. As prearranged, it would be Holmes on the phone. Rebus had told him to pretend to be anybody, to say *any*thing, so long as he kept Lady Deborah occupied for five minutes. Holmes had suggested he be a journalist seeking some quotes for a magazine feature. Rebus smiled now. Yes, there was probably vanity enough in Lady Deborah to keep her talking with a reporter for at least five minutes, maybe more.

Still, he couldn't waste time. He had expected to have to do a lot of searching, but the computer seemed the obvious place to start. There were floppy discs stored in a plastic box beside the monitor. He flipped through them until he came to one labelled GC DISC. There could be no doubt. He slipped the disc into the computer and watched as the display came up. He had found the records of The Gentlemen's Club.

He read quickly. Not that there was much to read. Members must attend every week, at four o'clock on Tuesday. Members must wear a tie. (Rebus looked quickly in a drawer of the desk and found five ties. He recognised them as belonging to various clubs in the city: the Strathspey, the Forth Golf Club, Finlay's Club. Stolen from the girls' fathers of course, and worn to meetings of a secret little clique, itself a parody of the clubs their fathers frequented.)

In a file named 'Exploits of the Gentlemen's Club', Rebus found lists of petty thefts, acts of so-called daring, and lies. Members had stolen from city centre shops, had carried out practical jokes against teachers and pupils alike, had been, in short, malicious.

There were many exploits attributed to Suzanne, including lying to her parents about what she did on Tuesday after school. Twenty-eight exploits in all. Hazel Frazer's list totalled thirty at the bottom, yet Rebus could count only twenty-nine entries on the screen. And in a separate file, the agenda for a meeting yet to be held, was a single item, recorded as 'New Business: can suicide be termed an exploit of the Gentlemen's Club?'

Rebus heard steps behind him. He turned, but it was not Lady Deborah. It was Hazel Frazer. Her eyes looked past him to the screen, firstly in fear and disbelief, then in scorn.

'Hello, Hazel.'

'You're the policeman,' she said in a level tone. 'I saw you at the school.'

'That's right.' Rebus studied her as she came into the room. She was a cool one, all right. That was Hawthornden for you, breeding strong, cold women, each one her father's daughter. 'Are you jealous of her?'

'Of whom? Suzanne?' Hazel smiled cruelly. 'Why should I be?'

'Because,' answered Rebus, 'Suzanne's is the ultimate exploit. For once, she beat you.'

'You think that's why she did it?' Hazel sounded smug. When Rebus shook his head, a little of her confidence seeped away.

'I know why she did it, Hazel. She did it because she found out about you and her father. She found out because you told her. I notice it's too much of a secret for you to put on your computer, but you've added it to the list, haven't you? As an exploit. I expect you were having an argument, bragging, being competitive. And it just slipped out. You told Suzanne you were her father's lover.'

Her cheeks were becoming a deep strawberry red, while her lips drained of colour. But she wasn't about to speak, so Rebus went on at her.

'You met him at lunchtime. You couldn't meet near Hawthornden. That would be too risky. So you'd take a bus to Murrayfield. It's only ten minutes ride away. He'd be waiting in his car. You told Suzanne and she couldn't bear to know. So she killed herself.' Rebus was becoming angry. 'And all you can be bothered to do is write about her on your files and wonder whether suicide is an "exploit".' His voice had risen and he hardly registered the fact that Lady Deborah was standing in the doorway, looking on in disbelief.

'No!' yelled Hazel. 'She did it first! She slept with Daddy months ago! So I did it back to her. *That's* what she couldn't live with! That's why she –'

Then it happened. Hazel's shoulders fell forward and, eyes closed, she began to cry, silently at first, but then loudly. Her mother ran to comfort her and told Rebus to leave. Couldn't he see what the girl was going through?

He'd pay, she told him. He'd pay for upsetting her daughter. But she was crying too, crying like Hazel, mother and child. Rebus could think of nothing to say, so he left.

Descending the stairs, he tried not to think about what he had just unleashed. Two families broken now instead of one, and to what end? Merely to prove, as he had always known anyway, that a pretty face was no mirror of the soul and that the spirit of competition still flourished in Scotland's well-respected education system. He dug his hands deep into his jacket pockets, felt something there and drew out Suzanne's note. The crumpled note, found discarded in her bin, sticky on one side. He stopped halfway down the stairs, staring at the note without really seeing it. He was visualising something else, something almost too horrible, too unbelievable.

Yet he believed it.

Thomas McKenzie was surprised to see him. Mrs McKenzie had, he said, gone to stay with a sister on the other side of the city. The body had been taken away, of course, and the bathroom cleaned. McKenzie was without jacket and tie and had rolled up his shirt-sleeves. He wore half-moon glasses and carried a pen with him as he opened the door to Rebus.

In the drawing-room, there were signs that McKenzie had been working. Papers were strewn across a writing desk, a briefcase open on the floor. A calculator sat on the chair, as did a telephone.

'I'm sorry to disturb you again, sir,' Rebus said, taking in the scene. McKenzie had sobered up since the morning. He looked like a businessman rather than a grieving father.

McKenzie seemed to realise that the scene before Rebus created a strange impression.

'Keeping busy,' he said. 'Keeping the mind occupied, you know. Life can't stop because ...' He fell silent.

'Quite, sir,' Rebus said, seating himself on the sofa. He

reached into his pocket. 'I thought you might like this.' He held the paper towards McKenzie, who took it from him and glanced at it. Rebus stared hard at him, and McKenzie twitched, attempting to hand back the note.

'No, sir,' said Rebus, 'you keep it.'

'Why?'

'It will always remind you,' said Rebus, his voice cold and level, 'that you could have saved your daughter.'

McKenzie was aghast. 'What do you mean?'

'I mean,' said Rebus, his voice still lacking emotion, 'that Suzanne wasn't intending to kill herself, not really. It was just something to attract your attention, to shock you into ... I don't know, action I suppose, a *re*action of some kind.'

McKenzie positioned himself slowly so that he rested on the armrest of one of the upholstered chairs.

'Yes,' Rebus went on, 'a reaction. That's as good a way of putting it as any. Suzanne knew what time you got up every morning. She wasn't stupid. She timed the slashing of her wrists so that you would find her while there was still time to save her. She also had a sense of the dramatic, didn't she? So she stuck her little note to the bathroom door. You saw the note and you went into the bathroom. And she wasn't dead, was she?'

McKenzie had screwed shut his eyes. His mouth was open, the teeth gritted in remembrance.

'She wasn't dead,' Rebus continued, 'not quite. And you knew damned well why she'd done it. Because she'd warned you she would. She had told you she would. Unless you stopped seeing Hazel, unless you owned up to her mother. Perhaps she had a lot of demands, Mr McKenzie. You never really got on with her anyway, did you? You didn't know what to do. Help her, or leave her to die? You hesitated. You waited.'

Rebus had risen from his seat now. His voice had risen, too. The tears were streaming down McKenzie's face, his whole body shuddering. But Rebus was relentless.

'You walked around a bit, you walked into her room. You threw her note into the waste-bin. And eventually, *eventually* you reached for a telephone and made the calls.'

'It was already too late,' McKenzie bawled. 'Nobody could have saved her.'

'They could have tried!' Rebus was yelling now, yelling close to McKenzie's own twisted face. '*You* could have tried, but you didn't. You wanted to keep your secret. Well by God your secret's out.' The last words were hissed and with them Rebus felt his fury ebb. He turned and started to walk away.

'What are you going to do?' McKenzie moaned.

'What can I do?' Rebus answered quietly. 'I'm not going to do anything, Mr McKenzie. I'm just going to leave you to get on with the rest of your life.' He paused. 'Enjoy it,' he said, closing the doors of the drawing-room behind him.

He stood on the steps of the house, trembling, his heart pounding. In a suicide, who was to blame, who the victim? He still couldn't answer the question. He doubted he ever would. His watch told him it was five minutes to five. He knew the pub near the circus, a quiet bar frequented by thinkers and amateur philosophers, a place where nothing happened and the measures were generous. He felt like having one drink, maybe two at most. He would raise his glass and make a silent toast: to the lassies.

Monstrous Trumpet

John Rebus went down onto his knees.

'I'm begging you,' he said, 'don't do this to me, please.'

But Chief Inspector Lauderdale just laughed, thinking Rebus was clowning about as per usual. 'Come on, John,' he said. 'It'll be just like Interpol.'

Rebus got back to his feet. 'No it won't,' he said. 'It'll be like a bloody escort service. Besides, I can't speak French.'

'Apparently he speaks perfect English, this Monsieur ...' Lauderdale made a show of consulting the letter in front of him on his desk.

'Don't say it again, sir, please.'

'Monsieur Cluzeau.' Rebus winced. 'Yes,' Lauderdale continued, enjoying Rebus's discomfort, 'Monsieur Cluzeau. A fine name for a member of the *gendarmerie*, don't you think?'

'It's a stunt,' Rebus pleaded. 'It's got to be. DC Holmes or one of the other lads ...'

But Lauderdale would not budge. 'It's been verified by the Chief Super,' he said. 'I'm sorry about this, John, but I thought you'd be pleased.'

'*Pleased?*'

'Yes. Pleased. You know, showing a bit of Scots hospitality.'

'Since when did the CID job description encompass "tourist guide"?'

Lauderdale had had enough of this: Rebus had even stopped calling him 'sir'. 'Since, Inspector, I ordered you to do it.'

'But why *me?*'

Lauderdale shrugged. 'Why not you?' He sighed, opened a drawer of his desk and dropped the letter into it. 'Look, it's only a day, two at most. Just do it, eh? Now if you don't mind, Inspector, I've got rather a lot to do.'

But the fight had gone out of Rebus anyway. His voice was calm, resigned. 'When does he get here?'

Again, there was a pause while that missing 'sir' hung motionless in the air between them. Well, thought Lauderdale, the sod deserves this. 'He's already here.'

'What?'

'I mean, he's in Edinburgh. The letter took a bit of a time to get here.'

'You mean it sat in someone's office for a bit of time.'

'Well, whatever the delay, he's here. And he's coming to the station this afternoon.'

Rebus glanced at his watch. It was eleven-fifty. He groaned.

'*Late* afternoon, I'd imagine,' said Lauderdale, trying to soften the blow now that Rebus was heading for the canvas. This had been a bit of a mess all round. He'd only just received final confirmation himself that Monsieur Cluzeau was on his way. 'I mean,' he said, 'the French like to take a long lunch, don't they? Notorious for it. So I don't suppose he'll be here till after three.'

'Fine, he can take us as he finds us. What am I supposed to do with him anyway?'

Lauderdale tried to retain his composure: *just say it once, damn you! Just once so I know that you recognise me for what I am!* He cleared his throat. 'He wants to see how we work. So show him. As long as he can report back to his own people that we're courteous, efficient, diligent, scrupulous, and that we always get our man, well, I'll be happy.'

'Right you are, sir,' said Rebus, opening the door, making ready to leave Lauderdale's newly refurbished office. Lauderdale sat in a daze: *he'd said it! Rebus had actually ended a sentence with 'sir'!*

'That should be easy enough,' he was saying now. 'Oh, and I might as well track down Lord Lucan and catch the Loch Ness monster while I'm at it. I'm sure to have a spare five minutes.'

Rebus closed the door after him with such ferocity that Lauderdale feared for the glass-framed paintings on his walls. But glass was more resilient than it looked. And so was John Rebus.

Cluzeau had to be an arse-licker, hell-bent on promotion. What other reason could there be? The story was that he was coming over for the Scotland-France encounter at Murrayfield. Fair enough, Edinburgh filled with Frenchmen once every two years for a weekend in February, well-behaved if boisterous rugby fans whose main pleasure seemed to be dancing in saloon bars with ice-buckets on their heads.

Nothing out of the ordinary there. But imagine a Frenchman who, having decided to take a large chunk of his annual leave so as to coincide with the international season, then has another idea: while in Scotland he'll invite himself to spend a day with the local police force. His letter to his own chief requesting an introduction so impresses the chief that *he* writes to the Chief Constable. By now, the damage is done, and the boulder starts to bounce down the hillside – Chief Constable to Chief Super, Chief Super to Super, Super to Chief Inspector – and Chief Inspector to Mr Muggins, aka John Rebus.

Thank you and *bonne nuit*. Ha! There, he did remember a bit of French after all. Rhona, his wife, had done one of those teach-yourself French courses, all tapes and repeating phrases. It had driven Rebus bonkers, but some of it had stuck. And all of it in preparation for a long weekend in Paris, a weekend which hadn't come off because Rebus had been drawn into a murder inquiry. Little wonder she'd left him in the end.

Bonne nuit. Bonjour. That was another word. *Bonsoir.* What about *Bon accord?* Was that French, too? Bo'ness sounded French. Hadn't Bonnie Prince Charlie been French? And dear God, what was he going to do with the Frenchman?

There was only one answer: get busy. The busier he was, the less time there would be for small-talk, xenophobia and falling-out. With the brain and the body occupied, there would be less temptation to mention Onion Johnnies, frogs'-legs, the war, French letters, French kissing and French & Saunders. Oh dear God, what had he done to deserve this?

His phone buzzed.

'*Oui?*' said Rebus, smirking now because he remembered how often he'd managed to get away with not calling Lauderdale 'sir'.

'Eh?'

'Just practising, Bob.'

'You must be bloody psychic then. There's a French gentleman down here says he's got an appointment.'

'What? Already?' Rebus checked his watch again. It was two minutes past twelve. Christ, like sitting in a dentist's waiting-room and being called ahead of your turn. Would he really look like Peter Sellers? What if he didn't speak English?

'John?'

'Sorry, Bob, what?'

'What do you want me to tell him?'

'Tell him I'll be right down.' Right down in the dumps, he thought to himself, letting the receiver drop like a stone.

There was only one person in the large, dingy reception. He wore a biker's leather jacket and had a spider's-web tattoo creeping up out of his soiled T-shirt and across his throat. Rebus stopped in his tracks. But then he saw another figure, over to his left against the wall. This man was studying various Wanted and Missing posters. He was tall, thin, and wore an immaculate dark blue suit with a tightly-knotted red silk tie. His shoes looked brand new, as did his haircut.

Their eyes met, forcing Rebus into a smile. He was suddenly aware of his own rumpled chain-store suit, his scuffed brogues, the shirt with a button missing on one cuff.

'Inspector Rebus?' The man was coming forward, hand held out.

'That's right.' They shook. He was wearing after-shave too, not too strong but certainly noticeable. He had the bearing of someone much further up the ladder, yet Rebus had been told they were of similar ranks. Having said which, there was no way Rebus was going to say 'Inspector Cluzeau' out loud. It would be too ... too ...

'For you.'

Rebus saw that he was being handed a plastic carrier-bag. He looked inside. A litre of duty-free malt, a box of chocolates and a small tin of something. He lifted out the chocolates.

'Escargots,' Cluzeau explained. 'But made from chocolate.'

Rebus studied the picture on the box. Yes, chocolates in the shape of snails. And as for the tin ...

'Foie gras. It is a pâté made from fatted goose liver. A local delicacy. You spread it on your toast.'

'Sounds delicious,' Rebus said, with just a trace of irony. In fact, he was overwhelmed. None of this stuff looked as though it came cheap, meat paste or no. 'Thank you.'

The Frenchman shrugged. He had the kind of face which, shaved twice a day, still sported a five o'clock shadow. Hirsute: that was the word. What was that joke again, the one that ended with someone asking 'Hirsute?' and the guy replying 'No, the suit's mine, but the knickers are hers'? Hairy wrists, too, on one of which sat a thin gold wristwatch. He was tapping this with his finger.

'I am not too early, I hope.'

'What?' It was Rebus's curse to remember the endings of jokes but never their beginnings. 'No, no. You're all right. I was just, er, hold on a second, will you?'

'Sure.'

Rebus walked over to the reception desk, behind which stood the omnipresent Bob Leach. Bob nodded towards the bag.

'Not a bad haul,' he said.

Rebus kept his voice low, but not so low, he hoped, as to arouse Cluzeau's suspicions. 'Thing is, Bob, I wasn't expecting him for a few hours yet. What the hell am I going to do with him? I don't suppose you've got any calls?'

'Nothing you'd be interested in, John.' Leach examined the pad in front of him. 'Couple of car smashes. Couple of break-ins. Oh, and the art gallery.'

'Art gallery?'

'I think young Brian's on that one. Some exhibition down the High Street. One of the pieces seems to have walked.'

Well, it wasn't too far away, and it *was* a tourist spot. St Giles. John Knox's House. Holyrood.

'The very dab,' said Rebus. 'That'll do us nicely. Give me the address, will you?'

Leach scribbled onto a pad of paper and tore off the sheet, handing it across the counter.

'Thanks, Bob.'

Leach was nodding towards the bag. Not only omnipresent, thought Rebus, but omniscrounging too. 'What else did you get apart from the whisky?'

Rebus bent towards him and hissed: 'Meat paste and snails!'

Bob Leach looked disheartened. 'Bloody French,' he said. 'You'd think he'd bring you something decent.'

* * *

Rebus didn't bother with back-street shortcuts as they drove towards the Royal Mile. He gave Cluzeau the full tour. But the French policeman seemed more interested in Rebus than in the streets of his city.

'I was here before,' he explained. 'Two years ago, for the rugby.'

'Do they play a lot of rugby down your way then?'

'Oh yes. It is not so much a game, more a love affair.'

Rebus assumed Cluzeau would be Parisian. He was not. Parisians, he said, were – his phrase – 'cold fish'. And in any case the city was not representative of the real France. The countryside – that was the real France, and especially the countryside of the south-west. Cluzeau was from Périgueux. He had been born there and now lived and worked there. He was married, with four children. And yes, he carried a family photo in his wallet. The wallet itself he carried inside a black leather pouch, almost like a clutch-purse. The pouch also contained identity documents, passport, chequebook, diary, a small English-French dictionary. No wonder he looked good in a suit: no bulges in the pockets, no wear on the material.

Rebus handed back the photograph.

'Very nice,' he said.

'And you, Inspector?'

So it was Rebus's turn to tell his tale. Born in Fife. Out of school and into the Army. Paras eventually and from there to the SAS. Breakdown and recovery. Then the police. Wife, now ex-wife, and one daughter living with her mother in London. Cluzeau, Rebus realised, had a canny way of asking questions, making them sound more like statements. So that instead of answering, you were merely acknowledging what he already seemed to know. He'd remember that for future use.

'And now we are going where?'

'The High Street. You might know it better as the Royal Mile.'

'I've walked along it, yes. You say separated, not divorced?'

'That's right.'

'Then there is a chance ...?'

'What? Of us getting back together? No, no chance of that.'

This elicited another huge shrug from Cluzeau. 'It was another man ...?'

'No, just *this* man.'

'Ah. In my part of France we have many crimes of passion. And here in Edinburgh?'

Rebus gave a wry grin. 'Where there's no passion ...'

The Frenchman seemed to make hard work of understanding this.

'French policemen carry guns, don't they?' Rebus asked, filling the silence.

'Not on vacation.'

'I'm glad to hear it.'

'Yes, we have guns. But it is not like in America. We have respect for guns. They are a way of life in the country. Every Frenchman is a hunter at heart.'

Rebus signalled, and drew in to the roadside. 'Scotsmen, too,' he said, opening his door. 'And right now I'm going to hunt down a sandwich. This cafe does the best boiled ham in Edinburgh.'

Cluzeau looked dubious. 'The famous Scottish cuisine,' he murmured, unfastening his seatbelt.

They ate as they drove – ham for Rebus, salami for Cluzeau – and soon enough arrived outside the Heggarty Gallery. In fact, they arrived outside a wools and knitwear shop, which occupied the street-level. The gallery itself was up a winding stairwell, the steps worn and treacherous. They walked in through an unprepossessing door and found themselves in the midst of an argument. Fifteen or so women were crowded around Detective Constable Brian Holmes.

'You can't keep us here, you know!'

'Look, ladies –'

'Patronising pig.'

'Look, I need to get names and addresses first.'

'Well, go on then, what are you waiting for?'

'Bloody cheek, like we're criminals or something.'

'Maybe he wants to strip-search us.'

'Chance would be a fine thing.' There was some laughter at this.

Holmes had caught sight of Rebus and the look of relief on his face told Rebus all he needed to know. On a trellis table against one wall stood a couple of dozen wine bottles, mostly empty, and jugs of orange juice and water, mostly still full. Cluzeau lifted a bottle and wrinkled his nose. He sniffed the neck and the nose wrinkled even further.

The poster on the gallery door had announced an exhibition of paintings and sculpture by Serena Davies. The exhibition was entitled 'Hard Knox' and today was its opening. By the look of the drinks table, a preview had been taking place. Free wine all round, glasses replenished. And now a squabble, which might be about to turn ugly.

Rebus filled his lungs. 'Excuse me!' he cried. The faces turned from Brian Holmes and settled on him. 'I'm Inspector Rebus. Now, with a bit of luck we'll have you all out of here in five minutes. Please bear with us until then. I notice there's still some drink left. If you'll fill your glasses and maybe have a last look round, by the time you finish you should be able to leave. Now, I just need a word with my colleague.'

Gratefully, Holmes squeezed his way out of the scrum and came towards Rebus.

'You've got thirty seconds to fill me in,' Rebus said.

Holmes took a couple of deep breaths. 'A sculpture in bronze, male figure. It was sitting in the middle of one of the rooms. Preview opens. Somebody starts yelling that it's disappeared. The artist goes up the wall. She won't let

233

anybody in or out, because if somebody's nicked it, that somebody's still in the gallery.'

'And that's the state of play? Nobody in or out since it went missing?'

Holmes nodded. 'Of course, as I tried telling her, they could have high-tailed it *before* she barricaded everyone else in.' Holmes was looking at the man who had come to stand beside Rebus. 'Can we help you, sir?'

'Oh,' said Rebus. 'You haven't been introduced. This is ...' But no, he still couldn't make himself say the name. Instead, he nodded towards Holmes. 'This is Detective Constable Holmes.' Then, as Cluzeau shook hands with Holmes: 'The inspector here has come over from France to see how we do things in Edinburgh.' Rebus turned to Cluzeau. 'Did you catch what Brian was saying? Only I know his accent's a bit thick.'

'I understood perfectly.' He turned to Holmes. 'Inspector Rebus forgot to say, but my name is Cluzeau.' Somehow it didn't sound so funny when spoken by a native. 'How big is the statue? Do we know what it looks like?'

'There's a picture of it in the catalogue.' Holmes took the small glossy booklet from his pocket and handed it to Cluzeau. 'That's it at the top of the page.'

While Cluzeau studied this, Holmes caught Rebus's eye, then nodded down to the Frenchman's pouch.

'Nice handbag.'

Rebus gave him a warning look, then glanced at the catalogue. His eyes opened wide. 'Good Christ!'

Cluzeau read from the catalogue. ' "Monstrous Trumpet. Bronze and multi-media. Sixteen –" what do these marks mean?'

'Inches.'

'Thank you. "Sixteen inches. Three thousand five hundred pounds." *C'est cher*. It's expensive.'

'I'll say,' said Rebus. 'You could buy a car for that.'
Well, he thought, you could certainly buy *my* car for that.

'It is an interesting piece, don't you think?'

'Interesting?' Rebus studied the small photograph of the statue called 'Monstrous Trumpet'. A nude male, his face exaggeratedly spiteful, was sticking out his tongue, except that it wasn't a tongue, it was a penis. And where that particular organ should have been, there was what looked like a piece of sticking-plaster. Because of the angle of the photo, it was just possible to discern something protruding from the statue's backside. Rebus guessed it was meant to be a tongue.

'Yes,' said Cluzeau, 'I should very much like to meet the artist.'

'Doesn't look as though you've got any choice,' said Holmes, seeming to retreat though in fact he didn't move. 'Here she comes.'

She had just come into the room, of that Rebus was certain. If she'd been there before, he'd have noticed her. And even if he hadn't Cluzeau certainly would have. She was just over six feet tall, dressed in long flowing white skirt, black boots, puffy white blouse and a red satin waistcoat. Her eye-makeup was jet black, matching her long straight hair, and her wrists fairly jangled with bangles and bracelets. She addressed Holmes.

'No sign of it. I've had a thorough look.' She turned towards Rebus and Cluzeau. Holmes started making the introductions.

'This is Inspector Rebus, and Inspector Cl ...' he stumbled to a halt. Yes, thought Rebus, it's a problem, isn't it, Brian? But Cluzeau appeared not to have noticed. He was squeezing Serena Davies' hand.

'Pleased to meet you.'

She looked him up and down without embarrassment, gave a cool smile, and passed to Rebus. 'Well, thank goodness the grown-ups are here at last.' Brian Holmes reddened furiously. 'I hope we didn't interrupt your lunch, Inspector. Come on, I'll show you where the piece was.'

And with that she turned and left. Some of the women offered either condolences over her loss, or else praise for what works remained, and Serena Davies gave a weak smile, a smile which said: I'm coping, but don't ask me how.

Rebus touched Holmes' shoulder. 'Get the names and addresses, eh, Brian?' He made to follow the artist, but couldn't resist a parting shot. 'You've got your crayons with you, have you?'

'And my marbles,' Holmes retorted. By God, thought Rebus, he's learning fast. But then, he had a good teacher, hadn't he?

'Magnificent creature,' Cluzeau hissed into his ear as they passed through the room. A few of the women glanced towards the Frenchman. I'm making him look too good, Rebus thought. Pity I had to be wearing this old suit today.

The small galleries through which they passed comprised a maze, an artful configuration of angles and doorways which made more of the space than there actually was. As to the works on display, well, Rebus couldn't be sure, of course, but there seemed an awful lot of violence in them, violence acted out upon a particular part of the masculine anatomy. Even the Frenchman was quiet as they passed red splashes of colour, twisted statues, great dollops of paint. There was one apparent calm centre, an extremely large and detailed drawing of the vulva. Cluzeau paused for a moment.

'I like this,' he said. Rebus nodded towards a red circular sticker attached to the wall beside the portrait.

'Already sold.'

Cluzeau tapped the relevant page of the catalogue. 'Yes, for one thousand five hundred pounds.'

'In here!' the artist's voice commanded. 'When you've stopped gawping.' She was in the next room of the gallery, standing by the now empty pedestal. The sign beneath it showed no red blob. No sale. 'It was right here.' The room was about fifteen feet by ten, in the corner of the gallery: only one doorway and no windows. Rebus looked up at the ceiling, but saw only strip lighting. No trapdoors.

'And there were people in here when it happened?'

Serena Davies nodded. 'Three or four of the guests. Ginny Elyot, Margaret Grieve, Helena Mitchison and I think Lesley Jameson.'

'Jameson?' Rebus knew two Jamesons in Edinburgh, one a doctor and the other ...

'Tom Jameson's daughter,' the artist concluded.

The other a newspaper editor called Tom Jameson. 'And who was it raised the alarm?' Rebus asked.

'That was Ginny. She came out of the room shouting that the statue had vanished. We all rushed into the room. Sure enough.' She slapped a hand down on the pedestal.

'Time, then,' Rebus mused, 'for someone to sneak away while everyone else was occupied?'

But the artist shook her mane of hair. 'I've already told you, there's nobody missing. Everyone who was here *is* here. In fact, I think there are a couple more bodies now than there were at the time.'

'Oh?'

'Moira Fowler was late. As usual. She arrived a couple of minutes after I'd barred the door.'

'You let her in?'

'Of course. I wasn't worried about letting people *in*.'

'You said "a couple of bodies"?'

'That's right. Maureen Beck was in the loo. Bladder trouble, poor thing. Maybe I should have hung a couple of paintings in there.'

Cluzeau frowned at this. Rebus decided to help him. 'The toilets being where exactly?'

'Next flight up. A complete pain really. The gallery

shares them with the shop downstairs. Crammed full of cardboard boxes and knitting patterns.'

Rebus nodded. The Frenchman coughed, preparing to speak. 'So,' he said, 'you have to leave the gallery actually to use the ... loo?'

Serena Davies nodded. 'You're French,' she stated. Cluzeau gave a little bow. 'I should have guessed from the *pochette*. You'd never find a Scotsman carrying one of those.'

Cluzeau seemed prepared for this point. 'But the sporran serves the same purpose.'

'I suppose it does,' the artist admitted, 'but its primary function is as a signifier.' She looked to both men. Both men looked puzzled. 'It's hairy and it hangs around your groin,' she explained.

Rebus stayed silent, but pursed his lips. Cluzeau nodded to himself, frowning.

'Maybe,' said Rebus, 'you could explain your exhibition to us, *Ms* Davies?'

'Well, it's a comment on Knox of course.'

'Knocks?' asked Cluzeau.

'John Knox,' Rebus explained. 'We passed by his old house a little way back.'

'John Knox,' she went on, principally for the Frenchman's benefit, but perhaps too, she thought, for that of the Scotsman, 'was a Scottish preacher, a follower of Calvin. He was also a misogynist, hence the title of one of his works – *The First Blast of the Trumpet Against the Monstrous Regiment of Women.*'

'He didn't mean all women,' Rebus felt obliged to add. Serena Davies straightened her spine like a snake rising up before its kill.

'But he did,' she said, 'by association. And, also by association, these works are a comment on *all* Scotsmen. And all men.'

Cluzeau could feel an argument beginning. Arguments,

to his knowledge, were always counter-productive even when enjoyable. 'I think I see,' he said. 'And your exhibition responds to this man's work. Yes.' He tapped the catalogue. ' "Monstrous Trumpet" is a pun then?'

Serena Davies shrugged, but seemed pacified. 'You could call it that. I'm saying that Knox talked with one part of his anatomy – *not* his brain.'

'And,' added Rebus, 'that at the same time he talked out of his arse?'

'Yes,' she said.

Cluzeau was chuckling. He was still chuckling when he asked: 'And who could have reason for stealing your work?'

The mane rippled again. 'I've absolutely no idea.'

'But you suspect one of your guests,' Cluzeau continued. 'Of course you do: you have already stated that there was no one else here. You were among friends, yet one of them is the Janus figure, yes?'

She nodded slowly. 'Much as I hate to admit it.'

Rebus had taken the catalogue from Cluzeau and seemed to be studying it. But he'd listened to every word. He tapped the missing statue's photo.

'Do you work from life?'

'Mostly, yes, but not for "Monstrous Trumpet".'

'It's a sort of ... ideal figure then?'

She smiled at this. 'Hardly ideal, Inspector. But in that it comes from up here –' she tapped her head, 'from an idea rather than from life, yes, I suppose it is.'

'Does that go for the face, too?' Rebus persisted. 'It seems so lifelike.'

She accepted the compliment, studying the photo with him. 'It's not any one man's face,' she said. 'At most it's a composite of men I know.' Then she shrugged. 'Maybe.'

Rebus handed the catalogue to Cluzeau. 'Did you search anyone?' he asked the artist.

'I asked them to open their bags. Not very subtle of me, but I was – *am* – distraught.'

239

'And did they?'

'Oh yes. Pointless really, there were only two or three bags big enough to hide the statue in.'

'But they were empty?'

She sighed, pinching the bridge of her nose between two fingers. The bracelets were shunted from wrist to elbow. 'Utterly empty,' she said. 'Just as I feel.'

'Was the piece insured?'

She shook her head again, her forehead lowered. A portrait of dejection, Rebus thought. Lifelike, yet not quite real. He noticed too that, now her eyes were averted, the Frenchman was appraising her. He caught Rebus watching him and raised his eyebrows, then shrugged, then made a gesture with his hands. Yes, thought Rebus, I know what you mean. Only don't let *her* catch you thinking what I know you're thinking.

And, he supposed, what he was thinking too.

'I think we'd better go through,' he said. 'The other women will be getting impatient.'

'Let them!' she cried.

'Actually,' said Rebus, 'perhaps you could go ahead of us? Warn them that we may be keeping them a bit longer than we thought.'

She brightened at the news, then sneered. 'You mean you want me to do your dirty work for you?'

Rebus shrugged innocently. 'I just wanted a moment to discuss the case with my colleague.'

'Oh,' she said. Then nodded: 'Yes, of course. Discuss away. I'll tell them they've to stay put.'

'Thank you,' said Rebus, but she'd already left the room.

Cluzeau whistled silently. 'What a creature!'

It was meant as praise, of course, and Rebus nodded assent. 'So what do you think?'

'Think?'

'About the theft.'

'Ah.' Cluzeau scraped at his chin with his fingers. 'A crime of passion,' he said at last and with confidence.

'How do you work that out?'

Cluzeau gave another of his shrugs. 'The process of elimination. We eliminate money: there are more expensive pieces here and besides, a common thief would burgle the premises when they were empty, no?'

Rebus nodded, enjoying this, so like his own train of thought was it. 'Go on.'

'I do not think this piece is so precious that a collector would have it stolen. It is not insured, so there is no reason for the artist herself to have it stolen. It seems logical that someone invited to the exhibition stole it. So we come to the figure of the Janus. Someone the artist herself knows. Why should such a person – a supposed friend – steal this work?' He paused before answering his own question. 'Jealousy. Revenge, *et voilà*, the crime of passion.'

Rebus applauded silently. 'Bravo. But there are thirty-odd suspects out there and no sign of the statue.'

'Ah, I did not say I could solve the crime; all I offer is the "why".'

'Then follow me,' Rebus said, 'and we'll encounter the "who" and the "how" together.'

In the main gallery, Serena Davies was in furious conversation with one knot of women. Brian Holmes was trying to take names and addresses from another group. A third group stood, bored and disconsolate, by the drinks table, and a fourth group stood beside a bright red gash of a painting, glancing at it from time to time and talking among themselves.

Most of the women in the room either carried clutch-purses tucked safely under their arms, or else let neat shoulder-bags swing effortlessly by their sides. But there were a few larger bags and these had been left in a group of their own between the drinks table and another smaller table on which sat a small pile of catalogues and a visitors' book. Rebus walked across to this spot and studied the bags. There was one large straw shopping-bag, apparently containing only a cashmere cardigan and a folded copy of the *Guardian*. There was one department store plastic carrier-bag, containing an umbrella, a bunch of bananas, a fat paperback and a copy of the *Guardian*. There was one canvas shopping-bag, containing an empty crisp packet, a copy of the *Scotsman* and a copy of the *Guardian*.

All this Rebus could see just by standing over the bags. He reached down and picked up the carrier-bag.

'Can I ask whose bag this is?' he said loudly.

'It's mine.'

A young woman stepped forward from the drinks table, starting to blush furiously.

'Follow me, please,' said Rebus, walking off to the next room along. Cluzeau followed and so, seconds later, did the owner of the bag, her eyes terrified.

'Just a couple of questions, that's all,' Rebus said, trying to put her at ease. The main gallery was hushed; he knew people would be straining to hear the conversation. Brian Holmes was repeating an address to himself as he jotted it down.

Rebus felt a little bit like an executioner, walking up to the bags, picking them up in turn and wandering off with the owner towards the awaiting guillotine. The owner of the carrier-bag was Trish Poole, wife of a psychology lecturer at the university. Rebus had met Dr Poole before, and told her so, trying to help her relax a little. It turned out that a lot of the women present today were either academics in their own right, or else were the wives of academics. This latter group included not only Trish Poole, but also Rebecca Eiser, wife of the distinguished Professor of English Literature. Listening to Trish Poole tell him this, Rebus shivered and could feel his face turn pale. But that had been a long time ago.

After Trish Poole had returned for a whispered confab

with her group, Rebus tried the canvas bag. This belonged to Margaret Grieve, a writer and, as she said herself, 'one of Serena's closest friends'. Rebus didn't doubt this, and asked if she was married. No, she was not, but she did have a 'significant other'. She smiled broadly as she said this. Rebus smiled back. She'd been in the room with the statue when it was noticed to be missing? Yes, she had. Not that she'd seen anything. She'd been intent on the paintings. So much so that she couldn't be sure whether the statue had been in the room when she'd entered, or whether it had already gone. She thought perhaps it had already gone.

Dismissed by Rebus, she returned to her group in front of the red gash and they too began whispering. An elegant older woman came forward from the same group.

'The last bag is mine,' she said haughtily, her vowels pure Morningside. Perhaps she'd been Jean Brodie's elocution mistress; but no, she wasn't even quite Maggie Smith's age, though to Rebus there were similarities enough between the two women.

Cluzeau seemed quietly cowed by this grand example of Scottish womanhood. He stood at a distance, giving her vowels the necessary room in which to perform. And, Rebus noticed, he clutched his pouch close to his groin, as though it were a lucky charm. Maybe that's what sporrans were?

'I'm Maureen Beck,' she informed them loudly. There would be no hiding *this* conversation from the waggling ears.

Maureen Beck told Rebus that she was married to the architect Robert Beck and seemed surprised when this name meant nothing to the policeman. She decided then that she disliked Rebus and turned to Cluzeau, answering to his smiling countenance every time Rebus asked her a question. She was in the loo at the time, yes, and returned to pandemonium. She'd only been out of the room a couple of minutes, and hadn't seen anyone ...

'Not even *Ms* Fowler?' Rebus asked. 'I believe she was late to arrive?'

'Yes, but that was a minute or two *after* I came back in.'

Rebus nodded thoughtfully. There was a teasing piece of ham wedged between two of his back teeth and he pushed it with his tongue. A woman put her head around the partition.

'Look, Inspector, some of us have got appointments this afternoon. Isn't there at least a telephone we can use?'

It was a good point. Who was in charge of the gallery itself? The gallery director, it turned out, was a timid little woman who had burrowed into the quietest of the groups. She was only running the place for the real owner, who was on a well-deserved holiday in Paris. (Cluzeau rolled his eyes at this. 'No one,' he said with a shudder, 'deserves such torture.') There was a cramped office, and in it an old bakelite telephone. If the women could leave twenty pence for each call. A line started to form outside the office. ('Ah, how you love queuing!') Mrs Beck, meantime, had returned to her group. Rebus followed her, and was introduced to Ginny Elyot, who had raised the alarm, and to Moira Fowler the latecomer.

Ginny Elyot kept patting her short auburn hair as though searching it for misplaced artworks. A nervous habit, Rebus reasoned. Cluzeau quickly became the centre of attention, with even the distant and unpunctual Moira becoming involved in the interrogation. Rebus sidled away and touched Brian Holmes' arm.

'That's all the addresses noted, sir.'

'Well done, Brian. Look, slip upstairs, will you? Give the loo a recce.'

'What am I looking for exactly – suspiciously shaped bundles of four-ply?'

Rebus actually laughed. 'We should be so lucky. But yes, you never know what you might find. And check any windows, too. There might be a drainpipe.'

'Okay.'

As Holmes left, a small hand touched Rebus's arm. A girl in her late-teens, eyes gleaming behind studious spectacles, jerked her head towards the gallery's first partitioned room. Rebus followed her. She was so small, and spoke so quietly, he actually had to grasp hands to knees and bend forward to listen.

'I want the story.'

'Pardon?'

'I want the story for my dad's paper.'

Rebus looked at her. His voice too was a dramatic whisper. 'You're Lesley Jameson?'

She nodded.

'I see. Well, as far as I'm concerned the story's yours. But we haven't *got* a story yet.'

She looked around her, then dropped her voice even lower. 'You've seen her.'

'Who?'

'Serena, of course. She's ravishing, isn't she?' Rebus tried to look non-committal. 'She's terribly attractive to men.' This time he attempted a Gallic shrug. He wondered if it looked as stupid as it felt. Her voice died away almost completely, reducing Rebus to lip-reading. 'She has loads of men after her. Including Margaret's.'

'Ah,' said Rebus, 'right.' He nodded, too. So Margaret Grieve's boyfriend was ...

The lips made more movements: 'He's Serena's lover.'

Yes, well, now things began to make more sense. Maybe the Frenchman was right: a crime of passion. The one thing missing thus far had been the passion itself; but no longer. And it was curious, when he came to think of it, how Margaret Grieve had said she couldn't recall whether the statue had been in the room or not. It wasn't the sort of thing you could miss, was it? Not for a bunch of samey paintings of pink bulges and grey curving masses. The newspapers in her bag would have concealed the statue quite nicely, too. There was just one problem.

Cluzeau's head appeared around the partition. 'Ah! Here you are. I'm sorry if I interrupt –'

But Lesley Jameson was already making for the main room. Cluzeau watched her go, then turned to Rebus.

'Charming women.' He sighed. 'But all of them either married or else with lovers. And one of them, of course, is the thief.'

'Oh?' Rebus sounded surprised. 'You mean one of the women you've just been talking with?'

'Of course.' Now he, too, lowered his voice. 'The statue left the gallery in a bag. You could not simply hide it under your dress, could you? But I don't think a plastic bag would have been strong enough for this task. So, we have a choice between Madame Beck and Mademoiselle Grieve.'

'Grieve's boyfriend has been carrying on with our artist.'

Cluzeau digested this. But he too knew there was a problem. 'She did not leave the gallery. She was shut in with the others.'

Rebus nodded. 'So there has to have been an accomplice. I think I'd better have another word with Lesley Jameson.'

But Brian Holmes had appeared. He exhaled noisily. 'Thank Christ for that,' he said. 'For a minute there I thought you'd buggered off and left me.'

Rebus grinned. 'That might not have been such bad idea. How was the loo?'

'Well, I didn't find any solid evidence,' Holmes replied with a straight face. 'No skeins of wool tied to the plumbing and hanging out of the windows for a burglar to shimmy down.'

'But there is a window?'

'A small one in the cubicle itself. I stood on the seat and had a squint out. A two-storey drop to a sort of back yard, nothing in it but a rusting Renault Five and a skip full of cardboard boxes.'

'Go down and take a look at that skip.'

'I thought you might say that.'

'And take a look at the Renault,' ordered Cluzeau, his face set. 'I cannot believe a French car would rust. Perhaps you are mistaken and it is a Mini Cooper, no?'

Holmes, who prided himself on knowing a bit about cars, was ready to argue, then saw the smile spread across the Frenchman's face. He smiled, too.

'Just as well you've got a sense of humour,' he said. 'You'll need it after the match on Saturday.'

'And you will need your Scottish stoicism.'

'Save it for the half-time entertainment, eh?' said Rebus, but with good enough humour. 'The sooner we get this wrapped up, the more time we'll have left for sightseeing.'

Cluzeau seemed about to argue, but Rebus held up a hand. 'Believe me,' he said, 'you'll want to see these sights. Only the locals know the *very* best pubs in Edinburgh.'

Holmes went to investigate the skip and Rebus spoke in whispers with Lesley Jameson – when he wasn't fending off demands from the detainees. What had seemed to most of them something unusual and thrilling at first, a story to be repeated across the dining-table, had now become merely tiresome. Though they had asked to make phone calls, Rebus couldn't help overhearing some of those conversations. They weren't warning of a late arrival or cancelling an appointment: they were spreading the news.

'Look, Inspector, I'm really tired of being kept here.'

Rebus turned from Lesley Jameson to the talker. His voice lacked emotion. 'You're not being kept here.'

'What?'

'Who said you were? Only *Ms* Davies as I understand. You're free to leave whenever you want.'

There was hesitation at this. To leave and taste freedom again? Or to stay, so as not to miss anything? Muttered dialogues took place and eventually one or two of the guests did leave. They simply walked out, closing the door behind them.

'Does that mean we can go?'

Rebus nodded. Another woman left, then another, then a couple.

'I hope you're not thinking of kicking me out,' Lesley Jameson warned. She wanted desperately to be a journalist, and to do it the hard way, *sans* nepotism. Rebus shook his head.

'Just keep talking,' he said.

Cluzeau was in conversation with Serena Davies. When Rebus approached them, she was studying the Frenchman's strong-looking hands. Rebus waved his own nail-bitten paw around the gallery.

'Do you,' he asked, 'have any trouble getting people to pose for all these paintings?'

She shook her head. 'No, not really. It's funny you should ask, Monsieur Cluzeau was just saying –'

'Yes, I'll bet he was. But Monsieur Cluzeau –' testing the words, not finding them risible any more, 'has a wife and family.'

Serena Davies laughed; a deep growl which seemed to run all the way up and down the Frenchman's spine. At last, she let go his hand. 'I thought we were talking about modelling, Inspector.'

'We were,' said Rebus drily, 'but I'm not sure Mrs Cluzeau would see it like that ...'

'Inspector ...?' It was Maureen Beck. 'Everyone seems to be leaving. Do I take it we're free to go?'

Rebus was suddenly businesslike. 'No,' he said. 'I'd like you to stay behind a little longer.' He glanced towards the group – Ginny Elyot, Moira Fowler, Margaret Grieve –'all of you, please. This won't take long.'

'That's what my husband says,' commented Moira Fowler, raising a glass of water to her lips. She placed a tablet on her tongue and washed it down.

Rebus looked to Lesley Jameson, then winked. 'Fasten your seatbelt,' he told her. 'It's going to be a bumpy ride.'

The gallery was now fast emptying and Holmes, having battled against the tide on the stairwell, entered the room on unsteady legs, his eyes seeking out Rebus.

'Jeez!' he cried. 'I thought you'd decided to bugger off after all. What's up? Where's everyone going?'

'Anything in the skip?' But Holmes shrugged: nothing. 'I've sent everyone home,' Rebus explained.

'Everyone except us,' Maureen Beck said sniffily.

'Well,' said Rebus, facing the four women, 'that's because nobody but *you* knows anything about the statue.'

The women themselves said nothing at this, but Cluzeau gave a small gasp – perhaps to save them the trouble. Serena Davies, however, had replaced her growl with a lump of ice.

'You mean one of *them* stole my work?'

Rebus shook his head. 'No, that's not what I mean. One person couldn't have done it. There had to be an accomplice.' He nodded towards Moira Fowler. '*Ms* Fowler, why don't you take DC Holmes down to your car? He can carry the statue back upstairs.'

'Moira!' Another change of tone, this time from ice to fire. For a second, Rebus thought Serena Davies might be about to make a lunge at the thief. Perhaps Moira Fowler thought so too, for she moved without further prompting towards the door.

'Okay,' she said, 'if you like.'

Holmes watched her pass him on her way to the stairwell.

'Go on then, Brian,' ordered Rebus. Holmes seemed undecided. He knew he was going to miss the story. What's more, he didn't fancy lugging the bloody thing up a flight of stairs.

'*Vite!*' cried Rebus, another word of French suddenly coming back to him. Holmes moved on tired legs towards the door. Up the stairs, down the stairs, up the stairs. It would, he couldn't help thinking, make good training for the Scottish pack.

Serena Davies had put her hand to her brow. Clank-a-clank-clank went the bracelets. 'I can't believe it of Moira. Such treachery.'

'Hah!' This from Ginny Elyot, her eyes burning. 'Treachery? You're a good one to speak. Getting Jim to "model" for you. Neither of you telling her about it. What the hell do you think she thought when she found out?'

Jim being, as Rebus knew from Lesley, Moira Fowler's husband. He kept his eyes on Ginny.

'And you, too, *Ms* Elyot. How did you feel when you found out about … David, is it?'

She nodded. Her hand went towards her hair again, but she caught herself, and gripped one hand in the other. 'Yes, David,' she said quietly. 'That statue's got David's eyes, his hair.' She wasn't looking at Rebus. He didn't feel she was even replying to his question.

She was remembering.

'And Gerry's nose and jawline. I'd recognise them anywhere.' This from Margaret Grieve, she of the significant other. 'But Gerry can't keep secrets, not from me.'

Maureen Beck, who had been nodding throughout, never taking her moist eyes off the artist, was next. Her husband too, Robert, the architect, had modelled for Serena Davies. On the quiet, of course. It had to be on the quiet: no knowing what passions might be aroused otherwise. Even in a city like Edinburgh, even in women as seemingly self-possessed and cool-headed as these. Perhaps it had all been very innocent. Perhaps.

'He's got Robert's figure,' Maureen Beck was saying. 'Down to the scar on his chest from that riding accident.'

A crime of passion, just as Cluzeau had predicted. And after Rebus telling him that there was no such thing as passion in the city. But there was; and there were secrets too. Locked within these paintings, fine so long as they were abstract, so long as they weren't modelled from life. But for all that 'Monstrous Trumpet' was, in Serena Davies' words, a 'composite', its creation still cut deep. For each of the four women, there was something recognisable there, something modelled from life, from husband or lover. Something which burned and humiliated.

Unable to stand the thought of public display, of visitors walking into the gallery and saying 'Good God, doesn't that statue look like ...?' Unable to face the thought of this, and of the ridicule (the detailed penis, the tongue, and that sticking-plaster) they had come together with a plan. A clumsy, almost unworkable plan, but the only plan they had.

The statue had gone into Margaret Grieve's roomy bag, at which point Ginny Elyot had raised the alarm – hysterically so, attracting all the guests towards that one room, unaware as they pressed forwards that they were passing Margaret Grieve discreetly moving the other way. The bag had been passed to Maureen Beck, who had then slipped upstairs to the toilet. She had opened the window and dropped the statue down into the skip, from where Moira Fowler had retrieved it, carrying it out to her own car. Beck had returned, to find Serena Davies stopping people from leaving; a minute or two later, Moira Fowler had arrived.

She now walked in, followed by a red-faced Holmes, the statue cradled in his arms. Serena Davies, however, appeared not to notice. She had her eyes trained on the parquet floor and, again, she was being studied by Cluzeau. 'What a creature,' he had said of her. What a creature indeed. The four thieves would certainly be in accord in calling her 'creature'.

Who knows, thought Rebus, they might even be in *bon accord*.

* * *

The artist was neither temperamental nor stupid enough to insist on pressing charges and she bent to Rebus's suggestion that the piece be withdrawn from the show. The pressure thereafter was on Lesley Jameson not to release the story to her father's paper. Female solidarity won in the end, but it was a narrow victory.

Not much female solidarity elsewhere, thought Rebus. He made up a few mock headlines, the sort that would have pleased Doctor Curt. Feminist Artist's Roll Models; Serena's Harem of Husbands; The Anti-Knox Knocking Shop. All as he sat squeezed into a corner of the Sutherland Bar. Somewhere along the route, Cluzeau – now insisting that Rebus call him Jean-Pierre – had found half a dozen French fans, in town for the rugby and already in their cups. Then a couple of the Scottish fans had tagged along too and now there were about a dozen of them, standing at the bar and singing French rugby songs. Any minute now someone would tip an ice-bucket onto their head. He prayed it wouldn't be Brian Holmes, who, shirt-tail out and tie hanging loose, was singing as lustily as anyone, despite the language barrier – or even, perhaps, because of it.

Childish, of course. But then that was men for you. Simple pleasures and simple crimes. Male revenge was simple almost to the point of being infantile: you went up to the bastard and you stuck your fist into his face or kneed him in the nuts. But the revenge of the female. Ah, that was recondite stuff. He wondered if it was finished now, or would Serena Davies face more plots, plots more subtle, or better executed, or more savage? He didn't really want to think about it. Didn't want to think about the hate in the four women's voices, or the gleam in their eyes. He drank to forget. That was why men joined the Foreign Legion too, wasn't it? To forget. Or was it?

He was buggered if he could remember. But something else niggled too. The women had laid claim to a lover's jawline, a husband's figure. But whose, he couldn't help wondering, was the penis?

Someone was tugging at his arm, pulling him up. The glasses flew from the table and suddenly he was being hugged by Jean-Pierre.

'John, my friend, John, tell me who this man Peter Zealous is that everyone is talking to me about?'

'It's Sellars,' Rebus corrected. To tell or not to tell? He opened his mouth. There was the machine-gun sound of things spilling onto the bar behind him. Small, solid things. Next thing he knew, it was dark and his head was very cold and very wet.

'I'll get you for this, Brian,' he said, removing the ice-bucket from his head. 'So help me I will.'

AUTHOR'S NOTE

There *are* Cluzeaus in and around Périgueux. Lots of them, and all spelt like that. You can find them in the Dordogne phone book. I did.

I.R.

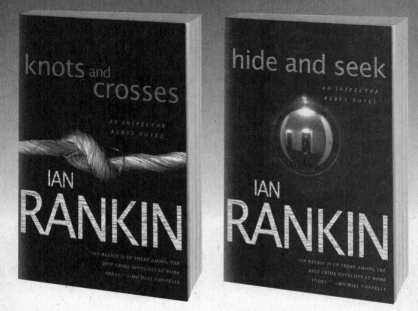